MURDER
AT THE
WHAM BAM
CLUB

MURDER AT THE WHAM BAM CLUB

CAROLYN MARIE WILKINS

KENSINGTON
PUBLISHING CORP.

kensingtonbooks.com

KENSINGTON BOOKS are published by

Kensington Publishing Corp.
900 Third Ave.
New York, NY 10022

All Kensington titles, imprints, and distributed lines are available at special quantity discounts for bulk purchases for sales promotion, premiums, fund-raising, educational, or institutional use. Special book excerpts or customized printings can also be created to fit specific needs. For details, write or phone the office of the Kensington Special Sales Manager: Attn. Special Sales Department. Kensington Publishing Corp., 900 Third Ave., New York, NY 10022. Phone: 1-800-221-2647.

Library of Congress Control Number: 2025932932

ISBN: 978-1-4967-5471-4
First Kensington Hardcover Edition: August 2025

ISBN: 978-1-4967-5473-8 (ebook)

10 9 8 7 6 5 4 3 2 1

Printed in the United States of America

The authorized representative in the EU for product safety and compliance
is eucomply OU, Parnu mnt 139b-14, Apt 123
Tallinn, Berlin 11317, hello@eucompliancepartner.com

This book is dedicated to Julian and Elizabeth Wilkins, who gave me the gift of storytelling.

ACKNOWLEDGMENTS

This book would not have been possible without the support of many people. I am grateful to all my beta readers, who patiently plowed through early drafts of this story and offered helpful suggestions. A special thank-you to my agent Lane Clark, my editor John Scognamiglio, and the people at Kensington Publishing who helped to bring this book into the world. As always, I offer a deep bow of gratitude to my husband John Voigt for his clear-eyed editorial insight, love and support.

MURDER
AT THE
WHAM BAM
CLUB

CHAPTER 1

Everything about the man ahead of me screamed "pimp," from the rakish tilt of his fedora hat to the diamond ring sparkling on his little finger. When you are psychic, as I am, being around the wrong people can make you very jumpy. The dark energy rolling off this man grated against my psychic senses like fingernails on a blackboard.

I was on my way home from dropping off my winter coat at Harry's Dry Cleaning. To cheer myself up on this gloomy October day, I'd chosen to wear my favorite outfit, a long-waisted yellow sweater and matching skirt with a fashionably short hemline. The cut of it showed off the generous curves I'd inherited from my mother, while its color complimented my caramel complexion. At the moment, however, I couldn't help wishing I'd worn something that didn't hug my hips quite so tightly.

As I approached the corner where he stood, I felt the pimp's eyes on me, sizing me up.

"Hey there, sugar," he said. He flicked his cigarette to the ground and sauntered toward me. "What's a pretty brownskin girl like you doin' out here, all by your sweet lonesome?"

I shot the man a dirty look, picked up my pace, and kept on walking.

"Suit yourself," he said, with a nonchalant shrug. "Plenty more fish in the sea."

Agate, Illinois, had been a sleepy river town when I grew up here, but all of that had changed since the Great War. New money, new ideas, and new people were flooding into town. It was 1922, and we were two years into a brand-new decade. Negroes were moving to Agate in droves, hoping to escape Jim Crow segregation in the South and make a better life for themselves. Every day the Illinois Central Railroad brought a fresh new crop of country girls from the Mississippi cotton fields to Agate where, they'd been told, the streets were paved with gold. As a result, my neighborhood had become a popular hunting ground for pimps, pickpockets, and other lowlife types.

Not to say that there weren't also plenty of ordinary, hard-working colored folks living here as well. Lincoln Avenue, the narrow and always congested street for which Agate's Lincolnsville neighborhood was named, was lined with stores offering to sell you everything from a fashionable new hat, to a tire iron for your Model T Ford. On this gray October day, the street was packed with Negroes going about their business. Women picking up stew meat at Harry's Butcher Shop. Men stopping off at Mo's Corner for a haircut, and to catch up with the latest gossip. Swift's Smoke Shop, with its bright red sign and cigar store Indian, was always crowded with people placing clandestine bets on the illegal numbers racket with Jimmy Swift, the store owner and local bookie.

At the corner of Sixth and Lincoln, a six-foot-tall red, white, and blue signboard blocked the sidewalk in front of the Black

Rooster Pool Hall, the thinly disguised speakeasy and gambling den that served as the unofficial headquarters for Republican ward boss Franklin C. Dillard. The sign read:

VOTE FOR
HARRY "HAPPY" SKELTON JR.
FOR U.S. CONGRESS
A TRUE FRIEND TO THE COLORED MAN.

Under the watchful eye of a beefy thug with a boxer's broken nose and cauliflower ears, a posse of street urchins in cloth caps and knee pants swarmed up and down the block shoving Skelton campaign flyers into the hands of people walking by.

"Election's in three weeks," a grimy boy reminded me as he stuck a flyer in my hand. "Don't forget to vote."

Congressman Skelton's opponent in the midterm election of 1922 was Jeremiah Saunders, a bespectacled white college professor from Peoria. Saunders was running on a reform ticket, which promised to clean up corruption and crime. Lincoln Avenue was peppered with speakeasies, gambling dens, and brothels. Prohibition, the federal law forbidding the sale of alcohol, had only made people drink more. These days, white and colored folks could be found staggering drunkenly down the street at all hours of the day and night. You might have thought an anti-crime candidate would be popular in my neighborhood, but Jeremiah Saunders had no chance of winning the colored vote. Franklin C. Dillard, the Republican boss of Ward Eleven, was a Harry Skelton supporter.

Boss Dillard was a former police detective who controlled a vast underground empire of illegal whiskey distillers, gangsters and thugs. If you wanted to do business in Lincolnsville, you needed to give Boss Dillard his cut, or risk having a brick thrown through your window or worse. Franklin C. Dillard was no ordinary hoodlum, however. He was also the City of Agate's only Negro lawyer. Dapper and articulate, Boss Dillard was never seen in anything but a handmade charcoal-gray three-piece suit with a fresh carnation in his lapel.

As I passed the pool hall, the clock at the top of First Episcopal Church struck eleven. I needed to hurry if I wanted to make it home in time to share a late breakfast with my Aunt Sarah before I left for work that afternoon. If I cut through the alley between Tenth and Water Street, I'd be home in ten minutes flat. The alley route was dangerous, of course. It was poorly lit and usually deserted, but I had already been hassled once that morning. What were the odds of lightning striking twice in the same day?

I was almost to the end of the alley when I saw a man and woman standing in front of me. The woman had her back to me, but I recognized her voice immediately. That high, icy, and penetrating soprano could only belong to Mrs. Sallie Wyatt, the last person in the entire city that I wanted to see. Mrs. Wyatt, a tall Negro woman with a high yellow complexion and intense hazel eyes, was the founder and headmistress of the Phyllis Wheatley Institute for Colored Girls. She was dressed in her customary impeccable style—a crisp gray suit, white gloves, and a pair of sensible but elegant English walking shoes.

When I lost both my parents to yellow fever in 1915, Mrs. Wyatt brought me to Phyllis Wheatley Institute, the live-in school she founded to help Agate's homeless colored girls. She encouraged me to learn a trade and maybe even go on to college one day. But I was a boy-crazed and rebellious teenager with a mind of my own. Mrs. Wyatt and the Phyllis Wheatley Institute were no match for the charms of William Bartholomew Jackson. Six feet tall with a cocksure grin and dreamy brown eyes, Will was visiting his cousin in Agate before returning to New York City to join the fabled all-Negro 369th Infantry

Regiment, known to colored folks all over the country as the Harlem Hellfighters. I was seventeen years old the third time Mrs. Wyatt read me the riot act for sneaking out after curfew. Determined to make my own way in the world, I ran away from Wheatley Institute, married Will Jackson, and moved to New York City.

How was I to know my new husband would be killed by a German artillery shell just six months later? How was I to know I'd end up coming back to live in Agate?

Although I'd been back nearly two years, I had not seen or spoken to Mrs. Wyatt. I had no desire to do so now. Yet, there she was, standing no more than a dozen feet away, giving the man in front of her a piece of her mind in that unmistakable voice of hers.

"I'm warning you, young man," she said. "If I catch you coming anywhere near the Wheatley Institute again, I will call the police. Is that clear?"

"It's a free country," the man replied. He had slick processed hair, rich brown skin, and a thin mustache. His mohair suit looked expensive, as did the two-tone patent leather shoes he wore. His gravelly voice made me think of whiskey, cigarettes, and other forbidden pleasures. "I got a right to advertise my show wherever I see fit," he said.

"A show at the Wham Bam Club?" Mrs. Wyatt shook her head in disgust. "If I had my way, the city would shut that horrid place down immediately. There's illegal drinking, gambling, and god knows what else going on in there."

The man laughed, the gold caps on his teeth flashing in the sun. "Quit foolin' yourself, lady. You and I both know these cops ain't gonna do nothing to me. My jazz band is the hottest thing in the Midwest. The way I see it, I'm doing the City of Agate a public service. Providing musical entertainment and good times to people who sorely need it."

"Do not trifle with me, young man," Mrs. Wyatt snapped. Despite her cultured manner, Mrs. Sallie Wyatt was quite strong, and not above giving you a good whipping if she felt you deserved it. Back when I was a misbehaving teenager, the very sound of Mrs. Wyatt's voice was enough to fill my heart with terror.

"You were not soliciting the general public, and you know it," she said, and wagged her finger in the man's face like an avenging angel. "For the last several nights, you've been hawking your wares directly in front of Phyllis Wheatley Institute, a place dedicated to protecting homeless colored girls from exactly this sort of temptation."

"A little bit of 'temptation' might be just what those lovely young things are looking for," he said, "a chance to get away from all that Bible reading and hymn singing you got them doing." His smile held more than a touch of malice. "At least that's what your girls tell me."

"Are you saying that residents of Wheatley Institute have been going down to the Wham Bam Club?" As Mrs. Wyatt stepped closer to the man, I detected a note of doubt in her voice.

"I can't be altogether sure about that," the man replied with an insolent grin. "Wouldn't want to get any of my little friends in trouble, right? I think I better keep mum on that one."

"Answer me, young man," Mrs. Wyatt demanded. "One of my girls has been missing since Friday. Her name is Lilly Davidson. Have you seen her?"

"If I had, do you think I would tell you?" he shot back. "Look, lady. I've got places to go and people to see. Can't waste no more time listening to your foolishness."

Mrs. Wyatt grabbed the lapel of his jacket. "Answer me," she said. "Have you seen Lilly Davidson? Do you know where she is?"

The man's eyes narrowed. "I don't have to tell you a damn

thing, old woman. Get your hands off me." He slapped at
Mrs. Wyatt's hand. When she did not let go, he gave her a
hard shove. As she lost her balance, tumbled to the pavement,
and lay motionless, the man turned and walked away without
looking back.

As I ran toward Mrs. Wyatt, I could see a small rivulet of
blood seeping through the gray hair of her elegant bun.

"Are you all right, Mrs. Wyatt?" I said. "Can you hear me?"
I knelt next to her on the pavement and touched her hand.

She nodded weakly, and winced in pain as she pushed herself
to a seated position.

"It's a good thing you happened to come along, Nola Ann
Jackson," she said. "Has that despicable man left the area?"

"Yes, ma'am," I said.

"In that case, we shall go to the police at once," she said,
sounding much more like the authority figure I remembered
from my teenaged years. "Help me up, please. I want to report
this assault as soon as possible."

When Mrs. Wyatt tried to stand, it was clear she was in no
condition to walk unaided. Once I'd gotten her upright, she
teetered and would have fallen if I had not been holding her up.

"You should have someone look at that cut on your head before you do anything," I said, though it felt strange to be telling
my former headmistress what to do. "My house is just a few
blocks from here. My Aunt Sarah can bandage you up and put
some herbs on your wound so it doesn't get infected. There
will be plenty of time to fill out a police report afterwards."

Mrs. Wyatt nodded, biting her lip against the pain. She
leaned heavily against me as I led her, step by step, out of the
alley and onto Cherry Street. The man who had pushed her was
nowhere to be seen as we made our way slowly down the
cracked sidewalk past a block of small wooden houses, their
tiny porches and barren dirt yards a testament to the poverty of
the Negroes in my neighborhood. We turned left at the corner

of Cherry and Upper Fifth Street. Although it was small, like all the others on the street, my aunt's house was surrounded by a white picket fence and neatly painted in a cheerful shade of light blue. My Aunt Sarah was sitting in a rocking chair on the front porch waiting for us as I pushed open the front gate and led Mrs. Wyatt up the walkway.

CHAPTER 2

Aunt Sarah is a tall woman with big bones, strong features, and the high cheekbones she inherited from her Cherokee grandmother. Her skin is the color of deep mahogany, and when you look into her eyes, you can sense a wisdom that goes all the way back to a time before slavery.

"Aunt Sarah, this is Mrs. Wyatt, the head of Phyllis Wheatley Institute," I said, as I helped Mrs. Wyatt over the doorstep and into the front room.

"Set her on the sofa," Aunt Sarah told me. "She is going to need a bandage for that head wound."

When Mrs. Wyatt opened her mouth to speak, Aunt Sarah told her to save her energy. "You've had yourself quite a shock," she said, "but it's nothing the Spirits can't put right."

Too weak to say anything, Mrs. Wyatt sat down and slumped against the back of the sofa. Her normally tan complexion was pale and her breathing was ragged and shallow.

"You rest, Mrs. Wyatt. I'll go and get you some tea," I said, and followed Aunt Sarah down the hallway and into the kitchen.

When I started to tell her what had happened, Aunt Sarah

put a finger to her lips. "No need to explain," she said. "My Spirits showed me the whole thing. Nasty piece of work, that young man."

My aunt's psychic abilities were a daily source of wonderment to me. I was psychic myself and able to see shapes, colors, and energies around people. On a good day, I could see bits and pieces of a person's future, and often felt a buzzing sound in my left ear when something important was about to happen. Aunt Sarah's skills were at another level. Her ability to see into the future, prepare potions for healing, and, on occasion stop evildoers in their tracks, was legendary.

Psychic ability ran in the family, something my Bible-believing mother had done her best to deny. For Mama, the fact that Aunt Sarah brewed potions, read tea leaves, and talked to the Spirits was a source of profound shame. These activities represented a throwback to a dark and ignorant past, a past my mother was determined to move beyond. Mama rarely spoke about her sister, and when she did, her tone was bitter.

"Your Aunt Sarah is an educated woman," she told me. "I can't understand for the life of me why she wastes her time on this superstitious mumbo-jumbo. She learned how to read, write, and do figures at Zion Missionary School for Negroes. She ought to know better." Mama gave her head an angry shake and frowned. "I have not spoken to your Aunt Sarah in fifteen years. If she wants to behave like an ignorant savage, I suppose that's her business. But I can't be around that kind of foolishness. It's un-Christian. It's ignorant, and it's devilish."

One thing about my mama. When she made her mind up about something, it stayed made up. Like all the women in my family, she was as stubborn as the day was long. When my parents moved to Agate, Mama cut my Aunt Sarah completely out of her life.

I never saw or heard from my Aunt Sarah while I was growing up. Not once.

The summer I turned fourteen, an epidemic of yellow fever swept through Agate. My mother and father died on the same day, within hours of each other. I was a sullen and disobedient teenager at the time, with raging hormones and a smart mouth. Mama tried to rein me in, but I rebelled. I wasn't even home the day my parents died. I was out running the streets with some of my bad-news friends, and never got to say goodbye.

I felt horrible. The pursed lips and disapproving glances I received from the adults at my parents' funeral only increased my sense of worthlessness. Aunt Sarah was not invited to my parents' funeral. None of Mama's friends in Agate even knew she had a sister. For all anyone knew, I was an orphan, alone in a friendless world.

Reverend Oates, the pastor of my mother's church, brought me to live with his family. When I spent the next month drinking moonshine, chasing boys, and generally wreaking havoc, I was sent to live in the orphanage at Phyllis Wheatley Institute.

Aunt Sarah did not write me during the two and a half years I spent at Wheatley Institute. She did not write me when I eloped with Will Jackson and moved to Harlem. But exactly one year after Will was killed in the war, my Aunt Sarah wrote me a letter:

Dear Nola,
You don't know me, but we are family. When
your parents moved to Agate, I stayed behind in
Mississippi. But times have changed, and so have
my circumstances. I own a house in Agate now.
My Spirits tell me that you have lost your
husband, that you are grieving and need a place
to heal. I am getting on in years and need help
around the house. Come back to Agate, Nola.
Stay with me for as long as you like. I've wired

money to the Western Union on 125th Street for
your train fare home.

Was my Aunt Sarah really that psychic? Perhaps she had
read of Will's death in the obituaries. Whatever had prompted
Aunt Sarah to write me at that moment, her timing was perfect.
I was struggling hard to make a life for myself in New York
City, but Harlem had been my husband's home, not mine.
Without Will Jackson in my life, I felt rudderless there—no
friends, no job, and no family. After reading Aunt Sarah's letter,
I felt I had been given a new start. Two weeks later, I boarded
the Illinois Limited and returned to Agate.

It had been nearly two years since my return to Agate. Aunt
Sarah and I had settled into a comfortable rhythm. Although
the woman had to be at least seventy, she was sharp as a tack
and great company.

"Mrs. Wyatt needs something on that wound to keep it from
getting infected," Aunt Sarah told me. "I think I still have some
comfrey leaves in my cabinet. I'll fix her a poultice."

She pulled out a large metal key from the pocket of her tattered cardigan and opened the door of the glass-fronted cabinet
next to the sink where she kept her herbs, tinctures, and potions. After rummaging around for a minute, she pulled a large
glass apothecary jar filled with comfrey leaves from the back of
the cabinet. As she pried open the jar, a horrible smell filled the
kitchen. The leaves of the comfrey plant are long and hairy, and
they smell like horse manure. As I held my nose, I reminded
myself that comfrey had powerful astringent properties that
would help Mrs. Wyatt's wound heal quickly.

"Don't just stand there, Nola," Aunt Sarah said sharply. She
reached into the cabinet above the kitchen sink, pulled down a
small black tin, and handed it to me. "Fix Mrs. Wyatt a pot of
Recovery Tea," she said.

I took the tin, measured out a generous spoonful of powdered herbs and dropped them into a blue porcelain teapot. Aunt Sarah's homemade teas were wonder-workers, designed to help with everything from a runny nose to a broken heart. Recovery Tea was made from ordinary black tea mixed with a powder made from ginger, sassafras, and dogwood bark. However, its real power came from the mysterious incantations Aunt Sarah muttered under her breath as she ground the herbs.

I filled the teapot with hot water, let it steep for a minute, and placed it on a tray with a cup, a spoon, and a jar of honey. When I was finished, Aunt Sarah nodded her approval.

"You're starting to get the hang of this work, Nola," she said. "Now take this out to Mrs. Wyatt and see that she drinks it."

When I returned to the living room, Mrs. Wyatt was slumped in the same position I'd left her in earlier, wan and semi-conscious. I set the tray on the end table and filled her cup, making sure to add a generous dollop of honey to the steaming black liquid. After letting the tea cool for a few minutes, I tapped Mrs. Wyatt gently on the shoulder and helped her sit up.

"Drink this," I said, and placed the cup between her hands.

Fifteen minutes later, Mrs. Wyatt had finished her tea and was sitting upright on the couch. After the second cup, Mrs. Wyatt's color had returned and her breathing was back to normal.

"No need to fuss over me," she said, placing her empty cup back on the tray. "It's just a small bump on the head. I'll be fine."

"Aunt Sarah is making you a poultice for your wound," I told her. "It will be ready in a minute."

"Tell her I'm fine," Mrs. Wyatt said firmly. "I don't want her to go to any more trouble on my account."

As Mrs. Wyatt continued to insist that she did not need any further treatment, Aunt Sarah bustled into the room carrying a bowl filled with warm comfrey paste and a long strip of white cotton.

"Nonsense," Aunt Sarah said firmly. "You need more healing for that wound."

Once the bandage was in place, Mrs. Wyatt began to look a lot more like the intimidating, take-charge school principal I remembered from my teenaged years.

"I read about your husband's death in the *Agate Daily Chronicle*, Nola. Please accept my condolences," she said. "When I heard you were back in town, I was hoping you'd stop by Wheatley Institute to see me."

Although I was nearly twenty-one, I squirmed in my seat like a schoolgirl who'd been caught playing hooky. "Given the circumstances of my departure, I didn't think you'd ever want to hear from me again," I said.

"I won't say you were the easiest resident I ever worked with at Wheatley Institute," she replied, "but you were certainly one of the brightest. You remind me of Lilly Davidson, one of my residents. It was my concern for Lilly that got me arguing with that horrible man in the first place."

"Why were you in that alley? What brought you back there, Mrs. Wyatt?" Since Mrs. Wyatt had already brought up the subject, I figured it was okay to ask for details.

"I'm a bit embarrassed to admit this," Mrs. Wyatt said. "But I was following the man you saw me with. He's a musician who plays down at the Wham Bam Club, that infernal sin parlor across the river from Wheatley Institute. His name is Eddie Smooth."

Aunt Sarah had been listening to our conversation without comment. But when Mrs. Wyatt told me about the man she followed into the alley, Aunt Sarah studied Mrs. Wyatt intensely for a moment.

"There is more to the story, isn't there, Mrs. Wyatt?" Aunt Sarah said.

When Mrs. Wyatt began to cry, I was stunned. I had only thought of her as an authority figure, someone to be feared, someone who was always in control. To see her this vulnerable was a shocking revelation. I pulled a handkerchief out of my pocket and handed it to her. She wiped her eyes, blew her nose, and took a deep breath.

"I don't know how you know all of this," she told my Aunt Sarah, "but you are absolutely right. I am in a desperate fix, and I can't talk about it to anyone. The future of Phyllis Wheatley Institute hangs in the balance."

"Your secrets are safe with us, Mrs. Wyatt," Aunt Sarah said. "Nola and I are in your corner. Tell us what you need."

"It's about Lilly Davidson, the girl I mentioned," Mrs. Wyatt said. "My friend Jim Richardson took her and three other girls from Wheatley Institute to the colored YMCA across the river in Craigsville to see James Weldon Johnson give a lecture on Negro voting rights. Jim is a personal friend of Mr. Johnson's. When he offered to drive the girls in his new car and introduce them to the author into the bargain, I was delighted. After the lecture, Jim took the girls up to shake Mr. Johnson's hand. That's when Jim noticed that Lilly was missing. He drove all over town looking for her, but she seems to have vanished into thin air."

"It's not exactly thin air, is it," Aunt Sarah said pointedly. "You think that Eddie Smooth fella knows where she is. Am I right?"

Mrs. Wyatt nodded. "He's been hanging around in front of Wheatley Institute. Pestering the girls, inviting them to come hear his jazz band at the Wham Bam Club."

"Is that really such a bad thing?" I asked. When I lived at Wheatley Institute, I'd chafed at the many restrictions placed upon the residents. For a lively teenager like me, the place had felt like a prison. No smoking. No drinking. No dancing, no cursing, and absolutely no staying out after nine at night.

As I spoke, Mrs. Wyatt shot me a frosty glare. "Phyllis Wheatley Institute is under the direction of the City Welfare

Board, a group that is dominated by members of the Ku Klux Klan," she said. "When I first proposed building a community center that included a residence hall for homeless colored girls, the board turned my application down. They said Wheatley Institute would serve as a magnet, attracting immoral, shiftless Negro girls and the men that prey on them. In order to secure the board's approval, I promised to keep the girls in line." She turned to look me directly in the eye. "Residents of Wheatley Institute must maintain the highest moral character at all times. And that, my dear Nola, includes staying away from illegal gin joints like the Wham Bam Club."

I had to admit Mrs. Wyatt had a point. Klan members held positions of power in both city and state government. Given the racial climate in Agate, it was a miracle that Mrs. Wyatt had been able to get the welfare board to approve anything that served Agate's Negro population.

"There is another complication," Mrs. Wyatt continued. "Lilly has a benefactor—an anonymous donor who pays Wheatley Institute a generous sum each and every month to take care of Lilly until she turns eighteen. I've never met this person, but their instructions are very explicit. We are to prepare Lilly for adulthood—teach her a viable trade, and find her proper employment. Above all, we are to see to it that Lilly is raised in a safe, wholesome, and morally upright environment."

Mrs. Wyatt took another sip of tea, sighed heavily and continued. "What do you think this donor will say when they find out that Lilly has disappeared? How can I possibly tell them that I have not only lost track of the girl, but have allowed her to loiter about, drinking in a speakeasy? Everything I've worked for in the past ten years will go straight down the drain once the board gets word of this."

"And that's why you haven't contacted the police?" I said.

"The *Agate Daily Chronicle* has a reporter who practically lives at the police station," Mrs. Wyatt replied. "They'd just love a juicy story to splash all over the front page."

"The police are not going to look very hard for a missing colored girl in any case," Aunt Sarah said. "Quite a few of those fellas would be perfectly happy to see all the Negroes in Agate disappear forever."

Mrs. Wyatt nodded her head in agreement. "That's why I followed Eddie Smooth today," she said. "I believe he knows something about Lilly's disappearance. I need to find out what it is."

"What about the other girls at Wheatley Institute?" I asked. "Lilly's friends must know something about where she is."

"Lilly was difficult to get along with at times," Mrs. Wyatt said. "Brenda Washington was her only friend at Wheatley Institute. Brenda swears up and down on a stack of Bibles she doesn't know where Lilly is." She wiped her mouth with a napkin and sighed. "Thanks for listening to my tale of woe," she said. "I'm feeling much better now, certainly well enough to walk to my car. It's parked just a few blocks from here."

Despite these brave words, Mrs. Wyatt's aura was still a weak and wobbly yellow blob. Until Lilly Davidson was found, the woman would not be at peace.

"I've got an idea," I said. "Girls never tell authority figures everything they know, especially in a case like this. But the girls at Wheatley Institute might be willing to talk to a fellow resident, someone who's been in their predicament and understands how their minds work."

Aunt Sarah nodded approvingly. "Why don't you go to the institute tomorrow, Nola Ann? You could spend the night, get to know the girls and ask them questions. You'd be able to get a lot more out of them than Mrs. Wyatt here. After all, you're barely out of your teens your own self."

I sat up straighter in my seat and shot my aunt an aggrieved look. "I'm nearly twenty-one years old," I said crisply, "but I know what you mean. I understand these girls. I know how they think, and I know what they're going through. They might open up to me and tell me something useful."

Mrs. Wyatt nodded thoughtfully. "I would love to know if Lilly has been sneaking out to the Wham Bam Club, and if Eddie Smooth knows where she is. I would be forever in your debt if you could find the girl and persuade her to come back to Wheatley Institute."

"I have to be at work in an hour," I said, "but I'll come out to the institute first thing tomorrow morning. I'll spend a night or two, and see what I can find out."

CHAPTER 3

Half an hour later, wearing a black dress and white pinafore with DELUXE CATERING stitched across the front, I said goodbye to Aunt Sarah and walked to the intersection of Lincoln Avenue and Water Street. I waited at the bus stop for nearly forty minutes as two trolleys passed me without stopping. I was over an hour late for my shift by the time I finally arrived at the offices of the DeLuxe Catering company.

My boss frowned and looked pointedly down at his pocket watch as I walked through the front door. "Where on earth have you been?" he said.

Tall and slender, with thinning gray hair, nut brown skin, and the erect bearing of a former soldier, Edward Layton and his buxom wife, Minty, ran the DeLuxe Catering company with military precision. In the eleven months I'd worked there, I'd never seen Mr. Layton wear anything but a black three-piece suit, even at the height of summer.

"Two streetcars refused to stop for me," I said. "If a white person hadn't been standing next to me when the next trolley arrived, I'd still be waiting."

"That's no excuse for tardiness, young lady," Mr. Layton replied crisply. "You should know by now how the white folks are here in Agate. You're not in New York City anymore."

"Yes sir," I said. "It won't happen again. I'll make sure to leave earlier next time."

"See to it," Mr. Layton said curtly. He picked up a ten-pound sack of flour, threw it over his shoulder, and carried it outside.

"We've got to get a move on," his wife said, and nodded toward a large crate filled with fresh vegetables sitting by the front door. "Take that box out to the truck, Nola."

Minty Layton was as bubbly as her husband was reserved. A short, round woman with a rich brown complexion and an impish smile, Minty loved food almost as much as she loved to talk. When it came to cooking, however, Minty Layton was dead serious. Everything in her kitchen needed to be just so, the countertops spotless, the pots and pans hung up in a certain order, and the knives precisely arranged by size next to the cutting board. Minty took enormous pride in her work and in the business she and her husband had created. As far as I knew, DeLuxe Catering was the only Negro-owned catering company in Southern Illinois.

As we loaded the delivery truck with the food and equipment we needed for tonight's job, Minty was all business. "Mrs. Ratcliffe is having a big to-do at her house tonight. Poor woman's been in a full-on tizzy all day, calling every other minute to make sure we're coming."

Ten minutes later, Minty and I sat squeezed together on the front seat as Mr. Layton piloted his aging Model T delivery truck toward the Ratcliffe mansion. As we wove in and out of the traffic on Main Street, Minty shouted to me over the street noise pouring in through the open window.

"Mrs. Ratcliffe is our best customer," she said. "We've been with her so long, she's almost like family. She's good people, so be sure you mind your *p*'s and *q*'s. Especially during the séance."

"The what?" I said, leaning in closer. I was having trouble hearing her clearly over the sound of the Model T's rumbling engine.

"Séance," Minty repeated, shouting even louder. "That's what she calls them. Ten people sit in a pitch-black room and talk to the dead. That part should be right up your alley, being as your Aunt Sarah works hoodoo." Minty cocked her head and studied me inquisitively. "She tells me you've got what those hoodoo folks call the Sight. Is that true, girl?"

I nodded a yes. I began to see shapes and colors hovering around people's heads the day my husband Will died. At first, I thought I was going crazy. When I moved in with my Aunt Sarah, she assured me the visions were perfectly natural.

"Your husband's death has opened your gateway to the Spirit World," Aunt Sarah told me. "Quite naturally, he wants to make contact with you. Just remember that visions work best when you keep them to yourself until the time is right. You don't go yapping about them all over town."

As I remained silent, Minty Layton nudged me in the ribs and winked.

"No need to say another word, Nola Ann," she said. "Hoodoo folks like you and your Aunt Sarah got secrets you prefer to keep to yourselves. Long as you know how to act around Mrs. Ratcliffe. That's the important thing."

As Mr. Layton's truck labored up the steep hill that led to Vista View Road, we left the clatter and clamor of the city behind. I gazed out the window at the trees in their autumn finery and the vast expanse of the Mississippi river below while Minty chattered on. "Mrs. Ratcliffe is married to one of the richest men in Agate," she told me. "She's always involved in some cause or other. She marched with the suffragettes and got herself arrested at a protest march for demanding that women be allowed to vote. She's also big in the temperance league, so don't even mention the subject of hard liquor when she's around. Mrs. Ratcliffe's biggest passion is these séances. She holds them once a month in her parlor, and always brings us out to serve a fancy dinner beforehand."

As we pulled into Mrs. Ratcliffe's driveway, it was easy to see why Minty was so eager to keep this particular client happy. The Ratcliffe mansion was set at the very top of Vista Bluff, overlooking the Mississippi river and surrounded by a six-foot-tall wrought-iron fence. Everything about the house screamed money, from the gabled roof and leaded windows to the neatly clipped hedges surrounding her manicured lawn.

When the three of us had finished unloading the necessary supplies from our truck, Mr. Layton carried the plates, serving utensils, and warming trays into the dining room as Minty handed me an apron.

"Come in the kitchen and help me get these potatoes peeled," she said. "We're having them au gratin tonight."

"Yes, ma'am," I said. Minty's down-home version of the classic French dish was always a big hit with the clients. In addition to the velvety cream sauce and generous amount of freshly grated cheddar cheese, Minty always spiced up the dish with tiny chunks of hot Cajun sausage, bell peppers, and onion. To be honest, I was looking forward to having a spoonful or two before the serving platters were taken out to the guests.

As Mr. Layton set up the buffet table in the dining room, Minty and I stayed in the kitchen, working in peaceful silence. Mrs. Ratcliffe had instructed us to prepare enough food for thirty hungry people, so there was plenty of peeling and slicing to be done before dropping the potato slices in boiling water for exactly five minutes. As the cooked potato slices cooled, Minty got to work preparing the sauce. A half pound of butter melted slowly in a heavy cast-iron frying pan as she added large handfuls of finely chopped green bell pepper and sweet onion, stirring the mixture until the onions turned translucent.

"Turn on the oven and set it to three-fifty," Minty said. "Then fetch me a quart of milk from the icebox, put it in a saucepan and heat it until it's nearly boiling."

As I heated the milk, Minty added two cups of flour, just a tablespoon at a time, to the butter mixture until it turned a golden brown.

"Hurry up," she snapped. "If the flour gets too dark, I'll have to throw it out and start all over again."

Minty Layton was normally the kindest, most sweet-tempered of souls. But once she stepped into the kitchen, she was not to be messed with. Like any true artist, Minty could be quite temperamental in the act of creating. Her sudden mood swings had upset me at first, but after eleven months of working at DeLuxe Catering, I'd gotten used to Minty's Jekyll-and-Hyde style of employee management.

When the delicate operation of integrating the milk was complete, she added half a pound of mild cheddar cheese, one handful at a time, while I greased a deep casserole and arranged half the potato slices on the bottom. Under Minty's watchful eye, I chopped up a cup of spicy Cajun sausage and spread it on top of the potatoes. When I was finished, Minty covered the entire first layer with the creamy cheese sauce. After we'd repeated the entire procedure to create the second layer, she sprinkled a dash of paprika and a fine layer of breadcrumbs on top and slid the casserole into the oven.

Once the dish was safely in the oven, we both heaved a sigh of relief.

Minty wiped her face on her apron and called to her husband in the dining room: "How's the buffet setup coming out there, Edward? You need Nola to help you with anything?"

"I am just about ready," he replied. "I'll be in in a minute to fetch the rest of the dishes."

"All right," Minty said, and turned toward me. "Thank goodness Mrs. Ratcliffe didn't wander in and distract us with all her talking while we were fixing the sauce. We've done her catering for so long, the woman thinks she's part of our family. If she does come in here, smile and agree with whatever she says, then leéave the rest to me."

An hour later, Mrs. Ratcliff wandered into the kitchen. Our employer was a majestic white woman nearly six feet tall with a pile of unnaturally bright red hair held by a diamond clip and gathered in a towering bun on top of her head.

"We've had another cancellation," Mrs. Ratcliffe announced. "However, tonight's séance will continue as scheduled, with Professor Samuel Pierce as our guest medium."

"Yes, ma'am," Minty replied.

"Professor Samuel Pierce is the most famous Negro Spiritualist in the country," Mrs. Ratcliffe continued. "Cancellations or not, I intend to host the first interracial séance ever held in the City of Agate, Illinois."

"That's just fine, Mrs. Ratcliffe," Minty replied with a bland smile. If I weren't psychic, I would have missed the small flash of red light that rippled through Minty's aura as our employer spoke. In Agate, interracial activities of any sort could spell trouble, not only for Mrs. Ratcliffe, but for Negroes foolish enough to associate themselves with her radical ideas.

"Colored and white spiritualists have worshipped separately for decades," Mrs. Ratcliffe said. "I believe it's time for a change. Apparently, some of my friends do not agree. Since I announced that Professor Samuel Pierce would be the medium this evening, ten of my regular guests have cancelled on some flimsy pretext or other."

She picked up the copy of the *Agate Daily Chronicle* lying on the kitchen table. "I suspect they've been paying attention to that bigoted windbag Timothy Gonsails. Why the *Chronicle* wastes so much ink on that man is beyond me." Mrs. Ratcliffe opened the paper and began to read:

"Local minister addresses Ku Klux Klan rally at Bright Horizons Spiritualist Temple.
"The Reverend Timothy Gonsails was the principal speaker at the '100% American Rally' hosted by the Agate Klavern of the Ku Klux Klan. At an event billed as 'a Fiery Cross Ice Cream social' on the lawn of the Bright Horizons Spiritualist Temple, Gonsails invited his audience to 'learn the real truth about Spiritualism.' Angels and Spirits support the hooded order in their work, he told an enthusiastic crowd of over 200 listeners. 'Christ was the first Klansman and was crucified for saying what He believed,' Rev. Gonsails stated."

Mrs. Ratcliffe scowled and tossed the newspaper on the kitchen table. "The Klan may be on the rise for the moment," she said. "But if anyone thinks I will be put off by a few no-shows, they've got another think coming."

"Let me take that for you, ma'am," Minty said. She picked up the offending paper by the tips of her fingers and dropped it in the rubbish bin. As she did so, a portly white man with muttonchop whiskers and a ruddy face strode into the kitchen. When he saw Minty Layton, he broke into a smile.

"Good to have you back at the house again, Minty," he said. "I can't wait to dig into some of your fabulous au gratin potatoes tonight."

"My pleasure, Mr. Ratcliffe," Minty said, answering his smile with one of her own. "You remember Nola, don't you?"

Mr. Ratcliffe nodded pleasantly in my direction, then turned to his wife. "I've been looking all over for you, Portia. Your friend Harriet Wallaby is on the telephone. She wants to know what time we're starting this evening."

"Did you say we'll begin at nine o'clock as always?" Mrs. Ratcliffe asked.

"I did not," Mr. Ratcliffe retorted. "I told her the truth, that I had absolutely no idea."

Mrs. Ratcliffe put a hand to her forehead and sighed dramatically. "Bayard, you are absolutely hopeless," she proclaimed, and swept out of the kitchen as her husband trailed along behind her.

When both of our employers were out of earshot, Minty Layton shook her head.

"This interracial séance thing is risky business," she said. "Doesn't that woman know there was a lynching in Agate not two years ago? There are a lot of white folks here who don't care to see race mixing in any shape or form."

"You have to admire her courage," I said. "If somebody doesn't speak up, things will never change." Agate, Illinois, was a backward, Dixie-assed town, without question. In case I'd had any doubts on that score, my inability to hail a streetcar earlier that day had provided a stark reminder of this fact.

Minty shook her head and said, "You may be right, but trouble is bad for business, and I've got a business to run. Speaking of which, you better get out to the dining room and help Edward get the warming trays set up."

CHAPTER 4

Mrs. Ratcliffe had instructed Minty Layton to prepare food for thirty people. When I walked into the dining room in my black dress, frilly white cap, and white pinafore apron, only four guests nibbled on the buffet of ham and au gratin potatoes laid out on the table.

Our employer's husband, Mr. Bayard Ratcliffe, stood in the center of the room, talking to a slim blonde with bobbed hair wearing a scandalously short dress. I could tell that the young man standing next to her was the blonde's date by the possessive way she clung to his arm.

When I returned to the kitchen, I asked Minty about the girl. "Her name is Abigail Everleigh, and she's Mr. Ratcliffe's niece," Minty told me. "The gal's a regular flapper. She chain-smokes cigarettes and carries a small flask of whiskey in her purse. She's always arguing with Mrs. Ratcliffe. You be polite, but stay clear of her if you can."

As I carried a tray of cups filled with hot apple cider into the dining room, I studied Abigail Everleigh discreetly. From the looks of things, Mrs. Ratcliffe's niece had already taken several belts from that flask of hers. Her voice was loud, and her gait unsteady.

"You are just too funny, Uncle Bayard," she said, clinging tipsily to her escort. "It's not true what they say, you know. There's nothing boyish about having short hair. Today's young men find the flapper look quite attractive. Isn't that right, Joe?"

With a wicked grin she turned and gave her date a loud, wet kiss on the lips.

"Va-va-voom!" he said. He smacked his lips hungrily, then pulled the girl close for a second kiss.

Mr. Ratcliffe turned beet red as the couple kissed. "We've not been introduced, young man," he said. "Have we met before?"

Suddenly remembering his manners, Miss Everleigh's gentleman friend extended his hand. "Joe Quincy," he said. His voice was high in pitch, almost girlish, and held the trace of an accent I didn't quite recognize. "Pleased to make your acquaintance. Abbie's told me a great deal about you. So has Congressman Skelton."

Bayard Ratcliffe lifted a bushy eyebrow. "You have met the Congressman?"

"He is an old family friend," Joe Quincy said. "He and my father were roommates at Harvard. The Congressman visits us whenever he's in Boston."

So that's where he's from, I thought. I could tell from his la-di-dah, patrician-sounding accent that the man was not from around here.

"Joe's spending the autumn in Agate to help with Congressman Skelton's campaign," Abigail said proudly. "I'm not sure exactly what he does, but he's a bigwig of some sort."

Joe Quincy frowned. "Don't exaggerate, Abigail," he said. Although he continued to smile, there was a touch of asperity in his tone. "At the moment, I'm just an intern on Congressman Skelton's public relations team. It's a part-time job, but I'm expecting a promotion any day now."

As Joe Quincy spoke, a tall, angular woman entered the room, accompanied by a tall and red-faced gentleman who looked old enough to be her father. Her sharp features and gloomy expression were offset by the bright crimson of her dress.

"Good evening, Bayard," she intoned in a deep and somber voice. "I thought you would be out at your factory in Carbondale this week. I'm so glad you could join us for the séance this evening."

"Harriet Wallaby, as I live and breathe," Mr. Bayard Ratcliffe exclaimed. "You're looking well this evening. You and Richard, both." He kissed the woman on the cheek, then shook Richard's hand. "Have you met my niece Abigail? I've been acting in loco parentis for her since her parents passed away last year. I'm keeping a strict eye out while she completes her coursework at Agate Female College."

"Don't be too strict, Uncle Bayard. Please," Abigail said, with a mischievous smile.

She snapped her fingers and waved in my direction. "Yoohoo," she called out. "Would you be a dear colored girl and bring me some more of that heavenly cider concoction?"

As I handed her a fresh cup of cider from my tray, Mr. Ratcliffe continued. "I have to be a little strict, dear. After all, it's what your dear mother and father would have wanted me to do, God rest their souls."

"Long as you don't keep me from my nights at the Wham Bam Club," she said gaily.

"The what?" Mr. Ratcliffe looked more than a bit panicked.

"The Wham Bam Club, silly. It's utterly the place in Agate. The hottest Negro jazz joint in Southern Illinois. I bet your serving girl here knows all about it," she said, jerking her thumb in my direction. "Isn't that right, colored girl?"

"Don't be rude, Abigail," Mr. Ratcliffe said stiffly. "Her name is Nola."

"Whatever," the girl replied. She shrugged and turned to face me. "Tell this old fogey the Wham Bam Club is the best place to hear hot Negro jazz. Am I not right?"

"If you say so, miss," I replied. It was easy to see why Minty Layton had warned me to avoid talking to this girl. She was clearly trouble, with a capital T. Apparently, Abigail Everleigh went to the Wham Bam Club often. Could she have seen Lilly Davidson there? As I contemplated this possibility, Abigail hiccupped loudly, then giggled.

Mrs. Harriet Wallaby studied the girl for a moment, then gave Mr. Ratcliffe a sympathetic pat on the arm. "You're going have your work cut out for you," she said drily. She took her husband by the arm. "Come, Richard. Let's see what's on offer at the buffet table."

At precisely nine o'clock, Mrs. Ratcliffe appeared, dressed for her performance as the evening's resident mystic in a purple floor-length evening gown that complimented her flaming red hair.

"Now's the time for us to begin," she announced. "There will be no talking, eating, or smoking once we enter the séance room." She leveled an icy stare at Abigail Everleigh. "Absolute decorum must be observed out of respect for the Spirit World and our visiting medium. Please act accordingly."

"Yes, ma'am," Abigail muttered sarcastically.

As the six participants walked through the large double doors that led to Mrs. Ratcliffe's séance room, Minty Layton turned to me and whispered, "Mrs. Ratcliffe wants us to stay in the séance room in case anybody needs anything. But no matter what happens, do not react. Understand?"

I followed Minty into the séance room. It took a minute for my eyes to adjust to the dim light. Three tall candles set in a silver candelabra illuminated the room, while an antique grandfather clock ticked away loudly in one corner. The other corner of the room held a floor-to-ceiling bookshelf stuffed with leather-bound volumes. In the center of the room stood a heavy mahogany table surrounded by ten ornately carved wooden chairs. Facing the table, twenty additional chairs had been arranged in two rows, presumably to accommodate additional spectators.

Motioning for me to follow her, Minty positioned herself next to the lacquered Chinese cabinet that occupied the back wall. We were close enough to be summoned if needed, yet far enough away to be discreet. After the participants took their seats, the door on the opposite side of the room swung open to reveal a heavy-set colored man with a dark complexion, a thick handlebar mustache and large, commanding eyes. His aura was huge, a large and brilliantly colored violet oval that radiated out into the room.

As the man took his seat at the table, Mrs. Ratcliffe remained standing, her diamond hair clip sparkling in the candlelight. "Welcome to my Spirit Gathering," she said. "This is the first time I've had a colored medium sit in my circle. I can assure you that Professor Samuel Pierce will not disappoint. He gave me an amazing reading when I sat for him in Carbondale last month. I trust you will treat our guest with the courtesy and respect for which our fair city is known." She paused for a moment, giving each member of the group a stern look.

"Welcome to our circle, Professor," she said. "We are ready to begin."

After a moment of silence, Professor Samuel Pierce took a deep breath, looked around the table, and spread his arms wide.

"In the world of Spirit, there is neither Greek nor Roman,

neither master nor slave," he intoned. As befitting his status as the most well-known colored medium in America, Professor Samuel Pierce wore a black three-piece suit that must have cost more money than I would make in a year. A neatly folded white handkerchief protruded from his left breast pocket.

"All people are equal in the world of Spirit," he continued. "Tonight, I will be your messenger. I can already feel your deceased loved ones in the Spirit World gathering close. Let us sing a song to welcome them."

> *"There's a Sweet Spirit in this place*
> *The love of Summerland is near*
> *Join us Sweet Spirits*
> *Loved ones from beyond the Veil, Grace us.*
> *We are ready. We are waiting. Come, Spirit, come.*
> *We are ready, we are waiting.*
> *Come Spirit, come."*

Reluctantly at first, but then, with increasing enthusiasm, the rest of the participants joined in the refrain:

> *"We are ready. We are waiting. Come, Spirit, come."*

After repeating the refrain several times, the group settled into silence. The only sound to be heard in the dimly lit room was the ticking of the grandfather clock in the corner. Suddenly, I began to hear what sounded like an army of hornets buzzing in my left ear. Startled, I looked around, but no one else seemed to have noticed the sound. As my psychic sight kicked in, gauzy circles of light began to form in front of Harriet Wallaby's head, and a white, mist-like apparition entered the room. Slowly, a ghostly figure began to take shape in the flickering light.

Professor Pierce nodded his head and said quietly, "Someone's mother is in the room with us. She is elderly and wears an old-fashioned black bonnet. This mother wants to thank her daughter for the Bible she slipped into her coffin at the funeral. Does this make sense to anyone here?"

Harriet Wallaby's face turned dead white. "How could you possibly know that?" she said. "I waited until everyone else at the funeral had left. Nobody saw me put it there."

Professor Samuel Pierce nodded. "Your mother's spirit has come to greet you," he said. "Surely you can feel it."

As he spoke, the nebulous light in front of Harriet Wallaby's head grew larger.

"I do feel something," she said. Tears streamed down her face as she asked in a small, little girl's voice: "Is it really you, Mama?"

Professor Samuel Pierce rocked gently from side to side as he spoke. "The ring you lost last winter will be found in the left-hand pocket of your sable coat. It is the ring your husband gave you to celebrate your tenth anniversary. You told him it was at the jeweler's for repair when you were unable to find it."

"By Jove," Richard Wallaby muttered. "You mean that sapphire has been lost all this time?"

As Harriet Wallaby stared at Professor Pierce in open-mouthed surprise, the bright circle of energy in front of her began to fade.

"Your mother's love for you will never die," Professor Pierce said. "She wants you to look for her in the early mornings as you brush your hair. Her spirit sits in the maple tree just outside your window. You cannot see her, but she is there, just the same."

The medium's voice trailed off into silence. Seconds later, Abigail Everleigh's raucous laugh startled us all.

"This whole thing is a humbug," Abigail said loudly. "Can't you see he's making it up?" She crossed her arms over her chest and glared. "Bring *me* a message, Professor Pierce. I dare you."

"Hush, Abigail," Mrs. Ratcliffe said irritably. "Spirit is not a servant to be summoned on command. If our medium has a message for you, he'll call on you when he's ready."

Professor Samuel Pierce was now deep in trance, his eyes rolling upward as though searching for answers on the ceiling. Suddenly, he sat upright and stared at the gray cloud of psychic energy blossoming over Abigail's left shoulder.

"Your mother is with us, young lady," he told her. "She thinks you are walking down a very dark road. Tread carefully, lest you lose your way and fall."

Abigail Everleigh gave the medium a knowing smirk. "What's your gimmick, Prof?" she said. The cloud of energy around her grew larger as she spoke. "Did Portia Ratcliffe put you up to this?"

Mrs. Ratcliffe scowled. "Don't be impertinent, Abigail. There are Spirits among us."

The girl glared at Mrs. Ratcliffe and shook her head. "I don't believe you," she said. "I don't believe any of this. Not for a single minute."

Professor Samuel Pierce began to hum quietly, as if lost in another world. "The Spirits wish to offer the young lady a message," he announced. "To prove their existence, they will now lift our séance table and turn it to the left three times. Stand back, please."

Richard and Harriet Wallaby pushed their chairs back and stood, as did the rest of the guests. After a minute, even Abigail staggered to her feet.

Only Joe Quincy remained seated. Arms crossed over his chest, he glared angrily at Professor Pierce. "Maybe you can fool the others, but you can't pull the wool over my eyes, Professor." He smirked and looked up at his date. "Don't fall for this voodoo hokum, Abbie. The whole thing is just a hoax."

"Quiet, you foolish boy," Bayard Ratcliffe said angrily. "The Spirits are working."

All at once the heavy mahogany table lifted a foot off the ground, hovered in midair and spun around three times. I had never seen anything like this before. Along with the rest of the participants, I gasped in astonishment as the table hovered in midair for a few seconds before returning gently to its original position on the floor.

Joe Quincy jumped to his feet, his thin face tight with anger. "You must take me for some kind of fool," he hissed in his high-pitched, aristocratic voice. "I'll have you know that I am a *Quincy*, Professor. We are not taken in by bunco artists. I've seen better shows at the circus." His eyes glittered with rage as he took hold of Abigail's elbow. "Nobody pulls the wool over Joe Quincy's eyes, understand? *Nobody.*"

When Abigail continued to stand motionless, Joe tightened his grip on her elbow. "Time to skedaddle, Abbie," he said. "If we hurry, we can still catch Eddie Smooth's first set at the Wham Bam Club."

Could it be a coincidence that Eddie Smooth's name had been mentioned twice that evening? From the way my psychic senses were behaving, I doubted it. The Spirits were letting me know I was on the right track. First thing tomorrow morning, I would go out to Wheatley Institute, talk to the residents, and find out what they knew.

As Joe Quincy led Abigail out of the séance room, the girl looked more than a little confused. Bayard Ratcliffe followed the couple into the hallway, berating them in a loud voice.

"The two of you have spoiled our séance," Mr. Ratcliffe shouted. "And what's worse, you have shown disrespect to my wife and to my guests."

Richard and Harriet Wallaby exchanged a look. "Perhaps it's time we went home," Mrs. Wallaby said.

"Indeed," Richard answered. He stood, and offered Harriet his arm. "Unfortunate business, this. Portia Ratcliffe will be mortified."

After the couple had left the room, Minty Layton turned to me and rolled her eyes. "I've been to a few of these séances, but never one this crazy," she whispered. "We might as well start putting the food away. Doesn't look like these folks are going to eat anything more tonight." With a small shrug, she turned and walked back into the living room.

I started to follow her, but noticed that Samuel Pierce was still in trance, rocking back and forth in his chair with his eyes closed.

"Are you all right, Professor Pierce?" I said, gently touching the sleeve of his jacket. "Can I get you anything?"

The medium opened his eyes and looked around, as if seeing his surroundings for the first time. "Nola Ann Jackson," he said, fixing me with an eerie stare. "You have the gift of second sight, just like your Aunt Sarah. Your husband, Will, sends you greetings from the Spirit World. He wants you to know that he's all right, and that he will always love you."

There were so many questions I wanted to ask, but when I opened my mouth, not a single word came out.

"A young girl is missing and her life is at stake," Professor Pierce continued. "Without your help, she may die. But be careful. Once you enter her world, there will be no turning back." As Professor Pierce spoke, I felt the room grow ice-cold. "Heed my words," he continued. "There is danger and trouble ahead, Nola Ann Jackson. You could lose your life."

Without another word, Professor Samuel Pierce pushed back from the table and walked out of the room.

Shivers raced up my spine as I stood alone in the empty séance room. Had I really just received a warning from my dead husband? Was my life really in danger? What on earth had just happened?

Whatever it was, I needed to snap out of it and get back to work. I shook my head vigorously and headed back into the living room where Richard and Harriet Wallaby were in the process of saying their goodbyes to Mr. and Mrs. Ratcliffe. As I made my way to the kitchen, I watched Samuel Pierce collect his coat from Mr. Layton and slip quietly out the front door.

For the rest of the evening I went through my tasks as though I were sleepwalking.

"You all right, Nola Ann?" Minty said.

"Sure," I said weakly. "Just tired, I guess."

It was after midnight by the time I got home. I'd hoped to share my strange experience with Aunt Sarah, but she had fallen sound asleep in her favorite rocking chair in front of the fire. *I'll talk to her about it tomorrow*, I thought, and tiptoed down the hallway to my bedroom in the spare room next to the kitchen.

I was exhausted, yet at the same time I felt strangely stimulated. Some of Professor Pierce's spirit message was clearly about Lilly Davidson, the girl who had disappeared from Phyllis Wheatley Institute. The professor had said I would be putting my life in danger. As I contemplated this unnerving prediction, I also thought about the other message he'd given me. On August 10, 1918, my husband, Will Jackson, marched off to war. As he boarded the train with the rest of his unit, I saw a gray mist hovering over his head. I tried desperately to talk him out of going, but he wouldn't hear of it. He'd been so proud to be a Harlem Hellfighter—determined to prove his all-Negro regiment could lick the Germans as well as any white battalion on earth. From the moment I saw that mist, I was unable to shake the sensation that my husband would not return home alive, and, of course, he hadn't.

When I thought about what Professor Pierce had told me, I felt a certain comfort in knowing Will was doing all right up in the Spirit World.

"I miss you, Will," I whispered, and blew him a kiss. As if in reply, I felt something brush against my face. The sensation only lasted for a second or two, but it was enough. Whatever the future held, I knew that Will Jackson was with me, watching over me from the other side of life. Caught between apprehension and excitement, I tossed and turned restlessly before drifting off to sleep just before dawn.

CHAPTER 5

The next morning, Aunt Sarah was not surprised to hear that I had received a psychic message about a missing girl from Professor Pierce. "The Spirits are concerned about her, Nola," she said. She paused and took a sip of coffee before continuing. "The Spirits are concerned about you, too. There's some very nasty energy floating around this Wham Bam place. Lots of people going in and out of there, each one bringing his own demon. Be sure you put some Protection Oil on your head and across your belly before you do any more investigating."

After a hearty breakfast of black coffee, bacon, and hominy grits, I packed a small valise, took the streetcar to Wells Coal Mine at the end of the line, and hiked the remaining three miles to Wheatley Institute. Biting gusts of wind tugged at my thin woolen coat, making me wish I had worn something heavier.

I had initially thought to bring the beaver coat my husband, Will, gave me for our first anniversary, but Aunt Sarah cautioned me against it. "You don't want these girls thinking you've got money," she'd said. "Remember. You are going in there as just another poor, homeless colored girl, fresh from the country and down on her luck. If you give the appearance that you might be different from the rest, no one is going to talk to you."

Phyllis Wheatley Institute for Colored Girls was located ten miles from downtown Agate in a fortress-like building made of red granite. It was bordered by a white picket fence and surrounded by open fields on three sides. Behind the building, thick underbrush and a ragged line of pine trees concealed the murky waters of the Pigeon River. The opposite side of the river appeared uninhabited. The only building I could see was a ramshackle wooden farmhouse in dire need of paint.

As I approached the Wheatley Institute, I was flooded by memories of the time I'd spent there four years ago. After my parents died, Mrs. Wyatt brought me to live at the institute so that I could finish elementary school, learn enough about cooking and sewing to make a living, and maybe even go on to college someday. Once I got there, however, I'd been nothing but trouble, cutting classes, staying out late, and generally making a ruckus. When Will Jackson asked me to elope with him to New York City, I thought I was leaving behind Agate and the confining rules of Wheatley Institute forever. Never in my wildest dreams did I imagine that I would ever return. As I walked up the freshly scrubbed steps, I felt a shiver that had nothing whatsoever to do with temperature. I squared my shoulders, took a deep breath, and rang the bell.

The woman who opened the door was nearly six feet tall, with sharp angular features and skin the deep brown color of chewing tobacco. Her hair was pulled back in a severe bun, and she wore an unfashionable black dress that reached nearly to the tops of her shoes.

"Good afternoon, Miss Jackson," she said in a deep, rumbling voice. "I am Maybelle Clark, Mrs. Wyatt's assistant." When I'd lived at the institute, Mrs. Wyatt had run the whole place by herself. Maybelle Clark was definitely not the schoolmarm type I would have expected at a place like this. Her hand was rough and calloused, and her grip was firm, almost to the point of being painful, as I shook her hand. "Mrs. Wyatt tells me you are here to mingle with the girls and to find out what's become of Lilly Davidson," she said.

"Yes," I replied. "My plan is to stay at least one night here, get other girls to talk to me, and see what I can find out."

Miss Clark gave me an icy stare.

"Mrs. Wyatt is a kind and generous woman," she said, "I am not. You're here to find out what happened to Lilly. I expect results, and I expect them on the double. And be discreet about it. Word gets around why you're here, I will see that you regret it. Got it?"

I glared right back at her. "There is no need to threaten me, Miss Clark. I have promised Mrs. Wyatt that I will do my best."

"I was not here when you were a resident at Wheatley Institute," she replied. "Perhaps if I were, you would not have escaped from here so easily. We run a tight ship here, Miss Jackson. See to it that you do not besmirch the name of Phyllis Wheatley Institute during your stay here." She held my gaze for a long minute, then gestured for me to step inside and closed the door. "The girls are just sitting down to lunch," she said. "Follow me."

As we walked down the long hallway lined with portraits of Frederick Douglass, Booker T. Washington, Mary McCleod Bethune, and other Negroes of distinction, the sound of our footsteps clattered against the bare wooden floor.

The dining room was at the end of the hall. It was long and narrow, with two windows that looked out onto a small vegetable garden. As I took my seat at the dining room table, nine teenaged girls of varying ages and sizes studied me with intense curiosity. No one spoke as a matronly woman in a white uniform ladled soup into our bowls.

Must be a new rule, I thought. No talking until after grace. When my grandmother lived with us years ago, we'd had to follow a similar regimen. With a look that warned the girls to stay silent or else, Miss Clark took her seat at the head of the table and began to pray: "Heavenly Father. Thank you for this bread that we take today. Thank you for the breath in our bodies and the strength in our hands. May we be forever grateful for the great sacrifice of your beloved Son, Jesus Christ, who gave his life that we might be saved. Let us stay true to his wishes, living a life of blameless adherence to his Holy Scripture in thought, word, and deed. Bless this food and bless our humble home. Amen."

I spooned down my soup, augmenting it with a roll from the bread plate in front of me.

"You from around here?" one girl said, peering at me suspiciously. She had long braids, buck teeth, and a tan complexion. "Mrs. Wyatt usually makes new girls wait till the evening before she lets them in. How come you get to walk in here in the middle of the day?"

Miss Clark gave the girl a disapproving look.

"Don't be impertinent, Minerva," she said crisply. "Why Mrs. Wyatt chooses to do or not do anything is absolutely none of your business."

"Yes, ma'am," Minerva answered. The gray cloud of psychic energy hovering around Minerva's head told me the girl was far from satisfied with Miss Cark's response. Just the kind of girl who might know something about Lilly's disappearance, I thought. I made a mental note to talk further with her when Miss Clark was not around.

"How long you gonna stay here?" another girl asked. She wore a plain dress made of blue gingham with a matching bow tied around a frizzy crown of dark brown hair. She looked to be one of the younger girls in the bunch, perhaps no more than thirteen.

"I'm leaving as quick as I can," I told her. "Got some relatives up in New York City who've promised to send for me soon."

When we were finished eating, Miss Maybelle Clark stood up and clapped her hands.

"It's time for sewing class, ladies," she said, then turned to me. "Leave that valise with me, Nola. I will make sure it's taken upstairs to the dormitory."

As I joined the rest of the girls and walked down the hall toward the sewing room, Miss Clark stood by the dining room door, watching. *That woman really doesn't like me*, I thought. *Good thing I'm not planning to stay here very long.*

A weak October sun filtered through the thin curtains covering the three large windows at the back of the room. Along one wall was a large blackboard. Ten sewing tables were arrayed in two neat rows along the center of the room. Next to each table was a wicker basket filled with white muslin.

Standing in front of the blackboard was an older Negro woman with thinning gray hair.

"Good afternoon, girls," she said.

"Good afternoon, Miss Jones," the girls chorused in reply.

"Please sit down. We have a lot of work to do this afternoon." As the girls took their places, I stood hesitantly at the back of the room.

"You sit there," the sewing teacher told me, and pointed to a table by the window.

As I took my seat, the girl at the table next to me gave me a friendly smile. "My name's Brenda Washington," she whispered. "This is my best friend Lilly's place. You can sit in her seat but you'll have to move when she gets back, okay?"

"You have my word," I told her solemnly. Brenda Washington was the girl Mrs. Wyatt told me about yesterday, the girl who was Lilly's only friend at Wheatley Institute. She had a light tan complexion, tightly curled reddish-brown hair, and freckles all over her face. Although Brenda Washington, like all the other residents of Wheatley Institute, was no doubt broke, homeless, and down on her luck, her aura radiated a cheery orange. When questioned by Mrs. Wyatt about Lilly's disappearance, Brenda claimed she had no idea where the girl was. Was Brenda telling the truth?

As I made a mental note to talk with Brenda further, our sewing teacher began her lecture. "Proper technique is the key to producing a quality product," she said in a clear, cultured voice. "The needle must be inserted at a forty-five-degree angle." She gestured with her hand to demonstrate the correct position. "Failure to do this will result in crooked stitching, which in turn will result in wasted time and fabric."

As she continued her lecture, my mind drifted back to the days when I'd been a resident here. "Colored girls who can sew are in high demand as seamstresses," Mrs. Wyatt had told me. "Something to earn you extra money while you finish your schooling here." Mrs. Wyatt was always on me about the importance of education, a subject that held little or no interest for me at the time. Nor was I thrilled with the idea of working as a seamstress. I'd hated sewing class when I was made to take it four years ago. Lining up all those teeny, tiny stitches in a row, making sure they were all the same size and evenly spaced. I found the whole process tedious in the extreme. I gazed out the window and allowed my mind to drift. I needed to find a time when I could speak to the girls alone, away from the watchful eye of Miss Clark. Surely there was time put aside during the day for recreation?

I was pondering my options when I suddenly noticed the sewing teacher standing directly in front of me.

"Why are you not sewing, Miss Jackson?" she said sharply. "Is there a problem?"

"No, ma'am," I said, and picked up my sewing needle. Brenda Washington giggled and rolled her eyes, but stopped when the teacher speared her with a look that would have melted the North Pole.

"The handkerchiefs you are embroidering will be given to the generous donors who support this institution at our fundraising gala next Sunday," she said. "They must be flawless. I expect you each to have finished three of them before supper this evening. Is that clear?"

"Yes, Miss Jones," we replied.

Dinner that evening was a stringy roast supplemented by a large mountain of mashed potatoes. Sitting at the head of the table, Miss Clark told each girl to share one thing she had learned during the day. Minerva Williams, the buck-toothed girl, spoke about the importance of matching the correct thread to each kind of fabric when sewing. "Your work will be sloppy otherwise," she said. "Miss Jones says that sloppy work is the sign of a sloppy mind."

"Quite right," Miss Clark said. As I began to lift a forkful of potatoes to my mouth, she turned to me. "What about you, Nola?" she said. "Tell us what you've learned today."

As she fixed me with a challenging stare, I put down my fork and fumbled for something appropriate to say. Why was this woman picking on me? She knew I had not come to Wheatley Institute to learn anything except the whereabouts of Lilly Davidson.

At a loss for words, I decided the best thing to do was to be honest. "I haven't learned very much so far," I told her. "I plan to learn something new tomorrow."

"Humph," Miss Clark said. "I certainly hope so."

When we'd finished our dinner, Miss Clark told us to gather in the parlor for what she described as the "evening social hour." The minute I walked into the room, I was flooded with memories. When I lived at Wheatley Institute four years ago, the parlor had always felt claustrophobic and overheated. The furniture was essentially the same as I remembered—three overstuffed sofas and two aging armchairs arranged in a semi-circle facing the gas fire. A battered Chickering upright piano stood along the wall, and a picture of Mary Church Terrell, the pioneering Negro educator, hung over the fireplace. The only thing new was the four-foot-tall walnut RCA radio console standing in the corner next to the piano.

As we took our seats, Mrs. Wyatt walked into the room. "As you can see, we have a new girl with us," she said. "For those who have not yet met her, her name is Nola Ann Jackson."

After a smattering of applause, Mrs. Wyatt took a seat in the armchair next to the gas fire, and told the girls to introduce themselves to me one at a time. Yesterday, Mrs. Wyatt had given me the names of the three other girls who'd accompanied Lilly Davidson to the poetry reading the night she disappeared. As the girls lined up to speak to me, I decided to focus on getting to know these girls first.

Marcia and Minerva Williams were the first of the trio to introduce themselves. The two girls were twins—both thin, with buck teeth and narrow eyes. Even as they said hello, I got the distinct sense they were not interested in making new friends. They barely bothered to shake my hand, and neither girl looked me in the eye. Had they been equally unfriendly toward Lilly Davidson?

Darlette Wilson rounded out the trio of girls who'd come to the poetry reading with Lilly. Unlike the twins, she seemed friendly. She gave my hand a warm squeeze and whispered "welcome" in a low, melodious voice. As I met the other six residents of Wheatley Institute, I tried to get a sense of which one might have known Lilly best. Betsey, Myra, and Helen were young and giggly. It seemed unlikely that Lilly would have brought them into her confidence. Ditto for Nancy, who carried a small leather Bible in her left hand and made it a point to sit next to Mrs. Wyatt on the sofa.

By the time I'd met all nine girls, their names and faces ran together in a blur. I tried to tune in to each girl with my psychic senses, but quickly became overwhelmed. When the introductions were finished, Mrs. Wyatt asked Brenda Washington, my new acquaintance from sewing class, to stand.

"Brenda is our resident musician, Nola," she explained. "The girl can play just about anything, as long as it's wholesome and uplifting, of course. It is our custom to sing together every evening after dinner. I hope that you'll join us."

With a mischievous smile lighting up her freckled face, Brenda Washington sat down at the piano and struck a celebratory chord. "Come on, everyone. Let's show Nola what we're made of. Sing along to the songs you know," Brenda said gaily. "And tap your foot to the ones you don't."

After a rousing hour of belting out old favorites like "Hail, Hail, the Gang's All Here," "I'm Always Chasing Rainbows," and "Yankee Doodle Dandy," even Miss Clark was nodding her head in time with the music, her knitting needles clacking as she worked her way around the arm of the sweater she was working on.

"I've picked all the songs so far," Brenda said. "Nola, would you like to sing something?"

As the rest of the girls clapped and whistled approvingly, Mrs. Wyatt gave me an encouraging nod. "Yes, Nola Ann. Sing us a song."

I stood up, cleared my throat, and launched into an off-key version of a raunchy song called "Hot Dog Blues." I knew it would infuriate Mrs. Wyatt, who detested any kind of popular music, but I hoped the song would win me points with the girls, particularly the rebellious ones most likely to know something about Lilly's disappearance.

"Yo' sausage is hot and greasy," I sang. "Slide it in my bun. This little girl is hungry, gonna lick it till the juices run."

Before I could finish the first verse, Mrs. Wyatt stood up and glared at me. "We do not sing that lowdown devilish music here," she said sternly. "As it is only your first day with us, I will excuse you on the grounds of ignorance." If she was aware that I'd chosen the song deliberately to ingratiate myself with the girls, she did not let on.

Miss Clark shot me a pointed stare. "Remember what I said to you this morning, young lady," she said. She put away her knitting and stood. "It's time you girls went to bed. You've got a big day tomorrow." She turned to Brenda Washington. "I've taken Nola's valise upstairs. Assist her with her things, Brenda. Show her where to hang her towel and which bed to sleep in."

As we walked up the staircase to the upstairs dormitory, Brenda whispered in my ear: "Don't mind that old battle-axe, Nola. I love the blues. If you promise not to tell, I'll show you a place where you can hear all the music you want and then some."

I began to reply, but she put a finger to her lips. "Not now," she told me. "Wait till you hear the clock chime midnight. Meet me in the bathroom, and bring your coat and shoes."

At nine o'clock, Miss Clark turned off the lights in the dormitory and retired downstairs. Strains of the nightly radio broadcast from the New York Philharmonic drifted through the floorboards, lulling my roommates off to sleep. Gentle snores could be heard coming from the corner where Marcia and Minerva slept. Darlette Wilson was the next to doze off, mumbling something about "Freddy" before settling into a restless sleep.

As the grandfather clock downstairs struck midnight, I slipped my feet over the side of the bed and crept across the bare wooden floor toward the doorway. As I passed Brenda's bed, I noticed with surprise that it was already empty. Holding my shoes in one hand and my coat in the other, I slipped out of the dormitory, scurried down the hallway and into the bathroom.

Brenda Washington, dressed in a threadbare cotton sack dress, a thin wool coat and serviceable black boots, was waiting for me. Flashing me a cautionary look, she raised the sash of the window overlooking the back garden and put her leg over the side.

It was only a short drop to the garden below. When I heard her land with a soft *thump* on the muddy flower bed below, I followed Brenda out the window.

"What about the window?" I whispered. "Won't anyone notice it's open?"

My fellow escapee shook her head. "We'll be back before daylight. The doors are locked but we can climb up the trellis and scoot back in the window. No one will ever know." She frowned and looked up at the moon. "Wish there was a bit more light out here, but we'll find our way well enough. The Wham Bam Club is just the other side of the Pigeon River. We're strictly forbidden to go there, of course, but you only live once. If we hurry, we can still catch Eddie Smooth and the St. Louis Stompers before they finish their set."

Bingo, I thought to myself. My investigation was already halfway to success. I'd learned that at least some girls were definitely sneaking out of Wheatley Institute, and exactly how they'd eluded detection so far. As the two of us scrambled over the rutted fields behind Wheatley Institute, Brenda told me that she and Lilly had made this same trip several times. She paused at the top of the riverbank to catch her breath. Bright lights glowed from the ramshackle farmhouse I had spotted on the opposite side of the creek earlier that day. "That's it," she said. "Isn't it beautiful?"

It hardly looked beautiful to me, but I was not going to argue. "How are we going to get across the water?" I asked.

"Oh ye of little faith." Brenda giggled. "Follow me and all will be revealed." She took my hand and led me through a thick tangle of weeds and down a set of wooden stairs to a small jetty. The dock was not visible from the shore or even from the riverbank where we had just stood.

I stood on the dock and looked across the river while Brenda took some matches and a kerosene lantern from a metal box hidden in the underbrush. She struck a match, lit the lantern, and waved it from side to side. Several minutes later, a dinghy piloted by a small dark-skinned boy in a cloth cap and dark coat pulled alongside the dock where we stood.

"Evenin', ladies," the boy said. "Can I offer you a lift?"

We were on the other side of the river in ten minutes. The boy helped us out of the dinghy with a great show of gallantry and led us up a rickety flight of stairs to a gravel pathway bordered by thick woods on either side. After several minutes of walking uphill, we emerged in front of the farmhouse I'd seen from the other side of the river. The building had appeared deserted when I'd seen it earlier that day. Now, there were over two dozen cars parked next to the building, and every light in the place was blazing. As we got closer, we heard the infectious sound of a jazz band in full swing pouring through the open windows.

"Welcome to the Wham Bam Club," the boy said, and doffed his cap.

CHAPTER 6

Brenda Washington grinned at me. "Isn't this something?" she said. "If it wasn't for Lilly, I'd never have figured out how to get over here without getting caught. She showed me everything—where the dock was, and how to signal for the boat. She made me swear a blood oath not to tell."

"Your secret is safe with me," I lied. "Lilly sounds like a real party girl. I sure would love to meet her someday."

Brenda studied me carefully before giving a satisfied nod. "I don't think Lilly would mind me sharing this place with you, Nola. You're not like the other girls. I knew that the minute you started singing the 'Hot Dog Blues.'"

"I can't wait to get away from Wheatley Institute," I said. That, at least, was the complete, unvarnished truth. "Too many rules and regulations. I completely understand why Lilly got sick of the place. Did Eddie Smooth help her escape from there?"

Brenda's aura clouded suddenly. "I really don't want to talk about it," she said. "All I know is that I miss her something awful." She grabbed my hand and pulled me through the front door of the Wham Bam Club. "Come on," she said. "The band's playing my favorite tune!"

Standing in the vestibule, we had an unobstructed view of the main room, with its large dance floor ringed by tables on three sides. A boisterous crowd filled the dance floor, shimmying furiously to the jazzy music provided by seven sweating Negro musicians standing on a stage at the back of the room.

Every table was filled. The customers were mostly colored, but to my surprise, there were also several white people in the crowd. Negro waiters in white dinner jackets held steaming platters of fried chicken aloft as they scurried between tables of people shouting to be heard over the music.

The volume of sights, sounds, and smells that surrounded me was overwhelming. All this sensory stimulation was putting my nerves on overload. One by one, I felt my psychic senses begin to shut down.

Brenda Washington, however, was vibrating with excitement. "Can I tell you a secret?" she said, shaking her hips in time with the music. "I'm going to be a musician myself someday. I play a pretty mean ragtime piano, but of course that's not allowed at Wheatley Institute. If I wasn't scared to death to get out and make my own living, I'd leave there tomorrow."

I nodded in reply, but Brenda had already turned her attention back to the band. After a dramatic cymbal crash, the drummer beat out an infectious rhythm. He was soon joined by the bass, banjo, and piano. One by one the clarinet, trombone, and trumpet joined in, until the whole band blared out a raucous melody that pulsed with the joy of being alive.

As the crowd stomped, whistled, and cheered, the man I'd seen arguing with Mrs. Wyatt in the alley stepped onto the stage. He wore a flashy green suit, and the pomade in his wavy black hair glistened in the light. In his hand, he held a shiny brass trumpet. "Good evenin', folks," he said. "I'm Eddie Smooth, and this is my band, the St. Louis Stompers. Hope you're enjoying the music. Here's a song for all those beautiful ladies in the house." With a wicked grin, he began to sing in a raspy, sensuous drawl:

> *"I need you, pretty mama*
> *Come on an' grease my pole*
> *Give me some jelly, baby*
> *Some jelly roll*
> *It's cold outside*
> *But yo' jelly keeps me warm"*

The crowd broke into raucous applause as the band swung into the next verse. With a small bow, Eddie Smooth put his trumpet to his lips and blew a soaring riff. Although there were no words, the pulsing rhythm of his music left no doubt as to the erotic intentions of his song. Eddie Smooth may have been a nasty skunk as a human being, but he sure knew how to sing and play that horn. As I listened, I felt a sinfully delicious shiver running up my spine.

I was tapping my foot in time to the music when a meaty black hand landed on my shoulder.

"Scram, jail bait." The speaker was dark and heavyset with a pockmarked face and a diamond stud in his ear. "No way in hell you're old enough to come in here."

I shot the man a withering glance. "I'm more than old enough to go wherever I please," I replied. I'd come too far to let some thug block my investigation. "My friend and I have an appointment with someone here. Take your hand off me or I'll report you to the owner of this establishment."

The heavyset man replied to my bluff with a snort of derision.

"You're talkin' to Tom Hoyt, little girl. I *am* the owner of this establishment." He grabbed me roughly by the arm and started to push me back out the door. I was about to give him a swift kick in the shin, when I spotted a familiar face. Abigail Everleigh, Mrs. Ratcliffe's wayward niece, was sitting at a table just inside the door.

"Hello, Miss Everleigh," I shouted. "I thought I'd never find you."

Abigail Everleigh peered into the vestibule where I stood, Tom Hoyt's heavy hand gripping me tightly by the arm. "Is that you, Nola?"

"Yes, miss," I said. "Would you mind telling this gentleman to take his beefy mitts off me? I told him I was coming here to meet you, but he refused to believe me."

Abigail Everleigh looked surprised, but I guess the desperation of my voice inspired her to play along.

"Let her go, Tom," she said sharply. Abigail Everleigh was a wild child and a rebel, but she was a *white* wild child, and a rich one at that. Recognizing the authority in her voice, Tom Hoyt grunted and removed his hand.

"Like I told you, my friend and I are here to meet someone," I said, making a great show of smoothing down the arms of my coat. "See that you are more courteous to your guests in the future."

As Brenda and I marched triumphantly into the dining room, Abigail waved toward the two empty seats at her table.

"Come join me," she said. "I'm all by my lonesome. My boyfriend, Joe Quincy, was supposed to meet me, but I guess he got sidetracked." She reached under the table and produced a small bottle of bootleg whiskey. "Drink, anyone?"

When Brenda and I shook our heads, Abigail shrugged and sloshed a generous portion into an empty coffee cup. "What brings you girls to the other side of the river?"

It was a fair question, but I had no intention of answering it. Fortunately, the musicians took that moment to start playing a lively two-step. Couples rushed to the dance floor in the center of the room. Although the majority of dancers were Negroes, there were also white couples sprinkled among the crowd, and even, to my great surprise, a pasty-faced college boy in a white tennis sweater cutting the rug with an attractive Negro girl with long legs, a short bob, and a wide, carefree smile.

"The Wham Bam Club is absolutely the place to be," Abigail told us, shouting over the sound of the music. She pointed to a balding, stoop-shouldered man sitting by himself at the table by the band. "Do you know who that is?"

Brenda and I shook our heads.

"That, my dears, is Joe's boss, Mr. Jeffrey Q. Fairchild," Abigail said. "Mr. Fairchild is Congressman Skelton's right-hand man. Nothing important gets done in Southern Illinois without Jeff Fairchild's say-so. He also happens to be Eddie Smooth's biggest fan."

That much I could see for myself. As Eddie Smooth and the St. Louis Stompers continued to play, Jeffrey Fairchild nodded his head and tapped his foot in time with the music.

Taking another swallow of whiskey from her coffee cup, Abigail said, "People complain about the type of crowd that comes here. They complain about the illegal drinking, the gambling, and the prostitutes. Mostly they complain because the Wham Bam Club is run by a colored man. But Eddie Smooth is the hottest horn player north of the Mason-Dixon Line, and Jeff Fairchild knows it. As long as Eddie Smooth works his musical magic, this party is never going to end."

She leaned in tipsily and nudged me in the ribs. "Eddie's a pimp, you know. Got a stable of girls turning tricks down in the basement."

I nodded blandly. If this man had anything to do with Lilly Davidson's disappearance, Mrs. Wyatt's worst nightmare had become a reality. "Doesn't he worry about getting arrested?" I asked.

"Not down here," Abigail replied. "Like I said, the man's got friends in high places. As long as Eddie Smooth keeps playing that sweet, hot, sexy music of his, the man can do whatever he likes."

I pondered my next step while I watched the dancers strutting their stuff in the center of the room. Whether Negro or white, the crowd at the Wham Bam Club was uniformly young, and determined to dance the night away, consequences be damned. Never had I seen the races mingle so freely. One thing was certain. I had to find a way to talk to Eddie Smooth and find out what he knew.

I noticed a heavyset dark-skinned man hovering near the bandstand. From his flat boxer's nose and cauliflower ear, I assumed he was some kind of bodyguard. He was not the kind of person I saw in the course of my daily routine. Yet, the man looked familiar. When he turned his face in my direction, I realized I'd seen him on Lincoln Avenue the day before, handing out campaign leaflets in front of Boss Franklin C. Dillard's pool hall.

"Isn't that one of Boss Dillard's thugs?" I asked Abigail.

The girl gave me an airy shrug. "I wouldn't be a bit surprised," she said. "All the gangsters come here, colored and white." She took another sip of bootleg whiskey from her coffee cup and scanned the crowd with hungry eyes. "Joe promised he'd be here ages ago," she told me. "Don't you think it's rude to leave a girl sitting at a table by herself?"

"Very rude," I replied. "Especially in a place like this. Hope he shows up soon."

Brenda paid no attention to us, and remained absorbed in the music as we spoke. At the end of the next song, she waved to the bass player, a short stocky man with dark skin and a pencil mustache. When the bass player grinned at her and waved back, Brenda clutched my hand.

"Did you see that?" she said breathlessly. "I do believe he likes me."

"Of course he likes you," Abigail said wryly. "You're the

perfect dish for a guy like that. You should invite him over to the table, let him give you a proper hello."

Abigail was right, I thought. Brenda Washington was clumsy, unsophisticated, and obviously a newcomer to the game of love, but she was beautiful in her own way.

As Brenda blushed and looked down at the table, Eddie Smooth picked up his trumpet and blew an attention-getting fanfare.

"This next number is dedicated to a very special friend of mine," he announced. "I'm not going to tell you her name, but when she hears this song, she'll get the message."

He nodded to the drummer, who beat out a slow funeral march on his snare drum. As the rest of the musicians joined in, Eddie Smooth began to sing:

> *"You're everybody's favorite coed*
> *The girl with the golden smile*
> *Why does your fella leave you all alone*
> *At your table on the aisle*
> *Doesn't he know you miss him*
> *Doesn't he know you're blue*
> *Smilin' on the outside*
> *Cryin' on the inside*
> *Poor little lonely you*
> *Poor little lonely you."*

Abigail's face twisted into a snarl. "You scum-sucking son of a bitch," she muttered under her breath. She brushed away a tear with the back of her hand before sloshing another shot of bootleg brew into the coffee cup in front of her. With an ironic grin, she raised her cup toward the bandstand in a mock toast before downing the contents in one long swallow.

As she did so, Eddie Smooth grinned and snapped his fingers in rhythm. Taking his cue, the band launched into the next tune, a lively up-tempo number that had the dancers gyrating furiously.

At the end of the song, Eddie Smooth took a deep bow. "You've been listening to the hot sounds of Eddie Smooth and the St. Louis Stompers," he announced, wiping the sweat from his face with a large white handkerchief. "I'm Eddie, and on behalf of myself and the rest of the band I'd like to thank Mr. Tom Hoyt, the owner of this fine establishment. We're gonna take a short break, but we'll be back. Don't you dare go anywhere!"

Brenda Washington looked at us, her round and freckled face glowing. "That bass player is truly wonderful," she said. "Handsome, too. I sure wish I could meet him."

"Today's your lucky day, honey," Abigail said. "The band hangs around out back between shows. Go out that back door over there, and you will find your Romeo."

"Come on, Brenda," I said, and stood up. "I'll keep you company."

As we left the table, Abigail Everleigh called out to us, "If you run into my boyfriend while you're out there, tell him to hurry up. I'm sick and tired of sitting here by myself."

Outside the kitchen door of the Wham Bam Club, three members of the St. Louis Stompers sat facing away from us in rickety wooden chairs. The banjo player, a portly man who looked to be in his late thirties, took a deep drag on his cigarette. "You're killin' it tonight, Corey," he said, giving the wiry young drummer an approving pat on the back.

"Amen to that," the bass player chimed in. "I never heard you beat those tubs with so much power. That's the way to get a groove on."

It had gotten colder in the past hour, and my thin woolen coat offered little protection from the late October chill. Outside the Wham Bam Club, away from the noise of the music and the crowd, my psychic senses began to return. Small orbs of rosy light danced over the heads of the three musicians as they continued their conversation. As Brenda and I watched them, Eddie Smooth walked up behind us.

"Good evening, ladies," he said. "You look mighty familiar. Have we met before?"

I had a sudden moment of panic. Had Eddie Smooth seen me standing in the alley as he argued with Mrs. Wyatt? Had he looked over his shoulder and spotted me running to her aid as he walked away?

"Of course we've met," Brenda Washington replied. "I was here just last week with my friend Lilly Davidson."

The trumpet player's eyes narrowed slightly. "Lilly Davidson? Can't say I recall that name."

"Sure you do," Brenda insisted. "You and Lilly had a long talk down in the basement the last time we were here."

"Is that so?" At the mention of Lilly's name, Eddie Smooth's aura shifted from bright yellow to a muddy brown. I was sure the man was hiding something.

As Brenda's face remained a study in puzzlement, the bass player ambled over to greet us.

"Don't pay Eddie no mind," he said. "My name's Larimer Betts, and I remember you perfectly. You were here with your girlfriend last week. I was hoping you'd come back."

Brenda grinned from ear to ear, a rosy glow rippling through her aura. "Really?" she said.

"Of course," he said. He offered Brenda his elbow and asked, "Will you take a walk with me? I'd love to know what a beautiful woman like you is doing out here in the sticks."

As the couple walked away, Eddie Smooth turned to me and winked. "My bass man just found himself a fat, sweet cherry, ripe for the picking," he said. He stepped back and studied me appraisingly. "You, however, are another flavor altogether. Much as I'd love to taste your cherry, I've got a strong feeling somebody else has beat me to it. Am I right?"

"My cherry is none of your business," I said crisply. The

man was disgusting, but his aura had shifted when I mentioned Lilly's name. Hoping I could get him to tell me something more, I decided to flirt shamelessly: "We both know that the sundae tastes sweet even after the cherry is gone. Maybe even better."

He licked his lips and grinned. "Sho 'nuff, little girl."

"Lilly Davidson told me about you," I said. "She told me you'd know where to find her if she ever ran away from Wheatley Institute." It was a wild shot in the dark, but worth a try. I wanted to find out what Eddie Smooth had said to Lilly last week, but if I appeared too eager, he was sure to clam up. I decided to play hard to get.

"I guess you're not the man Lilly said you were," I said, and stepped away from him. "No hard feelings, but I've got to get back to Wheatley Institute before sunup."

Eddie Smooth gave me a disarming smile, and spread his hands open in a gesture of apology. "Don't leave now, sugar. Now that I think about it, I do seem to remember this Lilly gal you're talking about. She's short and tan complected, right? With a sweet shape and hazel eyes?"

"That's my Lilly," I said. "If she's run away from Wheatley Institute to be with you, I wanna come, too. We always promised we'd stay together, no matter what."

"Got no other family to take you in?" As Eddie Smooth looked me over with an appraising stare, I could almost see the wheels in his evil little brain turning. Was I the type of girl he could sweet-talk into joining his stable of prostitutes? I was playing a dangerous game, but if I wanted to find Lilly Davidson, I couldn't afford to back out now.

"I'm an orphan," I said. "Lilly's my only friend in the whole wide world. She's like a sister to me."

Eddie Smooth's wolfish grin widened. "Don't you fret, little girl. Your friend Lilly's staying with me. Right here at the Wham Bam Club."

Just as I suspected. I sidled closer. "Can I see her?"

"I might be able to arrange it," he said, "but If I do, what are you gonna give me in return?"

"Wouldn't you like to know," I said. I winked and offered him a naughty grin. "Let me talk to Lilly first, and then maybe we'll negotiate."

I steeled myself not to push Eddie Smooth away as he ran his hand along my cheek. "What did you say your name was, sugar pie?"

I hesitated. If I gave Eddie my real name, Lilly wouldn't recognize it. "Just tell her it's her best friend from Wheatley Institute. She'll know who it is."

"You wait right where you are. I'll tell Lilly you're here," Eddie said, and strode away.

CHAPTER 7

For the next fifteen minutes, I waited for Lilly Davidson to come back. When I got tired of standing, I sat down in one of the rickety wooden chairs by the kitchen door and waited some more. Brenda and her bass-playing friend were nowhere to be seen, and the other musicians had apparently gone back inside. Other than the banter of the cooks in the kitchen and bursts of laughter and conversation coming through the open windows of the dining room, the area behind the kitchen of the Wham Bam Club was quiet. Quiet enough for me to hear footsteps approaching, and the shrill sound of Abigail Everleigh's voice. I stood up and moved into the shadows to avoid being seen.

"Now you listen to me, Joe Quincy," the girl said loudly. "I refuse to spend the rest of the night sitting at a table by myself while you go off to gamble and Lord knows what else."

"Stop bothering me, Abbie," Joe said. His voice was even more girlish than I remembered. "Can't you see I've got important business to take care of? I'll come sit with you soon, I promise."

"That's what you said three hours ago," Abigail said petulantly. "I've been absolutely miserable without you. I just spent an hour sitting with Mrs. Ratcliffe's colored *maid*, for Chrissakes!"

"Not my problem," he replied. "If I don't go out to the parking lot and hand out these campaign flyers, that bastard Jeff Fairchild is going to fire me." He pointed his chin toward the large sheaf of papers in his right hand. "Do you want me to lose my job?"

"Of course not, but people are starting to talk," Abigail said miserably. "Eddie Smooth made fun of me tonight in front of everybody." Tears glistened in her eyes as she grabbed Joe Quincy by the arm. "Don't leave me to sit at that table without you."

Joe Quincy jerked his arm away. "Didn't I just tell you that I'm *busy*?" The venom in his tone was palpable. "I am not just some servant boy you can order around, Abigail. I'm a *Quincy*, dammit. I have got important work to do." Clutching the campaign flyers tightly, he turned and strode toward the front entrance of the Wham Bam Club without looking back.

Abigail Everleigh stood sobbing for a long moment as Joe Quincy rounded the corner and disappeared into the darkness. Then with a small sigh, she pulled a silver flask from her handbag and took a long drink before stumbling back through the kitchen door.

Poor kid, I thought. *She needs to wise up to that stinker and find herself a new college boy to play with.* I was about to return to my seat by the kitchen door when a slender girl in a tight-fitting beaded dress emerged from the kitchen.

"Brenda, are you there? It's me, Lilly," she whispered. "Eddie says you've come to see me." Lilly Davidson was barely five feet tall, with a light copper complexion and striking hazel eyes. Her hair was a very light brown, nearly blonde, and arranged in curly ringlets that complimented her long nose and hazel eyes.

"Hello, Lilly," I said, and stepped into the light.

Lilly Davidson stared at me in confusion. "What is this? You're not Brenda. Eddie said Brenda was here to see me."

"I'm Brenda's friend," I said. "Please let me explain. It'll only take a minute."

"What the hell do you want?" Lilly replied.

"My name is Nola Jackson, and I really am a friend of Brenda's. I've come here to help you get away from Eddie Smooth, while you still can."

"And why should I want to do that?" Lilly Davidson's voice dripped with sarcasm. "Eddie loves me. He's going to marry me and take me out of here."

"Marrying you is the last thing he wants to do," I said. "Don't you realize the man is a pimp?"

"I know Eddie has girls working for him," Lilly said defiantly, "but I'm different. That's not what he wants for me."

Underneath her sarcasm and anger, I could see the girl was scared witless.

"I know what it's like to be on your own," I said, putting a comforting hand on her shoulder. "I've been homeless, just like you."

Lilly pushed my hand away and scowled. "Well, that's your sorry luck, and definitely not my problem. Eddie says he's going to take care of me. I'll never be homeless again."

As I looked at her, my psychic senses began to kick in. Clear as day, my intuition showed me an image of a six-year-old Lilly sitting alone on the edge of her bed in a white-walled dormitory, crying bitterly.

"It's no wonder you're looking for a sure thing," I said gently. "When you were little, grown-ups gave you things, then took them away. Like the time they took away your Raggedy Ann doll at the orphanage."

Lilly Davidson stared at me, her cupid's bow mouth a round O of amazement.

"How did you know that?" she said suspiciously. "You some kind of spy or something?"

"Of course not," I said. "I'm a psychic. I just know things about people, that's all."

"Really?" She cocked her head, crossed her skinny arms in front of her chest, and shot me a challenging stare. "Prove it. Tell me my future."

"All right," I said. "What do you want to know?"

Lilly's face softened. "Are Eddie and I going to get married? Tell me what you see."

"Only if you promise not to run away," I said. Now that Lilly was less angry, I could see just how beautiful she was. A wisp of curly brown hair peeked out from her stylish hat, complimenting a light tan complexion and hazel eyes. Though part of her wanted to play the rebel, another part of her remained a lonely child, naive and hungry for love. Normally I never boasted about my psychic abilities. Aunt Sarah had taught me long ago that the best way to stay out of trouble was to keep a low profile. But if I had to play the role of an all-knowing fortune teller to get Lilly away from Eddie Smooth, so be it.

"I promise I won't run away," Lilly said solemnly. "Cross my heart and hope to die."

"All right then," I said. "Your future will now be revealed. Give me your hand." Lilly dutifully extended her arm. I took her hand in mine, allowing my Spirit Guides to flood my mind with images. "You lost your mother the day you were born," I said. "All you have left of her is a cameo brooch containing a lock of her hair."

Lilly's eyes widened. "Go on," she said. "Tell me what you see about Eddie and me."

The answer was obvious. It didn't take a psychic to see that Eddie Smooth was about to ruin her life. Nonetheless I closed my eyes and pretended to consult the stars. Lilly was locked into her fictional belief in a happily-ever-after future with Eddie Smooth. It didn't look like I was going to be able to convince Lilly to return to Wheatley Institute. But maybe, just maybe, she would come with me to Aunt Sarah's house. If I could get Lilly away from Eddie Smooth, even for a few hours, I felt certain Aunt Sarah and I could talk some sense into her.

I squeezed her hand and said dramatically, "There's a cloud over your love life."

Lilly's eyes widened. "A cloud?"

I nodded. "There's another woman in Eddie's life. Someone whose identity he has kept hidden from you."

Though my answer was correct, it had not required much in the way of psychic wizardry. Eddie Smooth was a confirmed ladies' man, the type to have a girl or two waiting for him in every town. When Lilly frowned, I knew I'd struck a chord.

"If Eddie ever left me for another woman, I'd tear his heart out with my bare hands," she said with a fierce intensity. "If I can't have him, no one will. I need to get rid of this woman. Can you make her go away?"

I released Lilly's hand and gave her a consoling pat on the knee. "Did you ever hear of Mrs. Sarah Brown?"

"The old witchy-woman who lives on Upper Fifth Street? I've heard some of the local girls talk about her."

"That's right," I said. "Mrs. Brown is my aunt. If you want, I'll ask her to fix you a powerful Binding Potion. A potion to ensure that Eddie Smooth never looks at another woman again."

The smile Lilly Davidson gave me was like the sun coming

out after a storm. "Perfect," she said. "Have your aunt make the potion and bring it out to me tomorrow. I will pay you whatever you want."

"The hex won't work unless she gives it to you in person," I said, lying through my teeth. "If you come back with me now, we can do it right away."

"She can't do it here at the club?"

"I'm afraid not," I replied. As Lilly studied me silently, I could almost hear the gears whirring inside her mind.

"All right," she said finally. "Let me go get my coat. I'll meet you in the woods by the old toolshed where no one can see us, okay? Walk toward the river for about a hundred yards, then look to your right. You can't miss it."

Without waiting for my reply, Lilly Davidson turned and hurried back inside the Wham Bam Club.

Tonight was truly my lucky night, I thought to myself. I'd figured out how Mrs. Wyatt's girls were escaping from Wheatley Institute, and I'd found Lilly Davidson. Best of all, I had persuaded Lilly to leave Eddie Smooth's evil circle of influence for a few hours. Aunt Sarah always said that we were guided and supported by unseen forces in the Spirit World. Whenever I expressed any skepticism about this, she'd say: "Just you wait, Nola. When the time is right, you won't have to wonder about this. You will just know." As I walked down the path toward the river, I felt a new level of certainty begin to blossom in the depths of my heart. Perhaps everything was going to turn out just fine, after all.

Following Lilly's instructions, I walked toward the river until I spotted a dilapidated wooden lean-to on the right. Back when the Wham Bam Club had been a simple farmhouse, the shed had probably been used to keep rakes, shovels, and other gardening tools. These days, the toolshed had fallen into serious disrepair. If Lilly had not told me it was there, I would probably have missed it. The surrounding woods had begun to reclaim the space around it, enveloping the tumbledown shed in a thick jumble of weeds. I stepped off the path, picked my way gingerly through the underbrush and approached the building. Its wooden door had once been secured by a heavy iron lock, but now hung partially open. The remains of a sawed-off tree stump pressed against the back wall of the shed. I took a handkerchief from my coat pocket, spread it out on the stump, and sat down. If Lilly was true to her word, she would be here soon. For the moment, there was nothing for me to do but wait.

From this distance, the sounds from the Wham Bam Club were muted. In the woods behind me, a night owl hooted a mournful tune. *Poor Lilly*, I thought. *Head over heels in love with an absolutely worthless man. There must be some kind of cure for her condition.* I resolved to ask Aunt Sarah about this once I'd gotten Lilly safely away from the Wham Bam Club.

As I huddled alone in the darkness, I brooded about the many things that could possibly derail my plans. If Lilly did not come back to meet me, I had absolutely no idea what I would do. Meanwhile, Brenda Washington was still nowhere to be seen. Necking in the woods with that bass player, most likely. Mrs. Wyatt would not be happy with the way I was chaperoning the girl, but I could only be in one place at a time. *Calm down, Nola*, I told myself. *No use worrying about things you can't control.*

Aunt Sarah had been teaching me to sit in silence whenever I felt overwhelmed. "There are messages in the sound of the wind, the lapping of waves, the rustle of trees," she told me. "If you listen to them and wait long enough, the answer will come."

Remembering Aunt Sarah's advice, I sat on the tree trunk behind the old toolshed and fell into a peaceful silence.

The sound of running footsteps jolted me out of my reverie. The heavy-set man I'd spotted standing next to the bandstand was racing down the path toward the river, breathing heavily. As he ran past the toolshed, my senses went on high alert. Why was this man running like that? Did it have anything to do with Lilly? As the sound of his footsteps died away, the woods grew silent again.

Lilly should have come back by now, I thought. *Should I walk back into the Wham Bam Club and look for her?* On the one hand, this might be a good idea. On the other hand, if I left our agreed-upon meeting place, Lilly might come looking for me and give up if I was not there. I decided to wait another few minutes.

Suddenly I heard a woman scream. Was it Lilly's voice? I stood, pushed my way through the underbrush, and ran up the path toward the Wham Bam Club. I was within sight of the kitchen when a loud explosion rocked the earth beneath me. Stunned, I stood on the path and watched as customers, cooks, waiters, and musicians poured out of the building and ran helter-skelter toward the parking lot.

A Negro cook wearing a white apron called back over his shoulder as he rushed out the kitchen door. "Leave it, Henry. Nothing in this dump is worth dying for."

"Forget about your bag," a white man shouted as he dragged his date by the arm.

A crackling tower of flame shot out from the roof of the kitchen. In seconds, the entire building was engulfed in flames. I wanted to look for Lilly, but it was clearly too dangerous for me to go back into the Wham Bam Club now.

Desperate people pushed and shoved each other, screaming and shouting. Car doors slammed and tires squealed as those fortunate enough to have reached their cars raced away from the burning building.

I scanned the milling crowd frantically, hoping to catch sight

of either Lilly or Brenda. I spotted Jeff Fairchild, the Congressman's right-hand man, yelling at Tom Hoyt, the owner of the
Wham Bam Club. Hoyt's scarred face was a study in confusion
as Fairchild pointed toward the back of the building and shouted
something in his ear. As Hoyt nodded slowly, Jeff Fairchild
hurried away from him, climbed into a sleek black Studebaker,
and drove off. Out of the corner of my eye I saw Joe Quincy
standing at the far end of the parking lot with his arms crossed.
Though he was too far away for me to see him clearly, he seemed
to be smiling as black clouds of smoke billowed from the windows of the dining room. Abigail Everleigh, however, was nowhere to be seen, and neither was Lilly Davidson.

Was it possible that Lilly had not joined the crowd stamped-
ing into the parking lot? Perhaps Lilly had run away from the
Wham Bam Club in the other direction, heading down the path
that led to the river. And where was Brenda Washington?
When I'd last seen Brenda, she and her bass-playing Romeo
were walking downhill toward the river.

Maybe, just maybe, I'd find both girls by the river. And
maybe, just maybe, if the dinghy was still moored by the dock,
the three of us could use it to get away from the fire and return
to the safety of Wheatley Institute. The chances of this were
slim, I thought, but not entirely out of reach.

Taking a last look at the panicked scene unfolding in the
parking lot, I turned and hurried down the path that led to the
river, calling out to Brenda and Lilly as I ran. It was pitch-black
in the woods. I stumbled and nearly fell several times in the
dark. But after several minutes, I could hear the sound of water
lapping against the shore.

"Lilly? Brenda?" I shouted. Breathing heavily, I tumbled
down the riverbank to the water, my feet scrabbling for pur-
chase amid the mud and loose stones. I nearly fell again, but
somehow managed to keep myself upright. And then I was

there, the jetty and the expanse of the river emerging out of the fog in front of me like some ghostly manifestation made real.

There was only one problem.

The dinghy I needed to take the girls across the river to safety was gone. Exhausted, I sank to the ground in despair. Brenda was gone. Lilly was gone, and I was stuck in the woods between a raging fire and the wide expanse of the Pigeon River.

Chapter 8

As the first rays of dawn filtered through the trees, I sat next to the river, too tired to take another step. All my carefully laid plans had fallen apart. I had no idea where Lilly Davidson was. I had no idea where Brenda Washington was, and Eddie Smooth had most likely also disappeared. As I contemplated these gloomy developments, a round-faced policeman walked toward me with his gun drawn.

"Freeze!" he shouted, despite the fact that I was clearly not running anywhere. "Put your hands above your head and walk over here, nice and slow."

My heart thumped furiously in my chest as I followed his instructions. "What is it, Officer?" I asked. "What have I done?"

"There's been a murder," he said gruffly. "We're taking all possible suspects down to the station house for questioning."

"A murder?" In my exhausted state, I must not have heard the man correctly.

"That's right," he said. "Detective Anderson wants to talk with all potential witnesses."

The policeman grabbed my arm and led me up the hill toward what remained of the Wham Bam Club. As we got closer, the air reeked of creosote. Sad plumes of smoke still hovered over the charred remains of the dining room. The area next to the kitchen door where I had waited for Lilly Davidson just hours earlier was now swarming with cops.

As we passed, I caught a glimpse of Abigail Everleigh talking with a runty little white man in a crumpled felt hat. Miss Everleigh's aura blazed with an electric yellow I had not noticed around her earlier that night. Waving her arms wildly as she spoke, she chattered a mile a minute as the little man scribbled furiously in a small black notebook.

When I stopped to see what was going on, the policeman poked me with his nightstick.

"Keep moving, girlie," he said, and pointed toward the large black patrol wagon idling next to the ruined building. "Get in."

I squeezed myself onto a bench along the side of the wagon and heard the door slam shut behind me. Everyone in the wagon was colored. For a fleeting moment, I thought Lilly or Brenda might be among my fellow passengers, but I recognized no one.

"Ain't this a pip," an older man said. As he spoke, a gloomy gray mist hovered around his head. From the white apron he wore, I figured he was one of the many cooks I'd seen scurrying around the kitchen earlier that evening. "That no-good pretty boy Eddie Smooth gets himself shot and now we're all headed for jail."

Suddenly I felt cold all over. Even in my bleary-eyed state of exhaustion, I could feel the hairs rising on the back of my neck. "Eddie Smooth has been murdered?" I said.

"That's about the size of it, sister," the cook replied. "Jive-ass pimp musta pissed off the wrong dame. Anyone could see he was headed for trouble. Bragging 'bout how he had the white folks wrapped around his little finger. Making fun of Jeff

Fairchild and that girly-voiced assistant of his when he thought they wasn't looking."

"The police have any leads?" I asked.

"How the hell would I know?" the cook said. "All I know is, we're all headed down to headquarters. That should be enough bad news for a lifetime."

When I tried to question the man further, he turned away from me without answering.

Half an hour later, the Black Maria pulled up in front of Agate Municipal Police Headquarters, where a potbellied, red-cheeked patrolman herded us out of the paddy wagon, up the stairs and into the station. After having my fingerprints taken, I and five other bedraggled women were taken to a long hallway and told to take a seat on a bare wooden bench to await our fate. One by one, my bench mates were taken into a room for questioning.

I willed myself to stay awake and alert as I awaited my turn. The police were casting a wide net, and might not be too particular about who they caught. A Negro who happened to be in the wrong place at the wrong time could be arrested for merely looking suspicious. The fact that I was innocent was no guarantee I would escape a similar fate. Once in police custody, anything could happen. In the colored community, it was common knowledge that some cops had the habit of beating suspects until they confessed to the charges against them, regardless of their guilt or innocence. Desperate as I was to find out whether Lilly or Brenda had been hurt in the fire, or whether they'd been swept up in the police dragnet, I knew better than to ask these policemen anything. One wrong move or inadvertent slip of the tongue could lead to my being arrested for a murder I did not commit.

Time slowed to a crawl as I slumped against the bare concrete wall. After what felt like hours, a rumpled detective with a long narrow face and a cigarette dangling from his mouth emerged from the room at the end of the hallway. A younger policeman wearing a uniform and holding a clipboard followed behind him.

"Which one of you is Nola Ann Jackson?" the detective said. When I raised my hand, he continued: "Let me get a good look at you. Turn around so I can see you from the back."

After I walked up and down the hallway a couple of times, he grunted.

"She's too tall, and she's too fat," he said, and turned to the uniformed cop standing next to him. "The girl we're looking for is much smaller. You can let her go."

"I'm free?" I said. I'd never been so happy to be called fat in my whole life.

"For the moment," the detective said. "Some agitator from the Negro Voters League has been raising a ruckus about you all morning. He says he's going to organize a protest outside the station house unless we release you."

Fifteen minutes later, I stumbled, blinking and bleary eyed, out of police headquarters and into the brilliant sunshine. I felt weak, weary, and numb all over. Now that I was out of jail, I had no idea what to do next. When I tried to tune in to my psychic senses for answers, I got nothing. They'd shut down the minute I was taken to the police station and had not returned since. Should I go back to Wheatley Institute and try to explain what had happened to Mrs. Wyatt? Were Lily and Brenda all right? Had they been hurt in the fire, or had they somehow escaped? Should I search for them? Perhaps I should just go back home, crawl into bed and pull the covers up over my head, I thought gloomily.

As I stood on the sidewalk contemplating my options, a lanky, brown-skinned man emerged from inside police headquarters. He wore a gray wool overcoat with a fur collar and a matching gray fedora cocked at a jaunty angle.

"You must be Nola Jackson," he said in a deep voice as he approached me. "I'm Jim Richardson. Mrs. Wyatt sent me to get you out of here and bring you back to Phyllis Wheatley Institute." He touched me gently on the arm. "If you'll come with me, my car is just around the corner."

I nodded and allowed Jim Richardson to lead me away from the police station.

"I really appreciate your help, Mr. Richardson," I said. "How did Mrs. Wyatt know I was here?"

"She saw the explosion at the Wham Bam Club from across the river. When she discovered that you and Brenda Washington were not in your beds, she suspected you had gone there. She called me when she saw the police begin rounding up people."

Although our pace was slow, I struggled to keep up with Jim Richardson's long-legged stride. After a few steps, he turned to face me. "You look as though you could do with a cup of coffee and a hot meal, Miss Jackson. Are you hungry?"

I nodded. Now that he had mentioned it, I could not remember the last time I had eaten.

"There's no magic elixir like a strong cup of java," Jim Richardson said. He took off his hat and offered me a sweeping bow. "Will you allow me to buy you breakfast, Miss Jackson?"

The gesture was so ridiculous, I couldn't help but smile. What kind of man does such a thing on a public sidewalk in the middle of the day? "Only if you stop referring to me as 'Miss Jackson,'" I said. "My friends call me Nola."

"Well then, Nola, you can call me Jim. And now that these formalities have been taken care of, let's get some breakfast into you. I've learned from my years with the Negro Voters League that you get more done with a full belly than with an empty one. There'll be plenty of time to get you out to Wheatley Institute after breakfast."

As we turned the corner onto Fifteenth Street, Jim waved toward the silver Nash touring car parked in the middle of the block.

The car was sitting several feet out from the curb in front of a fire hydrant, its impossibly long hood gleaming in the sunlight. "Hop aboard my chariot," he said, and opened the passenger door with a flourish.

I pointed to the orange traffic ticket peeking out underneath his left windshield wiper. "Shouldn't you do something about that?" I asked. "Perhaps we can go back in the station and talk to somebody."

"Nonsense," Jim Richardson said grandly. He plucked the ticket from the windshield and shoved it into his pocket. "I'll have a little chat with Franklin Dillard tomorrow. I've known our esteemed Republican ward boss since we were both in knee pants. He'll take care of things for me," he said. "Right now, I've got more important things to attend to. A certain young lady I've just met is in dire need of a hot meal."

As Jim helped me into my seat, his body smelled like fresh soap and Mennen aftershave. I tried not to think about what I smelled like. I had not bathed in two days. My cotton dress was wrinkled, and my hair was matted and tangled from running through the woods. It was not the way I would have chosen to look or smell for a ride with a handsome man in a fancy car, but what could I do?

"Have you ever been to Mr. Dave's Soul Food Diner?" Jim asked. "The food there is quite good."

"I don't go to restaurants much," I replied. "My Aunt Sarah is a great cook. She fixes breakfast for me most mornings."

"Lucky girl," Jim said. "When you're a lonely bachelor like me, you've got to make do with whatever you can get." He eased his sports car into the morning traffic on Lincoln Avenue, pulled up to the entrance of the restaurant, and turned off the engine.

"The sign over there says NO PARKING," I told him. "Aren't you worried you'll get another ticket?"

"I never let the petty minions of officialdom control my

life," Jim replied. "If we Negroes are too scared to break a rule now and then, we will never get ahead."

"If you say so," I said doubtfully. "Seems to me it would just be easier to find a legal parking spot."

Jim Richardson flashed me a lopsided grin. "Why don't you let me worry about that, Nola. I don't want you to walk any further than is absolutely necessary. Anyway, we're only going to be here a few minutes."

As Jim and I walked into the restaurant, we were greeted by a short, stocky man in a white apron. His dark, round face and bald head reminded me of a Negro Humpty-Dumpty.

"Mornin', Dave," Jim said. "How's life treating you today?"

"Fair to middlin'," Dave replied in a surprisingly melodious tenor voice.

"Dave, this is Nola Jackson," Jim said. "She has had a very rough night. Bring us two large breakfast specials, and a pot of the strongest coffee you got. We need to get some nourishment in her blood before she goes out to face the day."

The world-weary shrug Mr. Dave offered Jim in reply indicated he'd seen and handled many such situations. "Sure thing, Jimmy," he said blandly. "I'll bring the coffee straightaway."

After two cups of Mr. Dave's double-strength hot coffee, I began to feel more like myself again. And when Mr. Dave set two steaming platters of food on the table in front of us, both Jim and I smiled appreciatively. For the next several minutes, silence reigned as Jim and I stuffed ourselves on scrambled eggs, thick Canadian bacon, and biscuits.

When he'd scraped his plate clean, Jim Richardson leaned back with a satisfied sigh and looked at me. "Good, right?"

I nodded and bit into my second biscuit. It was not quite as light as the ones my Aunt Sarah made, but it was plenty good enough, considering how hungry I was.

I looked across the table at Jim Richardson and smiled. "Thanks for taking me to breakfast," I told him. "I didn't even realize how worn-out I was until now."

"It's the least I could do," Jim replied. "Especially considering I was the one that lost track of Lilly in the first place." He shook his head ruefully. "The girl completely gave me the slip," he continued. "One minute she was there, sitting all quiet and demure as James Weldon Johnson gave his lecture. The next minute she was gone, vanished without a trace. As soon as I noticed she was missing, I searched the building. And when I couldn't find her inside the Y, I looked all over that godforsaken town for her."

"Lilly must have had help making her getaway," I said. "Eddie Smooth was probably out there, waiting for her."

"In Craigsville?" Jim said dubiously. "Outside of the colored YMCA, there's nothing in Craigsville but the coal mine, the company store, and Zion Baptist Church. No self-respecting hustler would be caught dead in a dreary coal mining town like that."

"It's the only explanation that makes sense," I insisted, shaking my head in frustration. "That girl has made an art form of disappearing. I've been worried sick about her. She and Brenda Washington both. Have you heard anything?"

"Not a word," Jim said. "Other than Eddie Smooth, no one else was killed or even injured in the fire. The girls must have managed to get away somehow."

"That's a relief," I said. "I sure wish I knew where they were. Is it true Eddie Smooth has been murdered?"

"Quite true," Jim replied. "He was found in his dressing room with a bullet through his head."

I shivered. I'd been standing there talking to the man just a few hours earlier, yet my psychic senses had not alerted me to his fate. Why this was so, I had no idea. I made a mental note to ask Aunt Sarah about this when I got back home. I took another sip of hot coffee and leaned forward. "Are they sure it's him? The body must have been badly burned in the fire."

"They're sure," Jim said. "Eddie Smooth had gold caps on

three of his front teeth. The club owner identified his body at the scene."

I tried not to think of how those teeth had sparkled in the sunlight just two days ago, when I'd seen him arguing with Mrs. Wyatt in the alley off of Lincoln Avenue.

"Do the police have any suspects?" I asked.

"Not that I know of," Jim said. "Of course, the police don't tell me everything. There will probably be more information in the *Agate Daily Chronicle* when it comes out this afternoon. No use worrying about it until then."

"What about Brenda Washington?" I said. "She's the other girl who came to the club with me. Has she been found?"

Jim Richardson shook his head. "Brenda has completely disappeared. Same thing for Lilly Davidson. No one's seen hide nor hair of either one of them."

"I was so close to persuading Lilly to come back with me," I said. I told him about the conversation I'd had with Lilly at the Wham Bam Club. "If it hadn't been for the fire, I believe that girl would be sitting in the parlor of Wheatley Institute this very minute."

"Don't be too hard on yourself, Nola. It was an impossible situation. For what it's worth, I think you handled yourself quite well." Jim took a long swallow of coffee and wiped his mouth with a napkin. "I see you scraped your plate clean, Nola. You want anything else before we leave?"

When I shook my head, he pulled a fifty-cent piece from his pocket, laid it on the table, and stood. "We better get going," he said. "Mrs. Wyatt wants to see you."

I nodded, but remained silent. My mission to return Lilly Davidson to the Phyllis Wheatley Institute had been a total failure, and I was not looking forward to seeing Mrs. Wyatt again.

"Mrs. Wyatt tells me you were a resident at Wheatley Institute as a teenager," Jim said, easing his sedan into the busy stream of traffic rolling down Lincoln Avenue.

"I stayed there for two years," I replied. "But I was far from being the best-behaved girl in the bunch. I ran off to New York City the very first chance I got."

Richardson's easygoing laugh reminded me of a cool glass of lemonade on a hot summer's day.

"Mrs. Wyatt did mention that your stay at Wheatley Institute was cut short," he said wryly. "Can't say I blame you, though. New York is a great town. More culture, more music, more energy than anywhere else in the world. May I ask what brought you back to Agate?"

"My husband was killed in the war," I said. "I had no job or friends up in Harlem. I was about to become homeless when my Aunt Sarah invited me back here to stay with her."

"My condolences," Jim said softly. "That must have been rough. Has it been difficult coming back to Agate after being away?"

"It has," I admitted. Ordinarily, I did not discuss my personal feelings with strangers, but something about the rose highlights at the edges of Jim Richardson's aura invited my trust. It felt good to talk to someone who seemed genuinely interested in listening to what I had to say.

"I was an hour late for work the other day because not one, but *two* streetcar drivers refused to stop for me," I said. "There's more race prejudice in Agate than there is in New York."

"I don't know about that," Jim said. "At this very moment, the Negro Voters League is investigating rumors of a new Klan cell operating in the heart of New York City."

I sighed and shook my head. "I suppose you're right," I said. "Things are tough all over. At least in New York, the streetcars stop for you, and no one makes you go sit in the back."

Jim studied me thoughtfully. "Do you miss living in Harlem, Nola? Ever think about moving back there?"

As I considered Jim's question, a wave of memories flooded over me. Harlem had felt like paradise when Will and I first moved there. We danced at the Sugar Cane Club, snuggled in the Lincoln Theater and feasted on chicken and waffles in the Marguerite Tea Room. We were two teenagers so deeply in love, we thought the honeymoon would never end. Until, of course, it did. The day Will Jackson died, I lost my breadwinner, my protector, my best friend, and my only family. Without Will, Harlem became a cold and lonely place where no one cared whether I lived or died.

Did I miss living there? I turned to Jim Richardson and shook my head.

"New York is a tough town for a girl with no money, no friends, and no family," I said. "Here in Agate, I've at least got my Aunt Sarah. Things here are not perfect by a long shot, but I'll be all right. I just need to learn how to handle these nasty old trolley drivers."

Jim Richardson smiled. "The Negro Voters League is circulating a petition to require the city to hire colored streetcar conductors," he said. "If we can get enough Negroes registered to vote, we can really change things in this town."

When we crossed the Tyler Avenue Bridge, we were overwhelmed by a stench so strong it made your eyes water.

"Welcome to the West Side," Jim Richardson announced. "As you have no doubt noticed, the Carlson Paper Mill is just up the road." As Jim's touring car jounced and juddered over the uneven roads, the air became thick with dust and reeked of something that smelled like a mixture of skunk and rotting cabbage.

"White folks have been building like crazy on the West Side now that the Great War is over," Jim explained, rolling up the window in a vain attempt to keep out the stink. "Jack Pepperell is putting up a new sawmill, right next to Handy's Furniture Company. And up ahead to the right is the Makin Lumber Company, the biggest mill in town. The factories are booming, Nola. There are more jobs for Negroes here than there have ever been."

I stared out the window at the vast sawmill squatting on a lot that sloped down to the banks of the Mississippi river. As far as the eye could see, the land was dotted with stacks of lumber, many rising as high as a two-story building. The hundreds of saws whining away inside the building could be heard from the street as we passed by, mingling with the shouts of the men and the clatter of the freight train rolling along the railroad tracks on the opposite side of the street.

"The factories may be booming," I said, "but crime in Agate is booming, too. The streets of Lincolnsville are crawling with hustlers. Agate's become a tough place to live for any colored girl who's down on her luck."

"Which is exactly why Mrs. Wyatt founded Phyllis Wheatley Institute in the first place," Jim said. "I admit she's a bit of a Puritan, but she's done a remarkable job with those girls." He looked at me and smiled. "Even you turned out pretty good, if you'll allow me to say so."

I smiled. "I suppose I've done okay, all things considered," I admitted.

Jim Richardson's Nash touring car was sleek and comfortable. After we passed the Wells Coal Mine, he turned off the main highway onto a narrow gravel road lined on both sides by corn fields. When I made this journey the day before, it took me over an hour to walk from the last streetcar stop at the Wells Coal Mine to Wheatley Institute. In Jim Richardson's sleek Nash touring car, we made the trip in just a few minutes. He pulled his car to the curb in front of Phyllis Wheatley Institute, turned off the engine, and helped me out of the car.

"Keep your chin up, Nola," he said. "You've had a rough night, but I do believe things are going to work out."

"Maybe," I said softly. "I just wish I knew how."

"Don't you worry," he said, then touched me gently on the shoulder. "Mind if I give you a hug?"

He pulled me close without waiting for an answer. As I rested my head against his broad chest, my mind whirled around in somersaults. Was Jim merely being compassionate, or was there something else going on here? Before I could even begin to process this unexpected gesture, he released me, walked back to the driver's side of his car and got in.

"You're not coming with me?" I said, trying not to let my disappointment show. I'd only known the man for a couple of hours, and already I was going to miss his company and support.

"I wish I could, but I've got a meeting at City Hall in half an hour," he said. "I'll have to drive like a maniac to make it back in time. Stay strong, Nola. I'll check in with you later this afternoon."

CHAPTER 9

I took a deep breath as I watched Jim Richardson's car drive away. I didn't need to use my psychic powers to know the conversation I was about to have with Mrs. Wyatt was going to be difficult.

The grim expression on Miss Maybelle Clark's long, horsey face as she opened the front door confirmed my worst suspicions.

"Good afternoon, Nola," Miss Clark said. There was enough frost in her voice to freeze the Sahara desert. "Mrs. Wyatt will see you in her office now. Follow me." Without waiting for me to reply, Miss Clark turned and started walking toward Mrs. Wyatt's office.

I followed her down the hallway. As I passed the front parlor, the voice of a woman caught my attention.

"Phyllis Wheatley started out as a humble slave, but by the end of her life, became a world-renowned poet," the woman said in a clear, high voice. "Presidents, kings, and queens praised the work of this talented Negro woman."

I stopped and looked inside the room. Marsha and Minerva

Williams, Darlette Wilson and the rest of the Wheatley Institute girls sat on two overstuffed couches facing the window and listened as a diminutive Negro woman in a stylish blue dress continued to speak: "You girls are going through tough times right now. Remember that you have the power to create a better life, no matter what your current circumstances. Just look at what Phyllis Wheatley, a lowly slave, was able to accomplish."

Intrigued, I paused outside the door to listen until Miss Clark looked back over her shoulder and beckoned impatiently. With a resigned sigh, I followed her to the end of the hallway and waited beneath the large oil portrait of Frederick Douglass as Miss Clark knocked on Mrs. Wyatt's door.

It had been four years since I'd been inside Mrs. Wyatt's office. When I lived at the Institute, a visit to Mrs. Wyatt's office could only mean one thing: I had misbehaved yet again and was about to be punished. Mrs. Wyatt's office seemed huge to me when I was a teenager, as large as the personality of the woman who inhabited it.

As I followed Miss Clark into the room, I was struck by how small it actually was. One narrow window looked out on the barren fields surrounding the building. A cherrywood desk overflowing with books and papers stood in the center of the room. A portrait of Harriet Tubman hung on the back wall. A large bookshelf, a locked metal filing cabinet, and two leather armchairs made up the remaining office furniture.

Mrs. Wyatt sat behind her desk. As was her custom, she wore a tailored gray business suit. Her silver hair was swept up in a French braid and pinned with a tortoiseshell comb that complimented the matching pearl necklace and earrings she wore. Despite the elegance of her outward appearance, however, Mrs. Wyatt's aura was a dancing collection of jittery colors—green flashes alternated with twisting yellow tendrils that circled and looped around her head like a cloud of buzzing gnats.

"Close the door, Miss Clark, and sit down, both of you," she said. Without looking up, Mrs. Wyatt gestured toward the two leather armchairs across from her desk. As soon as Miss Clark and I were seated, Mrs. Wyatt pointed wordlessly at the afternoon edition of the *Agate Daily Chronicle* lying on her desk.

I picked up the paper and began to read.

Wheatley Institute Resident Is Prime Suspect in Murder of Negro Musician, the headline read. Black and Tan Joy Joint Destroyed by Mysterious Fire.

"Oh no," I said softly. "They're saying Lilly did this?"

Mrs. Wyatt nodded grimly. "Go on, Nola. Read the rest of it."

The *Agate Daily Chronicle* was the only newspaper in town, well-known for its sensational treatment of even the most trivial of stories. As I continued to read, I felt my stomach tighten with anxiety.

Police are on the lookout for a 17-year-old mulatto girl, described as being under five feet tall with a fair complexion and light brown hair. Local student Abigail Everleigh, who was present at the time of the fire, has identified the mysterious suspect as "Lilly," a resident of our city's notorious Phyllis Wheatley Institute for Colored Girls. A frequent visitor to the Wham Bam Club, an illicit pleasure palace and music hall, "Lilly" was seen waving a pistol at the victim, colored bandleader Edward Smooth, earlier in the evening. "Lilly" is believed to be armed and is considered dangerous.

As if that weren't bad enough, the writer concluded his article with an editorial statement:

The Phyllis Wheatley Institute has failed in its charge to educate homeless Negro girls. To stem the tide of undesirable Negroes flooding into our city, this writer urges the City

Welfare Board to put an end to this ill-conceived experiment
once and for all.

When I had finished the article, I looked at Mrs. Wyatt in
disbelief. "Surely they can't be serious," I said.

"I received a telegram from the welfare board not twenty
minutes ago," Mrs. Wyatt said. "They plan to hold a hearing
next Monday to discuss the future of Wheatley Institute."

Miss Clark sucked her teeth in disgust. "Those folks at the
welfare board have been trying to shut us down for months,"
she said. "You were supposed to find the girl and bring her
back here, Nola. What in heaven's name happened?"

"I wish I knew," I replied. "I was with Lilly less than an
hour before the murder. All she could talk about was how
much she wanted to marry Eddie Smooth. She wanted my
Aunt Sarah to fix her a Binding Potion to make Eddie stay with
her. For better or for worse, Lilly was crazy about that man. I
can't believe she killed him."

Mrs. Wyatt sighed heavily. "Lilly Davidson is a smart girl
with a brilliant future ahead of her," she said. "Is the girl difficult? Yes, and temperamental, too. But to shoot a man in cold
blood like that? It's just not possible."

"Lilly is no killer," Miss Clark said impatiently. "I know it,
you know it, and Nola knows it. The question is, how do we
get the police and the City Welfare Board to agree with us?"

The three of us sat in glum silence for a long minute. Then, I
got a bright idea: "If we can come up with enough evidence to
point the police in the direction of the real killer, then we
should be able to persuade the welfare board to see things dif-
ferently. We need to get the welfare board and the City of
Agate to see us as the last bulwark of decency and justice. We
are protecting innocent girls just like Lilly from the evil influ-
ences of a corrupt and tawdry world."

"The board has been reluctant to consider anything that

challenges their preconception that all Negroes are criminals,"
Mrs. Wyatt said. "That is the problem. They are already convinced that Lilly Davidson is guilty."

"Eddie Smooth had a lot of enemies," I said. "If I do some
more investigating, I might be able to figure out which one of
them really killed him. Abigail Everleigh, the girl who told the
Daily Chronicle about Lilly, is the niece of one of the white
people Mr. Layton does catering for. I could talk to her and try
to find out what she actually saw the night of the murder."

Miss Clark gave me a skeptical look. "I thought you were
supposed to be psychic," she said scornfully. "Can't you just
look into your crystal ball and see who the murderer is?"

What on earth was this woman's problem? I had no idea why
Miss Maybelle Clark had it in for me. In that moment, I really
didn't care. It had been a difficult two days, and I was not in the
mood for sarcasm.

"Sometimes I see things, and sometimes I don't," I said. As I
spoke, I could feel my temper rising. "Do you want to know
what I see right now, Miss Clark? I see that you're furious with
yourself. Furious because you failed to prevent the girls sneaking out in the first place."

Stung, Miss Clark bit her lip and looked away.

"Please, ladies," Mrs. Wyatt said gently. "Let's not quarrel
amongst ourselves. We've got enough to worry about as it is.
Nola's idea has merit. If we can uncover the real perpetrator of
this sordid crime, we will clear Lilly's name and vindicate the
Wheatley Institute."

"Lilly could tell us what really went on that night," Miss Clark
said, "but with our luck, the girl has probably left town."

"There's a chance Lilly is still in the area," I said. "Can you
think of anybody else in Agate she might go to for help?"

"Miss Constant, the librarian at the public library on Lincoln Avenue," Mrs. Wyatt said. "I don't know why I didn't

think of her before. She and Lilly were working on some kind of writing project together."

Miss Clark nodded in agreement. "Miss Constant is giving a lecture in the front room this very minute," she said. "Shall I ask her to come in when she's finished?"

Mrs. Wyatt shook her head. "No, not just yet," she said. "If by some chance Miss Constant is sheltering Lilly, we don't want to spook either one of them by asking too many questions. This whole matter needs to be approached with the utmost delicacy."

I nodded. "Miss Constant knows both of you, but she doesn't know me at all," I said. "Perhaps I could tell her I want to be a writer, just like Lilly, get her to talk to me about the girl and ask a few questions."

Miss Clark gave me a dubious look. "Sounds pretty fishy to me," she said. "You really think your plan could work?"

"We have to start somewhere," Mrs. Wyatt said firmly. "The police are on the lookout for Lilly and it's only a matter of time before she is found. Unless we can turn up some other suspects, Lilly Davidson is going to be charged with murder."

CHAPTER 10

Miss Clark and I walked into the front parlor and stood in the back while Miss Eleanor Constant finished her lecture. The librarian was a tiny woman with thick horn-rimmed spectacles and skin the color of dark chocolate. She wore a fashionable long-waisted yellow dress and a cheerful smile.

"I know you're down on your luck right now, girls," she told her audience, waving her arms for emphasis as she spoke, "but the dark days of slavery are over. No matter how challenging your life may be at the moment, you are free. Free to choose your own destiny, no matter what others may say. Seize your moment, ladies!"

The eight residents of Wheatley Institute broke into applause as Miss Constant stepped away from the podium that had been set up in the center of the room. Her bookish appearance and tiny stature heightened her remarkable charisma. Girls who'd most likely never gotten past the fourth grade gathered around her, asking for recommendations from the array of books she'd brought to share with them from the shelves of the public library.

As Miss Clark and I stood at the back of the room, Minerva Williams eyed me curiously. Yesterday at lunch, she'd questioned why I was being allowed into the institute during the day, instead of waiting until dinner, as was customary. As she watched me, a welter of suspicious green question marks filled her aura.

"Where were you this morning, Nola?" she said. "You didn't show up for breakfast."

Miss Clark gave the girl a disapproving look. "Where Nola went and what she did this morning are absolutely none of your business, young lady," she said. "Go in the dining room and set the table for lunch."

"Yes, ma'am," Minerva replied sullenly, but didn't move.

Miss Clark tapped her foot impatiently. "Well?" she said. "You heard me, Minerva. Don't just stand there. That dining room table is not going to set itself!"

"Yes, Miss Clark," Minerva said. She shot me a dirty look and stomped out of the parlor.

When the last eager girl had chosen a book to read from Miss Constant's offerings, she put the remaining library books away in a small traveling case. As the librarian began to put on her coat, Miss Clark poked me in the ribs. "Go on, Nola," she whispered. "Talk to her before she leaves. Now's your chance."

I nodded and walked to the front of the room. "May I speak to you for a moment, Miss Constant?" I said.

"Of course," she replied. "By the way, the girls here call me Miss Eleanor. What can I do for you?"

"My friend Lilly Davidson told me about you," I said. "She said you were helping her to write a story. I want to be a novelist, just like Lilly. Do you think you could help me?"

The librarian raised an eyebrow at me as she buttoned up her coat. "And you are?"

"Nola Ann Jackson," I said. "Lilly said I should talk to you if I wanted to be a writer."

I never was a very good liar, and I couldn't be sure if Miss Constant believed me or not.

"Lilly Davidson is in a world of trouble, as you are no doubt aware," she answered. "Nonetheless, I'm quite fond of her. I've got to get back to the library now, but if you'll stop by tomorrow, I'll see what I can do to help you." As she walked toward the front door, I followed her.

"Are you going back to Lincoln Avenue?" I said. "I hope it's not impertinent of me to ask, but could you give me a lift? Miss Clark said I could go downtown to visit my Aunt Sarah this afternoon. Perhaps we could talk on the way."

"As long as it's all right with Miss Clark," Miss Eleanor said. She turned to Miss Clark, who hovered just within hearing range. "Do I have your permission, Miss Clark?"

For what it was worth, Miss Clark was a far better liar than I was. She actually pretended to think the matter over for a minute before grudgingly nodding her head in approval. "Very well," she said, "but see that you behave yourself, Nola."

Ten minutes later, I was riding down Tyler Avenue in Miss Eleanor Constant's car, a large Model T that coughed and sputtered. Fumes from the exhaust pipe filtered in through the half-open window, and the occasional sound of the engine backfiring punctuated our conversation. Despite these disturbances, Miss Eleanor maneuvered her way down the rutted street and onto Tyler Avenue with easy confidence.

"Why are you really here, Miss Jackson?" she said. "If I'm not mistaken, you are Sarah Brown's niece, and have recently moved here from New York City. I've known your Aunt Sarah for years. If you are half as good a psychic as she is, there has got to be a reason why you've suddenly arrived at Wheatley Institute. Has Sallie Wyatt brought you in to find out what really happened to Lilly Davidson?"

I laughed. "You sure you're not clairvoyant, Miss Eleanor?"

"Just my teacher's instinct," she told me. "Lilly Davidson was working on a special project with me. She wanted to have one of her stories published in *The Crisis*."

"*The Crisis* publishes famous Negro writers like Paul Lawrence Dunbar and W. E. B. Du Bois," I said. "Is Lilly really that good?"

"She's very talented," Miss Eleanor replied. "If she sticks with it, Lilly might end up becoming a successful writer—the next Ida B. Wells, or even Jessie Fauset."

Miss Eleanor stopped speaking for a moment to focus on passing the large lumber truck in front of us. When the truck was safely in the rearview mirror, she continued. "Lilly grew up in an orphanage in Joliet. She became obsessed with finding her birth parents and telling their story. She spent hours in my library, poring over old newspapers and birth records. Recently she'd come to believe that her real father was a white man from one of Agate's elite families."

"Mrs. Wyatt mentioned something about this," I said thoughtfully. "Any truth to this idea?"

"I doubt it, but it made a good story," Miss Eleanor said. "Lilly is a diehard romantic, you know. She was a dreamer who saw everything in her life as one big fairy tale. She was always hoping for that perfect happy ending, looking for some Prince Charming to rescue her."

For the next several minutes, Miss Eleanor and I drove in thoughtful silence. As the scenery along the road changed from mills and mines to scattered houses and finally, to the stone buildings and cobbled streets of downtown Agate, I brooded on the nature of the female heart. What was it about falling in love that caused even the brightest, most talented girls to turn into absolute idiots?

Love was a beautiful thing, but it could make you lose your natural mind. Four years ago, I'd been crazy about Will Jackson, crazy enough to follow him all the way to Harlem, only to lose him to a German artillery shell in the final days of the war. Will had been dead nearly four years, but I still missed him terribly. At the same time, I was beginning to think that it might be nice to have a man in my life once again. As Miss Constant pulled her Model T to the curb at the corner of Lincoln Avenue and Main Street, I wondered if Jim Richardson was married. I made a mental note to ask Aunt Sarah about this when I got home.

The Frederick Douglass branch of the Agate Public Library was the only one of the city's three branches that served Negroes. The large granite building was located in an otherwise dismal block that housed a warehouse, a steam laundry, a barbecue joint, and a run-down wooden tenement. As Miss Eleanor and I climbed the wide staircase leading to the front door of the library, I was struck by the number of people going and coming through the main entrance. The five long wooden tables that ran down the center of the reading room were packed. Students from Washington High School sat side by side with senior citizens and housewives, each engrossed in their own private literary world.

Holding a cautionary finger to her lips, Miss Constant led me into her office. Not surprisingly, her desk was covered with books. At the rear, a small barred window overlooked the street below.

"I'm glad that you are looking into this, Nola. If there is anything I can do to assist you, just let me know," she said. "Lilly has had a rough life and needs all the help she can get."

"Do you know where she is?" I asked. "Mrs. Wyatt tells me that you were the only adult that Lilly was close to. Sorry if I'm being rude, but I have to ask."

Miss Eleanor smiled. "No offense taken," she said. "And no. I have not seen or heard from Lilly in over a week."

"Was there anyone else around here that she was close to? Can you think of anywhere else she might have gone to hide?"

Miss Eleanor shook her head. "Not really. The only other adult she was at all friendly with was Jim Richardson, from the Negro Voters League. Have you spoken to him?"

I nodded yes, hoping that Mrs. Eleanor wasn't psychic enough to notice the pink in my aura when his name was mentioned. "He wasn't able to tell me anything more about her disappearance, except that it was sudden. One minute Lilly was sitting in the auditorium at the YMCA, listening to James Weldon Johnson give a lecture. The next minute she was gone. I suspect Eddie was hanging around there somewhere, and helped her get away."

"Makes sense," Miss Eleanor said. "Thanks to that scurrilous rag, the *Agate Daily Chronicle*, we now know that Lilly argued with Eddie Smooth at the Wham Bam Club on the night he was shot. I still don't think she killed him, though. Eddie Smooth was a pimp, after all. He worked in a speakeasy and associated with gangsters. Surely there must be other suspects."

"Exactly," I said. "I went to the Wham Bam Club the night of the murder, hoping to convince Lilly to return to Wheatley Institute. While I was there, I saw Boss Dillard's bodyguard run out of the club shortly before Eddie Smooth was killed."

"That could be an important clue," Miss Eleanor said thoughtfully. "Gangsters shoot people all the time. The trouble is, you can't just walk into Boss Dillard's office and ask him about it."

We contemplated this reality in thoughtful silence for a minute. Then Miss Eleanor said suddenly, "Maybe there's a way around this, Nola. If I'm not mistaken, Jim Richardson and Boss Dillard went to school together. Perhaps if Jim went with you, Boss Dillard would be more willing to answer a few questions."

"Now that I think of it, Jim did tell me that he knew Boss Dillard." I smiled as I remembered how unconcerned he'd been about receiving a parking ticket in front of the police station that morning. "I'll drop by and pay him a visit. Boss Dillard isn't likely to tell me the full truth about what happened the night of the murder, but he might let something slip. Even the smallest clue would be helpful."

Miss Eleanor nodded. "When you see Jim Richardson, give him my regards," she said. To my surprise, I saw a small blue cloud flit through her aura. Was it possible Miss Eleanor knew Jim Richardson more intimately than she was letting on?

As I turned to go, Miss Eleanor touched me on the arm. "This is absolutely none of my business, but I'm going to say it anyway, because I like you, Nola. Jimmy Richardson is a very charming man, but he can be a bit irresponsible where women are concerned. I wouldn't want you to get hurt."

I felt my face grow warm from embarrassment. How had she known I was attracted to the man? "No worries on that score," I told her. "He's nice enough, but he's really not my type. He's got to be at least thirty."

"Of course," Miss Eleanor said. I don't think she believed me, but she was kind enough to let the subject drop. "It's none of my business, and I hope you'll forgive me for intruding." She extracted a slim volume from the pile of books on her desk and handed it to me. "When you find Lilly, be sure to give her this."

When I saw the title, I gave a low whistle. *The Five Founding Families of Agate: An Illustrated History*, by Harry A. Skelton Sr.

"Was this written by Congressman Skelton's father?" I asked.

Miss Eleanor nodded. "Lilly's been asking me to find it for weeks. I was finally able to get hold of an old copy from the main library downtown."

"I'll be sure she gets it," I said.

I left Miss Eleanor's office and walked back through the reading room. I was a long way from proving Lilly Davidson innocent of murder, but at least I had a plan. Best of all, a plan that would require me to pay another visit to Mr. Jim Richardson. But as much as I wanted to see him again, it would have to wait until tomorrow. According to the clock on the wall, it was already three o'clock. I was due at DeLuxe Catering in an hour. If I hurried, I'd have just enough time to wash up, change into my work uniform, and say hello to my Aunt Sarah before heading off to work.

CHAPTER 11

When I got home, my Aunt Sarah was sitting in a rocking chair next to the kitchen stove, sipping a cup of tea.

"There you are, Nola," she said. "Why didn't you come home last night? You all right?" I leaned over and kissed her wrinkled forehead.

"I'm fine," I said. "The last few hours have been a whirlwind. I'm terribly sorry to worry you."

"I wasn't worried for too long," she said with a mischievous grin. "Not after my Spirits told me you were having breakfast with that handsome Jim Richardson fella."

Darn! I loved my Aunt Sarah to death, but it was impossible to keep secrets from her. "It's not what you think," I said. "I'll tell you all about it when I come home tonight. Right now I've got to get ready for work. If I show up late again, Mr. Layton is going to kill me."

I splashed some cold water on my face, put on my black dress, frilly hat, and white pinafore with the DeLuxe Catering emblem sewn across the front, and grabbed my coat.

"I'll be back by ten tonight," I said. "I'll fill you in on everything then, I promise."

I walked down to Lincoln Avenue, where to my great relief, the southbound streetcar stopped for me without incident. Fifteen minutes later, I walked into the offices of Deluxe Catering at the stroke of four, just in time for my shift.

Minty Layton was in a foul temper when I arrived, her aura a thundercloud waiting to explode.

"I don't see how this woman expects us to prepare a decent meal when she calls us at the last minute like this," she fumed. She yanked down a five-pound bag of flour from the storage cabinet and wedged it into an already overflowing crate of baking supplies.

"Put this in the truck, Nola," she snapped. "Get a move on. We are running late as it is."

I did not ask Minty who she was talking about or where we were going. I'd worked for Mr. and Mrs. Layton long enough to know this was no time to ask for clarification or details.

"Yes, ma'am," I said and carried the crate outside.

Ten minutes later, as Mr. Layton drove the DeLuxe Catering delivery truck down Lincoln Avenue, Minty explained that Mrs. Ratcliffe was hosting an early supper for the Agate Ladies Auxiliary at her home that evening. The roast chicken, green beans, and mashed potatoes Mrs. Ratcliffe wanted us to prepare was easy enough. The problem was that in the middle of the afternoon Mrs. Ratcliffe had developed a last-minute craving for Minty's oyster soufflé, a request that resulted in Mr. Layton making a frantic trip to Sam's Fish Market to grab the last remaining oysters from the day's catch.

"Lucky for Mrs. Ratcliffe, Sam Weatherston is a friend of mine," Minty said. "Soon as I called, he was able to put three dozen aside for us. Otherwise, I don't know what I would have done."

Just after the oysters were purchased Mrs. Ratcliffe had called again. Her neighbor's son was having a birthday party, and she wanted to give a popcorn ball to each of the children. Would Minty fix a dozen popcorn balls and bring them along?

"How am I supposed to find time to prepare the damn things," Minty fumed. "I already got the chicken and the soufflé to deal with."

Edward Layton reached over and patted his wife gently on the knee. "You will manage, my dear," he said calmly. "Just as you always do."

"Humph," Minty replied gloomily. "We'll see."

The moment we set foot in Mrs. Ratcliffe's kitchen, Minty Layton barked out orders to me at lightning speed.

"Bring me that roasting pan, Nola. No, not that one. The big one. How am I gonna cook a roasting chicken in something that small? Use your head, girl."

"Yes, ma'am," I said.

Like many great cooks, Minty Layton was a true artist with a temperament to match. When she got like this, the best thing to do was cooperate and then get out of the way. She usually calmed down once dinner was on the table.

After the chicken had been rubbed down with garlic, oregano, and thyme and placed in the oven to cook, Mr. Layton and I got busy slicing the green beans. Most folks liked their green beans plain. But to make Minty's fancy beans you had to cut off both ends and slice the beans lengthwise into thin strips. When sautéed in a pan with butter and slivered almonds, Minty Layton's French green beans were beyond delicious. While Mr. Layton and I cut up the beans, Minty began the delicate process of preparing the oyster soufflé. Soon, the smell of oysters simmering with butter, onion, mushrooms, and garlic filled the kitchen.

Mrs. Ratcliffe walked into the kitchen a few minutes later. In her typical style, she launched into conversation, starting in the middle of a subject, assuming that those around her knew what she was talking about.

"That man is an absolute disgrace," she said angrily, "an utter embarrassment to the religion of Spiritualism."

"What man might that be?" Mr. Layton said mildly, and continued slicing string beans as Mrs. Ratcliffe spoke.

"That so-called 'reverend' Timothy Gonsails, of course." Sparks of anger flew out of Mrs. Ratcliffe's aura and danced around the room. "That hood-wearing moron is holding Klan rallies on the front lawn of his church."

"Lots of folks joining the Klan these days," Minty said, as she added flour to the oysters simmering on the stove. "Sad but true."

"Lots of folks may be joining, but this one has the absolute nerve to call himself a Spiritualist minister," Mrs. Ratcliffe said. "I sent him a telegram demanding that he cease and desist from holding these ridiculous events at once. And do you know what he said?" Without waiting for a response, she pulled a yellow telegram from her pocket and began to read:

"My Fiery Cross Ice Cream Socials are 100% American and very good fun," he says. "Disparage them at your peril. Woe to the enemies of True Americans!"

She balled up the telegram in her fist and hurled it to the floor in disgust. "Good fun, he calls it! Can you imagine?"

Minty Layton shook her head sadly as she cracked a dozen eggs one by one, deftly separating the egg yolks from the whites and dropping them into a bowl. "It's a crying shame what's going on," Minty said. "The Klan has opened a new office in Agate, right on Main Street."

Mrs. Portia Ratcliffe pulled herself up to her full height. "I don't care how popular these Ku Kluxers are," she announced. "I refuse to be intimidated. Congressman Skelton is coming here for dinner tomorrow night. I will demand that he take action."

A yellow wave of panic bubbled just beneath Mr. Layton's calm exterior. "I was not aware you were planning to entertain tomorrow evening," he said. "Did you want us to cater it for you?"

"Naturally," Mrs. Ratcliffe said grandly. "I will expect the three of you here tomorrow afternoon at four thirty on the dot."

"Yes, ma'am," Mr. Layton replied stoically. "Will there be other guests?"

Mrs. Ratcliffe paused for a moment, then clapped her hands together. "An excellent idea," she said. "I'll invite the Congressman's assistant, Mr. Fairchild, and his wife. To round out the party, I'll see if Richard and Harriet Wallaby can join us." Mrs. Ratcliffe's aura sparkled with excitement. "This is going to be fun," she exclaimed. "When tonight's guests have left, the three of us will plan out the menu."

When Mrs. Ratcliffe had left the kitchen, Minty Layton looked at her husband and sighed. "That woman is going to be the death of me," she said. "I could get heart failure from all this pressure. How can I possibly get a fancy dinner ready in one day? We've got to buy the food, prepare the food, and clean the dining area. Then there's the fresh flowers, the clean linen, and making sure the silver is polished. It's absolutely impossible."

"We'll manage," Mr. Layton replied calmly. "Just like we always do."

Minty nodded and sighed again. "I suppose so," she said. "Meanwhile, let's get tonight's meal out on the table." Using the dish towel in her hand as a pot holder, she pulled the chicken out of the oven and placed it on top of the stove. "Nola, set this roast on a platter and garnish it with parsley," she said. "Make sure it looks nice and pretty. We'll wait till the last minute to bring out the oyster soufflé."

Despite the drama taking place in the kitchen, Minty's dinner was a huge success. As I served the coffee, Mrs. Ratcliffe's guests raved about the soufflé and begged her for the recipe.

"Scrumptious," one woman maintained, while another of the guests said she had never tasted an oyster dish this wonderful, not even on her last visit to New Orleans.

When the dinner dishes had been cleared away, Mr. Layton brought out a large bowl of popcorn balls sweetened with corn syrup and studded with tiny marshmallows and handed them to Mrs. Ratcliffe. "For the birthday party of your neighbor's son," he explained. "We made one dozen, as you requested."

"Perfect," Mrs. Ratcliffe said. "I'll have my husband take them next door for the children."

I was cleaning the marble countertop next to the sink half an hour later when Mr. Layton walked up behind me.

"One of the cooks at the Wham Bam Club told me he saw you there the night it burned down," he said. "What were you doing there?"

"A friend invited me," I replied, hoping he would not probe further. "I had never been there, and I was curious."

"You picked a strange night to indulge your curiosity," Mr. Layton said. "My friend tells me he saw you being taken away." He gave me a hard look. "What do you have to say for yourself, Nola?"

"I didn't do anything wrong," I told him. "The police took just about everyone they could find down to headquarters for questioning. They let me go right away."

"And that's all there is to it?" he asked.

"Yes sir," I said.

He cocked his head and studied me for a minute. "Are you sure?"

I nodded, avoided eye contact and scoured the marble countertop with renewed vigor. Mr. and Mrs. Layton took great pains to assure their wealthy white customers that anyone employed by DeLuxe Catering was not only qualified, but one hundred percent trustworthy. If Edward Layton thought I was mixed up with any of the shady characters at the Wham Bam Club, he would fire me on the spot.

"Have it your way, Nola," Mr. Layton said. "If you want to continue working for DeLuxe Catering company, you'll need to stay away from gin joints like that in the future."

Minty Layton touched her husband gently on the arm. "Now, now, Edward," she cooed. "Nola is a good girl. She's not going to do anything that brings disrepute to our company." Minty put a hand on her hip, then flashed me a no-nonsense look. "You would never do anything like that, would you, dear?"

"You can count on me," I said gravely. "I will be on my best behavior in the future, I promise."

"I certainly hope so," Minty replied. Before she could say anything more, Mrs. Ratcliffe sailed into the kitchen.

"The dinner menu for tomorrow night needs to be extraordinary," she announced. "Tell me what you think we should prepare."

As Mrs. Ratcliffe and the two Laytons huddled around the kitchen table, I excused myself and stepped outside for some fresh air.

Edward Layton was not to be trifled with, I thought glumly. I needed to stay on the straight and narrow if I wanted to keep my job, which did not bode well for my plan to pay Boss Dillard a visit at the Black Rooster Pool Hall the following day. I could only hope that none of Mr. Layton's nosey friends would spot me going inside.

I was standing brooding on the sidewalk in front of Mrs. Ratcliffe's house when a taxicab pulled to the curb in front of me. When I saw Abigail Everleigh stagger out of the car, I suddenly felt hopeful. Abigail claimed she saw Lilly Davidson waving a gun at Eddie Smooth on the night of the murder. If I played my cards right, I could get the girl to tell me all about it.

I walked over to the girl and smiled. "Good evening, Miss Abigail," I said.

Miss Everleigh staggered closer and peered at me. "That you, Nola?"

"Yes, miss."

"My goodness, it's dark out here. Cold too," she said. "You wouldn't happen to have any Stark's Headache Powder on you, would you? I've got a real doozy of a hangover."

When I shook my head, Abigail pulled a silver flask from her handbag. "A girl's got to fortify herself if she's going to be out in this kind of weather." She took a quick nip, screwed the cap back on and replaced the flask in her purse. "Have you seen Mrs. Ratcliffe today?"

"She's in the kitchen," I said. "Planning the menu for tomorrow night's dinner with Congressman Skelton."

"How very la-di-dah," Abigail said. "Do you think the old bag is still angry with me?"

I suspected Mrs. Ratcliffe would never forgive Abigail for her disruptive behavior at Thursday's séance. In the hopes of pumping Abigail for information, I opted for a more neutral response.

"I really couldn't say, miss," I told her.

"Not that I give a hoot about Portia Ratcliffe," Abigail said sourly. "She could drop dead for all I care. That woman's got my Uncle Bayard wrapped around her little finger, and dear Uncle Bayard controls my inheritance. If Portia Ratcliffe tells him to cut me off, I'm done for." Abigail Eveleigh sighed, pulled out her flask and took another long swallow. "At least until I turn twenty-one. When that day comes, I'm gonna jump up and shout hallelujah!"

In a drunken imitation of a Negro preacher, she bugged out her eyes, stared up to heaven, and waved her hands in the air. "Yes, Lawdy," she shouted in an imitation Southern accent. "Gonna sing and dance like your people did when Lincoln freed the slaves."

I cringed inwardly, but did not react. I had no time to bother with Abigail's nonsense. I had a murder to solve.

"You told the reporter from the *Daily Chronicle* you saw Lilly Davidson fighting with Eddie Smooth the night of the murder," I said. "How did you know it was Lilly? Did Eddie Smooth introduce you?"

"Eddie? Don't be ridiculous," she replied archly. "I barely knew that man."

"I don't mean to pry, Miss Abigail," I lied. I absolutely did mean to pry, but there was nothing to be gained by advertising this fact. "You will remember that I was sitting at your table when Eddie Smooth sang that song about the lonely girl," I told her. "That song was about you, Miss Abigail. Eddie Smooth was goading you with it, trying to hurt you." I stepped in closer and looked her in the eye. "Did you speak to Eddie Smooth afterwards? Did you let him know how angry you were?"

Abigail Everleigh looked down at the ground for a minute. "I might have had words with Eddie last night," she admitted. "Or maybe the night before. My nights tend to run together sometimes."

"It's not every night your favorite speakeasy burns to the ground," I said. "Not every night your favorite trumpet player is murdered."

"Ask me if I care," she shot back. "No offense, but you coloreds are known to be violent. I'm not at all surprised that Lilly Davidson shot him. Eddie Smooth was the type of man that could drive a woman to murder."

If I hadn't been paying attention, I'd have missed the tiny streak of pink that peeked through her aura as she spoke. "What type of man was that, Miss Abigail?"

"Handsome," she said softly. "Attractive, in a dangerous sort of way. The kind of man who could charm the knickers off a nun. I don't fancy colored men, but I could see why other girls wanted to be with him."

I was about to ask Abigail more about Eddie Smooth and his women when she suddenly began to cry.

"This is all Lilly's fault," Abigail said, wiping away a tear with the back of her hand. "That black bitch has ruined everything." Abigail Everleigh was talking to me, but her eyes were focused inward, as though lost in the past.

"Tell me what happened, Miss Abigail," I said softly.

"Eddie and I had a big fight that night," she replied. "I wanted him to keep Lilly Davidson away from Joe. If he wanted to have Lilly turning tricks at the Wham Bam Club, that was his own affair. I'm as broad-minded as the next girl when it comes to these things, and not above having an adventure or two myself. But Joe was completely besotted with the girl, absolutely obsessed. He was always sneaking down to the basement, hoping to get a glimpse of her. He thought I didn't know, but a girl's got intuitions, you know? I was *not* going to lose my man to some colored whore. I told Eddie I wanted it to stop."

"What did Joe have to say about all this?" I asked. "Did you confront him about his interest in Lilly?"

As I waited for her reply, Abigail bit her lip and looked down at the sidewalk.

"No," she said. "Joe has not spoken to me in two days. When I came home from the fire, I thought sure he'd at least stop by to see if I was all right, if I was even alive. But I haven't heard from him. Nothing, not a single word."

Now we were getting somewhere, I thought. Abigail Everleigh and Joe Quincy both knew Eddie Smooth well. Could one of them have been angry enough with Eddie to kill him?

"Where were you when the fire broke out, Miss Abigail?" I asked.

"I was downstairs," she said softly.

"In Eddie Smooth's dressing room?" It was a wild guess, but Miss Abigail did not dispute my statement.

"I told Eddie to make Lilly Davidson go away, or else," she said. "I told him my Uncle Bayard was friends with the police commissioner. I said I'd blow the whistle on Eddie's entire pimping operation if he didn't keep Lilly away from my Joe."

Now that I'd gotten Abigail to talk to me, I didn't want to do anything to cut off the flow. I was barely breathing when I asked the next question. "And what was Eddie's reply?"

"He laughed in my face, and said that boys will be boys," she said bitterly. "He said that a man can't control the things he does when a beautiful woman gets her hooks into him."

"And then?"

"He kissed me."

My eyes widened in amazement. Eddie Smooth must have been completely off his rocker. In these parts, a Negro man could be lynched for even looking at a white woman.

"Really?" I said. "What did you do then?"

"I slapped the black bastard in the face," Abigail said. "Lucky for him I'm not buddies with the local Klan boys."

"Eddie must have been angry when you slapped him," I said. "What did he do then?"

"He laughed even harder," Abigail replied. "He told me he had a gun, and that if I didn't stay out of his business, I'd be sorry."

"He pulled a gun on you?"

"No, but I knew he had one," Abigail told me. "He used to brag about what a good shot he was."

A chubby white boy carrying a box wrapped in shiny red paper and tied with a silver bow walked over to us as she spoke. "I'm looking for Bobby Johnson's birthday party," the boy said. "Can you tell me if this is the right house? I'm already late as it is."

"How should I know," Abigail snapped. "Beat it, kid. Go on, scram."

Shocked, the boy burst into tears and ran off. "I'm gonna tell my mommy on you," he shouted over his shoulder.

As the boy's footsteps clattered away from us, Abigail looked around as if emerging from a trance. Her bleary eyes narrowed as they settled on me.

"I don't want to talk about this anymore," she said. "Suffice it to say that Eddie Smooth was a nasty piece of work. I wasn't the one who killed him, but I am not sorry he's dead."

Squaring her shoulders, Abigail Everleigh turned away and marched up Mrs. Ratcliffe's front steps without a backward glance.

CHAPTER 12

It was after ten when I got home from work that night. I thought my Aunt Sarah would probably be asleep, but she was sitting at the kitchen table when I arrived.

"You look like you've been through the ringer," she said. "Tell me what's going on, Nola."

I fixed myself a cup of chamomile tea and told my Aunt Sarah everything. I described the fire at the Wham Bam Club, and told her that Lilly Davidson was now a suspect in the murder of Eddie Smooth. When I told her about my visit to see Miss Eleanor Constant at the public library that morning, my aunt frowned.

"If Eleanor was really that close to Lilly, she may know more than she's letting on," Aunt Sarah said. "What do your Spirits have to say? Did you consult them after you spoke to her?"

"No," I admitted. "For the past two days, I've been running around like a chicken with my head cut off. I've barely had time to eat or sleep, let alone talk to my Spirit Guides." I shook my head in frustration. "I'm no closer to finding Lilly than I was yesterday. If anything, things have taken a step backwards. At least yesterday, I knew she was at the Wham Bam Club. Now, only God knows where she's gone."

Aunt Sarah patted my hand. "Take it easy, Nola. You need to have a little more faith in yourself, and a lot more faith in your Spirits. That is the one big thing my mama taught me. Our Spirits are with us, every step of the way. Did I ever tell you the story about my mama and Old Man Pennington?"

"No, ma'am," I said. "Please tell me. I'd love to hear it." Aunt Sarah was a walking encyclopedia of stories, recipes, and charms that came from way back in slavery times. I took another sip of tea and smiled.

"I was probably no more than five years old at the time, but I remember it like it was yesterday. This was two years before your mother was born. It was just Mama and me back then." She fell silent and stared into her tea cup for a moment. "We were slaves on Marse Pennington's plantation ten miles outside of Natchez, Mississippi. Marse Pennington was always a mean old coot, but after his wife Effie died, he got much worse. He'd get mad over the smallest thing, accuse people of things that were untrue, and lash out at anyone unlucky enough to be around him. When he was in one of his moods, even his own children stayed away."

"It must have been horrible," I said.

Aunt Sarah nodded. "We were slaves, Nola. We had no choice in the matter, no choice at all. My mama was his cook, and I was mama's little helper. I'd fetch the water, mind the fire, and help stir the pots to keep the stew from sticking to the bottom. On this particular day, Marse Pennington received a bill for the new horses he had bought to pull his buggy. He was already using the horses and real happy with them. The only problem was, he'd bought the animals on credit."

I nodded and took another sip of my tea. My aunt's voice had developed a slow, hypnotic quality, pulling me back with her to a dark and troubled time.

"When the bill for those horses came due, Marse Pennington didn't have the money to pay it," Aunt Sarah continued. "He comes into the kitchen and starts yelling at Mama, picking at her about this and that. The food wasn't seasoned right, he said. The biscuits were too heavy, and the dishes hadn't been washed properly. The man stood in the middle of the kitchen, holding that bill for the horses in his hand while he yelled at my mama for a full half hour. All the time, my mama just stands there looking down at the floor without saying a word."

As I listened, I saw the scene clearly in my mind's eye. The potbellied, ruddy-faced Marse Pennington waving his arms and yelling; the steamy, hot kitchen; Aunt Sarah's mama standing silently, enduring the old man's tirade.

"Suddenly Marse Pennington spots me sitting over in the corner playing with my doll," Aunt Sarah said softly. "He points at me and says, 'No wonder you can't do your work. This here pickaninny is distracting you from your duties. She's nothin' but a waste of resources,' he tells my mama. 'I'm not paying to feed and clothe her just so she can play games and lay around. I'm taking her to Natchez in the morning.' He gives my mama another dirty look and stomps out of the kitchen without another word."

Transported in her mind to a time before the end of slavery, Aunt Sarah stared silently into space. After a minute, she continued. "I was just a little girl, but I was old enough to know what he meant when he said he was taking me to Natchez. Natchez was where the slave market was. Folks he took to Natchez never came back. They were sold to traders and taken away to work in the cotton fields, never to be seen again."

In the past two years, I'd spent hundreds of hours talking with Aunt Sarah. In all that time I'd never once heard her talk about slavery. I reached across the table and squeezed her hand. "I didn't know you got sold," I said. "It must have been terrible to be auctioned off like a piece of furniture."

Aunt Sarah nodded. "When Marse Pennington walked out

of that kitchen that night, Mama's face got real serious. So serious it scared me to look at her. When we got back to our cabin, she told me to get in bed and stay there, no matter what I heard or saw."

Spellbound, I waited on the edge of my seat while Aunt Sarah took another sip of her tea.

"That night at the stroke of midnight," Aunt Sarah continued, "my mama went out into the woods alone. I was scared to death but I did just what she told me. I pulled the cover over my head and stayed on my pallet. When she came back, I heard her chanting, saying something in a language I'd never heard her speak before. At the same time, she was sewing some kind of doll out of burlap. She chanted and she sewed all night. After a while, I could have sworn I heard a man's voice talking back to her."

"A man's voice?" I asked. "Whose voice was it? Did your father live with you?"

Aunt Sarah shook her head. "No, child. There was only the two of us in that cabin. Just my mama and me. But somehow the chanting and the singing grew louder and louder until it sounded like an entire choir singing."

"Did you peek?" I asked her. "I know I would have. Weren't you curious to know what was going on?"

"You would think so," Aunt Sarah said, "but the truth was, I was terrified. Whatever was going on was something so strange, and scary, I was too afraid to know what it was." She paused for a moment, then chuckled softly. "My mama was one tough woman, Nola. If she told you to stay somewhere, you did it— no questions asked."

"Then what happened?" Although my tea had grown cold, I didn't want to leave my chair to refill it for fear I'd break the hypnotic spell Aunt Sarah's story had cast over me.

"The singing voices grew louder and louder," Aunt Sarah said. "Then just before dawn, the singing stopped. It didn't slowly die away. It just stopped suddenly in the middle of a phrase. When Mama and I went to work that morning, Marse Pennington was dead. Keeled over in the middle of the night from a heart attack."

A chill ran up my spine. I knew that hoodoo was powerful, but I'd never heard a story like this before. "You think your mama's hoodoo killed that man?" I said.

"I truly can't say, Nola," Aunt Sara replied. "All I know is, Marse Pennington was a healthy man one day, and a dead man the next."

"Was your mama the one who taught you how to talk with the Spirits?"

"Eventually," Aunt Sarah said, "but not until I was much older, after the Civil War. I suppose she was already teaching me little things—how to recognize different plants, how to prepare healing potions, things like that. It was a few years before she taught me about the Ancestors."

"The voices you heard singing that night?" I asked.

Aunt Sarah nodded. "The Ancestors come when they are really needed, Nola. They came to help my mama and me, and when the time is right, they will come to help Lilly Davidson." She patted me gently on the hand. "Your Spirits are closer than you think, Nola. So stop your fretting and get some sleep."

CHAPTER 13

I had planned to get up early the next morning. Instead, my lack of sleep over the last few days finally caught up with me. It was after ten when I finally crawled out of bed.

When Aunt Sarah offered to fix me breakfast, I shook my head. If I skipped breakfast, there was still time for me to stop by Jim Richardson's office before my shift at DeLuxe Catering began. The more I thought about it, the more suspicious it seemed that Mr. Dillard's bodyguard was running away from the Wham Bam Club minutes before the fire broke out. Boss Dillard would probably not be willing to tell me everything he knew about what had happened at the Wham Bam Club that night. But with a little coaxing from his old buddy Jim Richardson, he might relax his guard enough to let an important clue slip through.

On the other hand, a visit to Boss Dillard's office might turn out to be a wild-goose chase. If I was being honest with myself, I had to admit that even a wild-goose chase would not necessarily be a bad thing, as long as it was a goose chase that involved me spending time with Jim Richardson.

On an impulse, I decided to wear an orange dress I hadn't put on in months. The hemline was fashionably short, just below the knee. Not short enough to be scandalous, but eye-catching nonetheless. I pinned a tortoiseshell comb in my hair and checked my reflection in the mirror. *Not bad*, I thought to myself. With my generous hips, full bosom, and shapely legs, I could still turn a man's head when I needed to. Not that I was really interested in turning Jim Richardson's head, I told myself firmly. Still, it never hurt for a girl to look her best.

I stepped outside. It was a beautiful late October day. A westerly breeze kept the stink from the drainage ditch behind Miller's Slaughterhouse from blowing in my direction. Even the grimy brick storefronts along Lincoln Avenue sparkled in the morning sun. The field office of the Negro Voters League where Jim Richardson worked was located in the basement of Shiloh Methodist Church. If I walked briskly I'd get there in fifteen minutes.

Lincoln Avenue was teeming with colored folk, all in a hurry to get somewhere. As I passed the front door of Green's French-Fried Shrimp, the pungent scent of fried seafood and hot sauce filled the air. In my rush to get out of the house, I had skipped breakfast. Although my hungry stomach gurgled hopefully, I continued walking. First things first, I reminded myself. The sooner I got up to Jim Richardson's office, the better. I turned the corner onto Gray Street, and, to my surprise, spotted Jim Richardson striding down the sidewalk ahead of me.

"Jim," I called out.

He stopped walking, turned around, and smiled at me. "Nola Ann Jackson," he said. "May I say you are looking lovely today? That orange dress really suits you. I'd give you a hug, but as you can see, my hands are full." He pointed his chin at the greasy paper bag he held. "I was headed back to the office for a lonely bachelor's lunch. It would really brighten my day if you'd consider joining me."

I smiled. "I was just on my way to pay you a visit. Is that Green's french-fried shrimp?"

"Sure is," Richardson said with a grin. "A taste of down-home goodness, pulled fresh from the Mississippi."

When we arrived at Jim's cramped office in the basement of Shiloh Methodist Church, there was no one else in the building. Shoving the unruly pile of papers on his desk to one side, Jim opened the white paper bag and pulled out a cardboard carton piled to the top with crisp golden pieces of fried shrimp and a large Dixie cup filled with hot sauce. Propping his lanky frame against the side of his desk, Jim waved to the swivel chair behind it.

"Have a seat, beautiful," he said, and pried the lid off the cup with a flourish. "I've eaten in some of the best eateries in the world, but none of them hold a candle to Bettye Green when it comes to seafood. She got her start selling fried shrimp to travelers on the Illinois Central, hawking her wares on the platform at Union Station. These days, Mrs. Green runs her own restaurant and has more customers than she can handle."

Jim dipped a piece of shrimp in hot sauce, popped it in his mouth, then let out a satisfied sigh. "Life is good," he said with a grin. "A good meal and a beautiful woman to share it with. I'd sure like to do this more often, Nola."

This handsome man was definitely flirting with me. However, it had been so long since I'd been in this situation I barely knew how to respond. Perhaps sensing my awkwardness, Jim changed the subject. "How is your investigation going, Nola? Any new leads on the missing girl?"

I took a paper napkin from the bag, wiped a stray crumb off my mouth, and told Jim about my conversation with Eleanor Constant in the library the day before.

"I saw Boss Dillard's bodyguard come running past me at the Wham Bam Club just before the fire," I said. "Of course, there was a lot going on, and I only got a quick glimpse. But when I mentioned it to Miss Eleanor at the library, she reminded me that Boss Dillard was an old friend of yours."

Jim smiled. "Don't know if I'd call Franklin Dillard a close friend, but we do go back a long way," he said. "Whenever I need my traffic tickets fixed, he helps me out."

"I want to talk to Mr. Dillard," I said. "Would you be willing to come with me? I'd love to know what his bodyguard was doing at the Wham Bam Club that night. It's just possible the man may know something that could clear Lilly and point us in the direction of the real killer."

Jim nodded slowly. "It's possible Franklin knows something about this murder," he agreed. "On the other hand, we could be sticking our noses into something really dangerous. What if Franklin's bodyguard is the one who killed Eddie Smooth?"

"I won't ask him straight out whether his bodyguard killed Eddie Smooth," I explained. "My plan would be to ask a few gentle questions and see how he reacts. It could be dangerous, but it's worth a try."

"In a less corrupt city, this would be a job for the police," Jim told me. "But of course, this is Agate, Illinois. It's quite likely that several officers are already being paid to look the other way regarding Franklin Dillard's activities."

"If no other suspects turn up, the police are going to charge Lilly with murder," I said. "Will you help me get in to see Boss Dillard? If there's even the smallest chance he can help us find out who really killed Eddie Smooth, I've got to try, don't you think?"

"All right, Nola," Jim said. "Let's take a walk down to the Black Rooster Pool Hall and pay my old school chum a visit."

Jim Richardson and I made a good team. The man was easy on the eyes, sophisticated, and capable, too. As he reached for another piece of fried shrimp, I studied Jim's left hand covertly. When I saw he was not wearing a wedding ring, I smiled inwardly.

Jim looked at his watch and frowned. "Damn!" he said. "I've got a meeting at the Board of Commissioners in an hour. I can't come with you right now, but we can go tomorrow if you want."

I felt my left ear begin to buzz. "The police are going to find Lilly soon, and tomorrow may be too late. I have to talk to Boss Dillard right away. Can you call Boss Dillard and ask him if he'll agree to see me this afternoon?"

"Girl, you are really something," he said. "Beauty, brains, and courage to boot." He leaned forward and took my hands in his. "When all this is over, I'd sure like to spend some more time with you, Nola Ann Jackson. What do you say?"

Before I could answer, Jim kissed me on the mouth. The kiss only lasted for a moment. But the touch of his lips on mine sparked a fire inside me that had not burned for nearly four years. *Careful, Nola Ann*, my inner voice said. *This is exactly what Miss Eleanor warned you about.*

"I don't want you to get the wrong impression," I said hastily. "I don't usually go around kissing people I've barely met."

Jim smiled. "If I have my way, we'll be getting to know each other a lot better very soon," he said. When he kissed me again, I threw caution to the wind and kissed him back, hard. After a long, delicious minute, he pulled away.

"I could do this all day, Nola," he said, trailing his fingertips along my right cheek, "but we both have meetings to get to. I'll call Franklin Dillard and let him know you're on your way to see him."

CHAPTER 14

My feet barely touched the ground as I left Jim Richardson's office. I loved my late husband, and would revere his memory forever, but Will was in heaven now. I needed a real, flesh-and-blood man in my life. Someone who could kiss me, someone who could hold me the way Jim did. A nagging inner voice warned me against letting my passion overcome my common sense, but right now I was feeling too good to worry about anything. I'd ask Aunt Sarah what she thought when I got home.

What I had to do now was focus on the task at hand. Lilly Davidson was missing, and time was of the essence. I picked up my pace and turned onto Lincoln Avenue. At this moment, Jim Richardson was placing a call to Boss Franklin C. Dillard on my behalf. I could only hope he would be willing to meet with me.

When I arrived at the Black Rooster Pool Hall, two heavy-set colored men on ladders were hoisting a banner over the main entrance.

"It's sagging to the left," a third man shouted to them as he stood on the sidewalk looking up at them. "Pull up your end a little bit, Mike."

"Gotcha," the man on the left-hand ladder said, and pulled up his end so that the full banner was clearly visible.

BIG RALLY TOMORROW NIGHT!
SUPPORT CONGRESSMAN HARRY "HAPPY" SKELTON JR.! FREE
HOT DOGS! LIVE MUSIC!

I had never been inside a pool hall before. In my limited experience, pool halls were the province of loud-talking, tobacco-chewing men with an excess of time on their hands. Would I be stopped? Would I be questioned, asked who I was and what I was doing there?

I took a deep breath and walked through the door.

The light inside the pool hall was dim. The air was heavy with the smell of cigars and stale beer. On one side of the room, three large pool tables stood against the wall. In the center of the room, circular dining tables topped with red and white checked tablecloths formed a semicircle around a wooden dance floor. I walked toward the back of the room, noting with relief that no one seemed to be paying the slightest attention to me.

Three large men struggled to lift an upright piano onto a makeshift platform that had been set up against the back wall. There was a small metal door recessed into the wall on the right side of the platform. Next to this door, a heavy-set man with a boxer's broken nose, cauliflower ears, and a menacing attitude slouched against the wall. This was the same man I saw running from the Wham Bam Club the night of the murder. The man studied me without expression as I approached.

"My name is Nola Jackson," I told him. "I'm here to see Mr. Dillard. Jim Richardson just called here about me."

The man eyed me warily. "Wait here," he said.

He opened the door and went in, closing it firmly behind

him. When the man returned five minutes later, his tone was only slightly more civil. "Mr. Dillard will see you now," he said. "Follow me."

In sharp contrast to the gloomy atmosphere of the pool hall, Franklin C. Dillard's office was luxurious. Thick green carpeting covered the floor. The walls were paneled in dark wood and lined with pictures of Mr. Dillard fraternizing with an impressive number of Negro dignitaries, including W. E. B. Du Bois and Booker T. Washington.

Hanging on the wall behind Boss Dillard's desk was a photograph of him receiving his law license from William Harris, the president of the Alexander County Bar Association. Boss Dillard was the first Negro in the county to be admitted to the bar, and the event was widely covered in the Negro newspapers. The bar association had tried every trick in the book to keep Boss Dillard from becoming a member of the bar. On the streets around Lincoln Avenue, it was said that Boss Dillard received his license only after Congressman Harry Skelton had a quiet but persuasive talk with the president of the bar association.

Franklin C. Dillard was a small man, just barely over five feet, with a light brown complexion, curly hair and piercing gray eyes. It was rumored that his mother was an Irishwoman who had taken up with a Negro sailor, but no one was brave enough to question Boss Dillard directly on the subject.

"Have a seat," he said, and pointed to the green leather armchair in front of his desk. "Jimmy Richardson is an old acquaintance of mine. What can I do for you?"

"I'm looking for a girl named Lilly Davidson," I said. "She's accused of shooting Eddie Smooth down at the Wham Bam Club."

Boss Dillard's hawkish face remained expressionless. "Go on," he said.

"Lilly is innocent of this crime," I said. "I'm looking for the evidence that will clear her name, and I want to find her before the police do. I was hoping you could help me."

Boss Dillon's aura was an intimidating steel gray that surrounded him like a suit of armor. He was seeing me as a favor to Jim Richardson, but his goodwill would only extend so far. As he continued to study me without expression, I wished I'd taken the time to concoct a better strategy before my visit. But it was way too late to worry about that now.

"What makes you think I know where she is?" he said.

"Lilly was seen fighting with Eddie Smooth earlier that evening," I said. "I was hoping your bodyguard might be able to help me find out what happened to her."

Boss Dillon raised an eyebrow. "I don't follow you, little girl. What's my bodyguard, Jack Cross, got to do with anything?"

"He was at the Wham Bam Club that night," I said. "It's possible his testimony could prove the girl was nowhere near Eddie when he was killed."

"Nonsense," Boss Dillon snapped. "The Wham Bam Club is run by my competitor, Tom Hoyt. My employees are strictly forbidden to set foot anywhere near that dump. Jack Cross knows better than to disobey my orders."

"But I saw him there," I insisted. "Not once, but twice. I saw him standing near the stage during Eddie Smooth's first set, and I saw him running away from the club just before the fire." As I spoke, the slight waver in Boss Dillon's shiny steel aura told me that I was on to something.

"All I want to do is to talk to him," I said. "Your bodyguard may have seen something that could mean life or death for Lilly Davidson."

Boss Dillard rested his chin on his hands and looked up at the ceiling for a long minute. Then he stood up suddenly, strode across the room, and opened his office door.

"Get in here, Jack," he said. "Now."

The cauliflower-eared man I'd spoken to earlier appeared in Boss Dillard's office a minute later. "Yes, Mr. Dillard?" he said.

"Stand in the center of the room and let this girl get a good look at you," Boss Dillard said.

The man did as he was told. After a moment, Boss Dillard asked me if this was the man I had seen at the Wham Bam Club. When I nodded yes, Boss Dillard's face betrayed no emotion. "Shut the door, Jack," he said. "I want our little talk to be as private as possible."

Looking more than a little anxious, Jack Cross shut the door and returned to stand awkwardly in the middle of the room. Although he was a big man, at least six feet tall, Jack Cross shifted from one foot to the other like a guilty schoolboy who'd been called to the principal's office.

"I have instructed you on a number of occasions not to patronize the Wham Bam Club," Boss Dillard said. Although his voice was soft, there was no mistaking the menace it held. "And yet, this young lady says that she saw you there. What do you have to say for yourself, Jack?"

The man glared at me with daggers in his eyes. "She's wrong," he sputtered. "I was never there, Mr. Dillard. I swear it."

Boss Dillard studied his bodyguard silently for a full minute, then nodded his head, as if in conversation with himself. "I don't believe you," Boss Dillard said. "You have exactly one minute to tell me what you were doing at the Wham Bam Club before I ask Big Eddie and his friend Lorenzo to take you outside for a longer conversation. You don't want that to happen, do you?"

A bolt of yellow fear shot through Jack's aura.

"No, Mr. Dillard," he said.

"Excellent," Boss Dillard said. "At least there's one thing we can agree about." Although his tone was pleasant, the red tipped arrows of rage in Boss Dillard's aura told another story entirely. With the expectant air of a man waiting for a play to begin, Boss

Dillard crossed one leg over his knee, flicked a piece of lint off the knife-edged crease in his trousers, and smiled coldly.

"I only went to the Wham Bam to collect the money Eddie Smooth owed me," Jack Cross said, his scarred hands twisting awkwardly in front of him. "I won it off him in a crap game the night before. He promised to pay me after he got his gig money that night."

"I see," Boss Dillard said. His soft, noncommittal tone was far more terrifying than any screaming would ever be. "This young lady has some questions," he said. "You will now answer them."

It was now or never. It was not likely I'd get the opportunity to question this man again.

"You say that you waited by the side of the stage while Eddie and his band finished their set?" I asked.

"That's right," Jack Cross said. "I wanted to make sure the cheating little bastard didn't run off before I got my money. But the minute Eddie finished playing, Jeff Fairchild, the Congressman's assistant, asked Eddie to come sit at his table. Eddie told me to wait downstairs by his dressing room. He said he would give me my money then."

Boss Dillon shook his head sadly. "I bend over backwards to help Congressman Skelton win the colored vote," he said. "And how does the he reward me? He allows his right-hand man, Jeff Fairchild, to patronize the place owned by my competition." He turned to me and sighed. "Do you have any more questions?"

"When you went down to the basement, who did you see?" I asked Jack Cross. "Think carefully, please. It's important."

Jack gave Boss Dillard an imploring look. "Do I have to answer this?" he said. "There was a big crowd down there. I can't remember all the people I saw."

"Try," Boss Dillon said drily. "Or, if you prefer, Big Eddie and Lorenzo will be happy to jog your memory."

Jack shot me a sullen glare. "There was a poker game going on," he said. "There were a bunch of coloreds there. Harry Dodd, the fry cook. A couple of the musicians from the band. Oh, and that fancy-pants white boy who works for the Congressman."

"Joe Quincy?" I said. This must have been where Joe was while Abigail Everleigh sat alone at her table, waiting for him.

Jack grunted. "If you say so. Stuck-up little white boy with a fancy accent and voice like a girl."

"What about the women? " I said. "You see any women down there?"

"There's always women down there," Cross said dismissively. "Eddie Smooth keeps a couple of working girls around in case the boys need to relax."

"I'm looking for one girl in particular," I told him. "She's about four foot eleven, and light enough to pass for white, with short brown hair and hazel eyes. Did you see her?"

Jack laughed suddenly. "Sure, I saw her. No man with a working pulse is gonna miss a chick like that. I was waiting for Eddie and watching the poker game when she strolls in, smelling of fancy perfume. 'You seen Eddie?' she says. When I tell her Eddie's upstairs, she says she'll come back later."

"And did she?" I asked.

Jack shrugged. "How should I know? I was watching the poker game, remember? I was about to go back upstairs to look for Eddie when Jeff Fairchild shows up and starts giving that young kid Joe Quincy a piece of his mind. Chews the kid out good and proper for gambling when he was supposed to be passing out flyers in the parking lot. Chews him out right in front of everybody."

Jack Cross permitted himself a small smile. "It was pretty funny, to be honest. This white boy with his high little squeaky voice acting all offended, saying Mr. Fairchild didn't have no business talking to him like that. I'm a *Quincy*, he says, like that means something. 'I don't care who your daddy is,' Fairchild

says. 'If you don't wanna work, go back to Boston.' The kid
turned so red, I had to try real hard not to bust out laughing.
'You'll be sorry for this,' he says, and storms outta the room."

"What about Eddie Smooth?" I asked. "Did you see him
again?"

Jack gave Boss Dillard an imploring look. "Ain't I told her
enough, Boss? Don't seem right, me telling this broad all my
personal business like this."

"What's not right is you being at the Wham Bam Club when
I told you not to," Boss Dillard said coldly. "This young lady is
important to a friend of mine. Answer her questions, Jack. Tell
her when you saw Eddie Smooth next."

"Okay, Boss," Jack replied. "Eddie walks in while Jeff
Fairchild is yelling at Joe Quincy. 'Evenin', Joe,' he says to the
kid. 'Hard at work as usual, I see,' he says, and gives me a wink.
Then he tells me to step inside his dressing room, that he's
gonna give me my money. That's when this white girl marches
up to him. 'Eddie,' she says, 'we have to talk right away.' "

Abigail Everleigh, I thought to myself. She had admitted
being in Eddie's dressing room that night.

"Eddie takes her inside his dressing room and tells me to
wait in the hall for a minute, which I do," Jack continued.

"Could you hear what they were talking about?" I said.
"Were they arguing?"

"I don't know," Jack Cross told me. "The minute Eddie
took the white girl inside his dressing room, Tom Hoyt walks
up to me. He tells me he doesn't want anyone associated with
Boss Dillard inside his club. Before I have a chance to get a
word in, the black bastard pulls a gun on me. Tells me I've got
to the count of ten to clear out. I got the hell out of there in a
hurry."

"You didn't see either Lilly or Eddie Smooth again that
night?" I asked.

"Of course not," Jack said irritably. "I ran out the back door and down the path. I was halfway to the boat dock by the river when I remembered my car was in the parking lot. I didn't want Tom Hoyt to see me, so I sneaked back to the Wham Bam Club through the woods. I was in the parking lot when the fire broke out. Naturally, I jumped in my car and peeled out of there in a hurry."

Boss Dillard gave the man a hard look. "Some kind of body-guard you've turned out to be," he said, "disobeying my express orders like that. Running at the first sign of trouble. Based on what you've said, I don't see how I can entrust you with my personal safety." He sighed and shook his head sadly. "I'm going to need some time to think things over, Jack. Go outside and wait until I call for you."

It was an order, not a request. A band of queasy yellow rippled through Jack Cross's aura as he nodded silently and walked out, closing the door behind him.

Boss Dillard stood up. "It's time for you to leave, Miss Jackson," he said. "I don't expect that we will meet again. Be sure to give Jimmy Richardson my regards the next time you see him."

My left ear began to buzz the minute I left the Black Rooster Pool Hall. Soon, the buzzing sound in my left ear was drowning out all the other sounds around me. The shouts of the street vendors, the clang of the streetcar bell and even the honking of cars on Lincoln Avenue seemed far away.

My psychic senses were sending me an SOS. The problem was, I had no idea why. Was I receiving a warning about Boss Dillard and his bodyguard, Jack Cross? I felt overwhelmed, exhausted, and desperately in need of advice. My shift with DeLuxe Catering began in two hours. If I hurried, there was still time for me to talk things over with my Aunt Sarah before I left for work.

When I walked in my front door ten minutes later, Aunt Sarah was sitting at the kitchen table.

"Everything all right, Nola?" she said. Despite the relatively warm weather, she wore a heavy wool dress and a faded cardigan.

"Everything is just fine," I told her. I needed advice desperately, but I didn't want to sound like I was panicking.

My aunt eyed me skeptically. "If that's the case, what are those big yellow question marks doing in your aura?" she said.

I bent down and gave her a hug. "I suppose there's no use trying to fool a psychic," I replied. "I've got to be at work at four, but I really need your advice."

"My Spirits said you'd be coming," Aunt Sarah said. "I've been waiting for you to show up. Go on, then. Tell me what's going on."

As I changed into my DeLuxe Catering uniform, Aunt Sarah sat on my bed and listened as I told her about my meeting with Boss Dillard and his bodyguard, Jack Cross. "My left ear has not stopped buzzing since then," I said. "I'm worried I've done something wrong, but I can't for the life of me figure out what it is. Was it a mistake to ask Boss Dillard for help?"

Aunt Sarah closed her eyes and sat quietly for a minute. "Boss Dillard has got plans of his own," she told me, "plans that are not in your best interest."

My heart sank. No wonder my left ear was buzzing. "What should I do?"

"Nothing you can do but keep moving forward," she said. Then she touched me gently on the arm. "That's not the only thing that happened today, Nola Ann. Tell me the rest of it."

I felt my skin turn warm with embarrassment and looked away.

"Jim Richardson kissed me," I said sheepishly. "It's been so long since a man paid attention to me like that. Do you think I did wrong by kissing him back? I don't want him to think that I'm too eager."

Aunt Sarah looked at me and shook her head. "The day you moved in here, I promised you I wouldn't interfere with your personal life," she said. "Do you remember?"

"Yes, ma'am," I told her.

"Your love life is nobody's business but your own, Nola. It would be very wrong of me to meddle. But I will say this much." As I straightened my black dress and pulled the white pinafore with the Deluxe Catering logo over my head, Aunt Sarah stood up and looked me in the eye.

"Guard your heart, Nola Ann. You're still raw from losing your husband. Enjoy the attention, but try not to take this man too seriously."

I put on my coat and headed down to catch the southbound streetcar. Although I knew my Aunt Sarah was right, there was also no denying the ripple of excitement that shimmered through my body when I remembered the touch of Jim's lips against mine. *I'll pay Jim another visit tomorrow*, I thought. *Just to let him know how my investigation is proceeding.*

CHAPTER 15

When I arrived at the DeLuxe Catering office, Mr. and Mrs. Layton put me to work loading food and supplies into the delivery truck. When the boxes, bags, crates, and bottles were all inside, Mr. Layton carefully laid his black cutaway dinner jacket on top. For tonight's extra-special dinner with Congressman Skelton, Mr. Layton would dress even more formally than usual.

Minty Layton, who usually bubbled with gossip whenever we rode in the delivery truck together, was moody and withdrawn. After watching Minty stare out the window in silence for several minutes, I finally asked her if she was all right.

"No," she told me. "I am not all right, Nola. Edward and I are about to lose our best customer, and I am heartsick over it."

"Now, now," Mr. Layton said gently. "Don't fret yourself, Minty. We haven't lost any customers just yet. We're on our way to do an important job for Mrs. Ratcliffe this very minute. Don't make a mountain out of a molehill."

"Accuse me of exaggerating all you want," Minty said defensively, "but I know what I know, Edward. Last year, Mrs. Ratcliffe had us cater something at her house nearly every week-end. This year, we've only been out there five times. Now that she's getting these letters, who knows? It's quite possible she'll stop hiring us altogether."

Minty Layton's aura was usually a radiant green. When she'd said the word "letters," tiny streaks of yellow crept in to hover around the edges.

"Mrs. Ratcliffe is getting letters?" I said. As usual, the noise from the traffic on the street made it difficult for me to hear Minty clearly. "What kind of letters?"

"Hate mail," Mr. Layton told me. "Someone's been putting unsigned letters in Mrs. Ratcliffe's mailbox, letters warning her to keep away from Negroes. When she called me this morning to check on her order, she told me about them." He paused for a moment as he edged his delivery truck carefully into the left lane to pass a slow-moving car.

"Mrs. Ratcliffe only mentioned the letters in passing," he said. "She told me not to worry about them." He offered his wife a reassuring smile. "In all the years we've been going out to see Mrs. Ratcliffe, we've never had a lick of trouble from anyone."

Minty shook her head in disbelief. "Mrs. Ratcliffe told you the letter she received had a picture of a stick figure hanging from a noose with the words 'nigger lover' written on it," Minty said. "Does that sound like a joke to you?"

A chill ran up my spine. Minty was right. Just last spring, po-lice in Indianapolis had found the body of a Negro man next to a tree with his hands tied behind his back and a noose around his neck. The newspapers speculated that the murdered man had been seen with a white woman earlier that day. These ru-mors were never substantiated, and no one was ever arrested for the crime. Instead, the Marion County coroner listed the man's cause of death as "suicide."

"The police don't care about Negroes getting killed," I said, "but seeing as it's Mrs. Ratcliffe, I think they would definitely investigate. Has she called them?"

"Of course not," Minty said sourly. "That woman never wants to admit that anything or anyone has gotten the better of her."

"These letters are just a nasty prank," Mr. Layton said firmly. "Mrs. Ratcliffe is not taking them seriously, and neither should we."

Minty Layton's aura flared crimson. "You think not, Edward?" she said. "Have you forgotten that we are the only catering company in Agate that is owned by Negroes? Have you thought about what would happen to us if Mrs. Ratcliffe decided it was too dangerous to hire us? Have you thought about what would happen if she decided to hire a white-owned catering company instead?" Minty flashed her husband a challenging stare. "Have you thought about that, Edward? Have you?"

Mr. Layton did not reply. Instead, he concentrated on driving for several minutes without speaking. He knew better than to contradict his wife when she was in the middle of a tirade.

Raising her voice to be heard over the rumble of traffic on Main Street, Minty continued. "We need to take these letters very, very seriously, Edward. Mrs. Ratcliffe has a lot of enemies—that Ku Klux phony-baloney preacher Timothy Gonsails, for example."

"People like that are everywhere these days," I said. "Those letters could have been written by anyone. Yesterday's *Daily Chronicle* said that two hundred people attended a cross-burning ceremony at Bright Horizons Spiritualist Temple last Sunday."

"That's exactly my point," Minty said. "This whole situation is extremely worrisome. Our lives and livelihood are at stake."

Mr. Layton gave his wife a reassuring pat on the arm. "Mrs. Ratcliffe is one of the richest women in Agate," he said. "She's a tough old bird with a lot of powerful friends, not the least of whom is Congressman Harry 'Happy' Skelton. When she tells the Congressman what's going on, he will put a stop to it."

"We'll see," Minty said grimly. She slumped back in her seat and went back to staring out of the window.

Fifteen minutes later, we arrived at Mrs. Ratcliffe's house. For the next two hours, Edward, Minty, and I immersed ourselves in cooking, cleaning, preparing, and polishing. For dinner that evening, we were to prepare a standing rib roast accompanied by Parker House rolls, French onion soup, whipped sweet potatoes with butter-pecan topping, and creamed spinach. For dessert, Mrs. Ratcliffe had instructed Minty to make an apple pie.

"It's the perfect all-American dessert for a politician," she said. "Give the Congressman hot apple pie, and the man will be in heaven, I promise you."

All that afternoon, Mrs. Ratcliffe flitted nervously in and out of the kitchen to check on the dinner preparations, her aura oscillating between deep pink and jagged yellow.

Minty Layton was annoyed by the constant interruptions, but she held her tongue, offering Mrs. Ratcliffe a reassuring smile each and every time she came into the kitchen. "Don't you fret, ma'am," Minty told her. "Everything's going to be just fine."

By seven that evening, all was in readiness. The long cherry-wood dining room table had been covered with a white linen tablecloth and set with Mrs. Ratcliffe's finest gold-rimmed china. The silverware, freshly polished by Mrs. Layton and myself earlier that day, sparkled in the light provided by large candelabras placed in the center of the table between crystal vases filled with fragrant bouquets of red, white, and yellow roses.

Congressman Skelton's assistant, Jeffrey Fairchild, and his wife rang the bell promptly at eight. As I watched from my station next to the kitchen door, Mr. Layton, looking even more regal than usual in the black cutaway jacket and matching trousers he reserved for formal occasions, ushered the couple into the dining room.

"A pleasure to meet you, Mr. Fairchild," Mrs. Ratcliffe said, extending her hand in the manner of an English queen. "I'm so glad you and your wife were able to come on such short notice."

When I'd seen Mr. Fairchild sitting at his table at the Wham Bam Club, I hadn't realized he was such a small man. Soaking wet, Congressman Skelton's assistant couldn't have weighed more than one hundred thirty pounds. His shoulders hunched nearly to his ears, as if walking against a brisk winter wind, and his wire-rimmed glasses and thinning brown hair gave him a decidedly bookish air.

"Thank you for inviting us," he said in a slow and measured voice. "Allow me to present my wife, Penelope."

Like her husband, Penelope Fairchild was tiny and quite thin. Her pale complexion was set off by a thick mane of raven-black hair, which she wore in an elaborate bun on the top of her head. When she spoke, her voice was so soft that Mrs. Ratcliffe had to lean closer to hear it.

"I've heard about the Spiritualist séances you offer," Mrs. Fairchild said. "Perhaps someday I'll be able to attend."

As his wife spoke, Mr. Fairchild's aura shifted ever so slightly. If I hadn't been watching him closely, I might have missed it. I got the definite impression she had embarrassed him, though I had no idea why. I was distracted from thinking about this further by the arrival of Congressman Skelton and his wife.

"Good evening, Portia," the Congressman said in his resonant baritone. Harry "Happy" Skelton was slender, with penetrating hazel eyes, a long patrician nose and a tousled mane of curly gray hair. "I've been spending so much time away in Washington, D.C., these days, I don't get home to see old friends nearly as much as I'd like."

He clapped Mr. Ratcliffe on the back and shook his hand. "I'm looking forward to catching up on all the developments with that new glassware factory you're building, Bayard. Quite a project, I understand."

As Mr. Ratcliffe and the Congressman launched into their conversation, Mr. and Mrs. Wallaby arrived. Not to be outdone by Mrs. Ratcliffe's flamboyant lime-green evening gown, Mrs. Harriet Wallaby wore a dress made with shimmering pink sequins. If I didn't know we were in Southern Illinois, I would have thought I'd landed in the jungle amidst a colorful flock of tropical birds. Mr. Wallaby wore a black cutaway with the row of military ribbons he'd received during the Spanish-American War proudly pinned to his lapel. Although the war had been over for nearly thirty years, the old man never tired of telling anyone who would listen about how he charged up San Juan Hill with Teddy Roosevelt and his Rough Riders.

Millicent Skelton, the Congressman's wife, looked lost amidst all these flamboyant personalities. Although her black evening gown was equally expensive, it hung on her thin, gangly frame like a coat draped carelessly over a hanger. Still, she had been married to Congressman Skelton long enough to know the rules of engagement at affairs such as this. She smiled, nodded, and made pleasant small talk with the other women, as the men, grouped together at the other end of the room in front of the fireplace, talked business.

At precisely eight o'clock, Mr. Layton announced that dinner would be served and asked them to please take their seats at the long dining room table positioned in the center of the room.

For the next hour, little was said as the guests devoured one fabulous course after another. Minty Layton was a great cook at any occasion, but she had outdone herself for this very important dinner. As Mr. Layton and I served each guest, the only sounds to be heard were "oohs" and "aahs" of pleasure.

"This roast beef fairly melts in your mouth," Congressman Skelton said between bites.

"And these rolls," Mr. Wallaby said, slathering his third roll with a thick slab of butter. "They are absolutely heavenly!"

"Your cook is to be commended," Penelope Fairchild said. "The sweet potato dish was exceptional. She's added a wonderful combination of flavors that I do not fully recognize. Would she be willing to share her recipe, Mrs. Ratcliffe? I'd love to bring it home for my girl Susan to prepare."

"Of course," Mrs. Ratcliffe said. "I shall ask Edward to write it out before you leave."

After I had served the coffee, Mrs. Ratcliffe turned toward Congressman Skelton. "So glad to see you back in Agate, Congressman," she said. "While you were away, certain of the rougher element in town have taken advantage of your absence to assert their presence in ways that do not flatter our fair city or its values."

Harry "Happy" Skelton put down his coffee cup and eyed her warily. He must have known, politician that he was, that he would be asked to do something in return for Bayard Ratcliffe's large campaign donation. Nothing comes for free, especially not for people with his kind of influence in the corridors of power.

"I may be living in Washington, but I'm not out of touch with local affairs," he said. "Jeff Fairchild keeps a close watch on what goes on in my district."

"Has he told you about the cross burnings being held at Bright Horizons Spiritualist Temple?"

"He has," the Congressman replied. He took another sip of coffee before setting his cup down carefully in its saucer.

"These disgraceful affairs are attracting large crowds," Harriet Wallaby said. "I find it worrying, don't you?"

The Congressman shrugged. "Crude, perhaps, but certainly not illegal. Isn't that right, Jeff?"

"Reverend Gonsails is within his legal rights," Jeff Fairchild replied. "I looked into this myself. The church has received permission from the fire department in accordance with ordinance 24, section C of the municipal code."

Harry "Happy" Skelton spread his hands wide in a gesture of helplessness. "There you have it, ladies," he said. "The cross-burning services at Bright Horizons Spiritualist Temple are perfectly legal. Just people out having a good time. No harm in that, surely."

A plume of brilliant red light shot out from Mrs. Ratcliffe's aura, and her face turned beet red. "No harm? A Negro man was lynched after a similar cross-burning event in Indianapolis last month."

"Most regrettable," the Congressman said. "But sentiment is strong among the native-born white people of this city. There's a fear that what with all these Negroes pouring into town from down south, we'll be overrun with ignorant colored folk, bringing their criminal and immoral ways with them."

"Surely you don't countenance these cross burnings, Congressman," Mrs. Ratcliffe persisted. "They only incite the worst in people. Not only that, but they create an atmosphere of fear among the coloreds here."

Congressman Skelton shook his head and offered Mrs. Ratcliffe a patronizing smile. "Perhaps a little fear is not such a bad thing, Portia. Negroes are not like us, you know. They are just one step removed from the jungle and must be kept in their place."

Mr. Layton had continued to serve dessert as this conversation continued. He kept his face neutral and his eyes facing forward. If you didn't know him, you might have missed the tightening along his jawline as he silently clenched his teeth. I tried my best to follow his example as I poured the coffee. I wanted to dump the entire pot of coffee over the Congressman's head, but I held my temper.

Jeff Fairchild took a napkin and daintily wiped the last crumbs of Minty Layton's apple pie from his mouth. "Don't get the wrong impression, Mrs. Ratcliffe," he said. "Congressman Skelton is not a monster. In fact, he recently made a large donation to the Phyllis Wheatley Institute."

"Even after they lost that girl last week?" Mr. Ratcliffe asked. "That incident certainly hasn't done anything to inspire confidence, either in Mrs. Wyatt or in the institution."

"Harry and I are inclined to be patient about these things," Millicent Skelton answered. "The coloreds are not always as capable as we would like, but with proper guidance, they're coming along. We support colored causes, don't we, dear?"

"Absolutely," Harry "Happy" Skelton said. "As long as they keep to their proper place, we are happy to help our colored friends here in Agate."

Jeff Fairchild nodded in agreement. "There is a proper place for everyone in this town, a natural order decreed by God," he said. "The white man was destined to rule because of his superior intelligence and intellect."

Jeff Fairchild's wife, Penelope, followed the conversation as though watching a tennis match, her head swiveling from side to side to observe each speaker in turn. As the Congressman paused to take another bite of apple pie, she cleared her throat and spoke. Her manner was timid, as though afraid she would be interrupted or reprimanded for speaking.

"Negroes do have their place," she said. "For example, they're excellent at singing and dancing. Isn't that right, Jeff?"

"Yes, dear," Jeff Fairchild said, and patted her on the hand.

"Jeff and I love dancing to Negro music," Penelope continued, "especially that song Eddie Smooth used to play. What was it, dear?"

"'Comeuppance Time,'" Jeff Fairchild said with a wry smile. "It's a suitable anthem for anyone who works in politics. I went to the Wham Bam Club nearly every night to hear him sing it." He took a sip of coffee, then continued. "Eddie Smooth was a musical genius. Unfortunately, the man was also arrogant and high-handed, like so many Negroes nowadays. I was re-minded of this just yesterday while having a very difficult con-versation with that so-called 'boss,' Franklin Dillard."

"Is Mr. Dillard the Negro who came to the house yester-day?" Penelope Fairchild asked. "I thought I recognized his name. What did he want?"

"He wanted me to get Congressman Skelton to back legisla-tion that would close the loophole that allows for nightclubs within fifteen miles of the city limits," Jeff Fairchild said.

Bayard Ratcliffe shook his head. "Surely this is an excellent suggestion, even if it did come from Boss Dillard," Mr. Rat-cliffe said. "We've got Prohibition now. Those nightclubs are havens for illegal drinking, Jeff. Everybody knows that."

Jeff Fairchild gave Mr. Ratcliffe a bland smile. "So they tell me," he said. "All I know for sure is that Tom Hoyt, the owner of the Wham Bam Club, is a hardworking businessman. He's just giving Mr. Dillard a little healthy competition, that's all."

Harry "Happy" Skelton nodded in enthusiastic agreement. "Competition in business is the American way," he said firmly. "I intend to make this very same point when I speak at the Agate Rotary Club next week."

"Not that the Wham Bam Club matters anymore," Jeffrey Fairchild said with a note of sadness in his voice. "The place is nothing but ashes now."

"Which again points up the danger of fires," Mrs. Ratcliffe persisted stubbornly. "Surely you can do something to stop these disgraceful cross burnings, Harry."

Congressman Skelton put down his coffee cup and laughed loudly. "My, my, Bayard," he said. "Your wife is not a woman who gives up easily." Though his voice remained amiable, his aura told a different story. Irritation lurked just behind the edges of his genial smile.

"Persistence is one of Portia's strongest qualities," Mr. Ratcliffe said. He shot his wife a look of caution. "But enough of politics," he continued. "Let's abandon this discussion, shall we?"

"Hear, hear," Mr. Wallaby agreed. "Enough on the so-called 'burning questions' of the day, if you'll pardon my little pun." After laughing heartily at his own joke, Mr. Wallaby asked, "Will you be coming to our Veterans Day parade, Congressman? I understand that the Agate Ladies Auxiliary is preparing something special this year."

"Our little group have been getting together for months to work on the plans," Millicent Skelton said in a bright and cheerful tone. "Our event this year is going to be very special."

Penelope Fairchild clapped her hands together like a small child. "Is it true that you're planning to bring the Eighth Army Band all the way from Washington to perform?"

"That information is top secret, my dear," Mrs. Skelton said with a knowing wink. "Let us just say this year's parade is going to be spectacular."

I could feel Mrs. Ratcliffe sweltering with frustration as the conversation continued. While she played the role of gracious host for the rest of the evening, a gray cloud wrapped itself around her aura like a blanket. It was clear to her and everyone else at the table that Congressman Harry Skelton had no intention of putting a stop to Reverend Timothy Gonsails, his weekly cross burnings, or the growing popularity of the Ku Klux Klan.

When all the guests had all gone home, Minty Layton strode into the kitchen, took off her apron, and hurled it to the floor.

"What a hypocrite!" she exclaimed bitterly. "The Congressman claims to be a friend of the colored man, yet he does nothing to stop these hateful rallies."

Mr. Layton nodded grimly. "Mr. Skelton's behavior is the kind of thing that encourages race riots," he said. "I will never forget what happened here twelve years ago. White folks ran amok in our neighborhood, burning, killing, and looting for three days before the police put an end to it."

The race riot of 1910 had left a permanent scar on the psyche of every colored person in Agate who was old enough to remember. Although I was barely ten years old at the time, my memories of the riot were vivid. I was in my bed asleep when the mob started running up Lincoln Avenue. My mother and I hid in the cellar while Daddy kept watch in the darkened living room, a grim expression on his face and a shotgun in his hand. I will never forget what it felt like to sit in that tiny cellar listening to the sounds of glass shattering and feet running on the street outside. Lucky for us, none of the buildings on our block were set on fire. Our house was at the far end of the colored district, almost to the edge of town. The rioters must have run out of energy by the time they got to our street.

"The way things are going these days, there could be another race riot in Agate soon," Minty said sadly.

"With men like Congressman Harry 'Happy' Skelton running the show, another race riot is inevitable," Mr. Layton said. His dark face was grim. "It's only a matter of time."

CHAPTER 16

It was nearly midnight by the time Mr. Layton's delivery truck rattled up to the curb in front of Aunt Sarah's house. As I got out of the car, the dark and moonless night sky perfectly matched my mood. Despite his jovial moniker, Congressman Harry "Happy" Skelton was a cold-blooded, calculating man. With opportunists like the Congressman running the show, there was little hope things would get better for the colored man. Not for me, not for Boss Dillard, and certainly not for Lilly Davidson.

Disappointed and downhearted, I waved goodbye to Mr. and Mrs. Layton and trudged up the front stairs. Aunt Sarah's house was located in the most crime-ridden neighborhood in the city. In spite of this, she never locked her door. I'd lectured Aunt Sarah about this several times to no avail. Whenever I mentioned the many terrible things that could happen to a defenseless old woman in our neighborhood, she merely smiled.

"Don't you worry yourself about me," she told me. "My Spirits will take care of me just fine."

Aunt Sarah had made this statement so often and with such conviction that I had given up trying to change her. But as I pushed open the front door, I heard my aunt talking to someone in the kitchen. It was well after midnight, I thought. God knows what kind of riffraff may have decided to pay my aunt a late-night visit. Fearing the worst, I grabbed the poker from the fireplace and hurried down the hallway.

"Put that poker down, Nola Ann," Aunt Sarah said as I ran into the kitchen. "Have a seat. Lilly and I were just talking about you."

To my amazement, Lilly Davidson was sitting, bold as brass, at my Aunt Sarah's kitchen table. The girl's expensive dress was ripped at the shoulder and muddy at the hem. There were bags under her eyes, and a nasty purple bruise covered the left side of her face.

"Where in heaven's name have you been, Lilly?" I said. "I've been looking all over for you."

"I decided to take your advice about paying your aunt a visit," Lilly said brightly, as if it was the most normal thing in the world to show up at people's houses after midnight.

A wide range of emotions raced through me as I studied her. On the one hand, it was a relief to know that she was alive and had survived the fire. On the other hand, Lilly Davidson was wanted by the police. Her presence in Aunt Sarah's home would bring nothing but trouble.

"You can't stay here," I said bluntly. "You're going to get us all arrested."

In response, the girl put her head in her hands and burst into tears.

"Mind your manners, Nola," Aunt Sarah said sternly. "Can't you see Lilly needs help? You of all people should know what it feels like to be in her situation."

The old woman's words hit home. Four years ago I'd been a

war widow with no money and no prospects. If Aunt Sarah hadn't taken me in, I'd have ended up homeless on the streets of Harlem.

"Sorry, Lilly," I said. "I've had a rough day. I didn't mean to hurt your feelings."

"Apology accepted," Lilly said, offering me a tearstained smile.

"Put that poker back in the living room, Nola," Aunt Sarah said. "I'll fix you some tea."

"Yes, ma'am," I said.

When I had settled myself, Aunt Sarah poured all three of us a fresh cup of chamomile tea, then sat down and gave Lilly an encouraging nod. "Start from the beginning, child," she said. "Tell us how you came to meet Eddie Smooth in the first place. Tell us everything, and do not leave out a thing."

Lilly Davidson set down her teacup, pulled a handkerchief from her handbag, and blew her nose. "The first time I saw Eddie, I was at the library, working on my article," she said, and looked at each of us to make sure we'd heard. "I'm writing the story of my life, you know. It will be published in *The Crisis* when it's done."

"What was Eddie doing at the library?" I asked. "No offense, but he didn't strike me as being a bookworm."

"No offense taken," Lilly said. "Eddie never got the chance to finish eighth grade, so he wasn't much of a reader." Her face took on a dreamy, faraway expression. "I was sitting on the front steps of the library, reading a book, when Eddie just happened to walk by. He asked me what I was reading, and if I liked music. After we talked awhile, he invited me to hear him play at the Wham Bam Club."

"How did you plan to get there?" I asked.

"Eddie said he'd send a boy to fetch me," she said. "All I had to do was find a way to sneak out after curfew and this boy would be waiting to take me to the Wham Bam. When I discovered how easy it was to climb out that bathroom window, it felt like a sign from heaven."

"Or a sign from the other place," Aunt Sarah said wryly. "Weren't you worried about getting caught?"

"I didn't care," Lilly said. "I hated Phyllis Wheatley Institute. I would never have gone there if I hadn't gotten that letter."

I set down my cup and looked at her. "What letter?"

"I received an unsigned letter the day before my sixteenth birthday," Lilly said. "There was a ten-dollar bill inside, and directions for how to get to Wheatley Institute."

"You have no idea who sent you the letter?" Aunt Sarah said.

"Not really. To be honest, I didn't really care. The orphanage in Joliet only keeps you till you turn sixteen. After that, you've got to fend for yourself. It was either go to Wheatley Institute or live on the street."

She sighed, took a sip of tea, and wiped her eyes with the back of her hand.

"Eddie was so sweet," she said softly. "Every time I came to the club, he'd give me flowers and a box of chocolates. And the way he played that horn? It was pure magic." She paused and stared into her teacup. "Our love was so beautiful, like a dream. Until she came along."

Aunt Sarah and I exchanged a knowing look.

"Another woman?" Aunt Sarah said.

Lilly nodded and bit her lip to hold back her tears. "I never found out who it was. All that I know is Eddie began to treat me different, like he didn't care for me anymore."

"You must have been very angry," I said. "I know I'd be angry if something like that happened to me. Is that when you decided to kill him?"

Lilly Davidson recoiled as if she'd been hit, put her head down on Aunt Sarah's kitchen table, and began to cry.

"Hold your tongue, Nola," my aunt said sharply. "Let Lilly tell the story in her own way and her own time."

"Is that what you think?" Lilly said. "I would never. I could never. In spite of everything, I loved Eddie. I really and truly did." She raised her head to look me in the eye. "I came here because I wanted Aunt Sarah to make me a potion. A potion that would make Eddie stay with me forever."

"Why didn't you meet me by the toolshed like you promised?"

"I was planning to meet you," Lilly said. "Honest I was. But when I got back to the club, Eddie was waiting for me in the hallway outside his dressing room. He was mad as a hornet, yelling at me, wanting to know where I'd been. I tried to explain, remind him that he was the one who'd sent me out to see you in the first place. But that only made him madder." She sighed and wiped away a tear with the back of her hand. "That's when he hit me. Then he stuck his gun in my face and said he'd kill me if I ever left him."

"You must have been terrified," Aunt Sarah said gently.

"I was more shocked than anything," Lilly said. "I just stood there, crying like a dope. We stayed that way for at least a minute, just staring at each other. Then all of a sudden, Eddie hands me the gun and tells me to put it on top of the dresser. He tells me he's sorry and kisses the place where he hit me. 'I love you, baby,' he says. 'Go up to the kitchen and put some ice on that pretty little face before it swells up.'"

"That's the last time you saw him?" I said.

Lilly nodded, then stared down at the table, her eyes wet with tears. Wordlessly, I handed her a napkin, then sipped my tea thoughtfully.

If she was telling us the truth, Lilly Davidson was one of the last people to see Eddie Smooth alive that night. She must have seen something that could help me identify the real killer. But the girl's aura was badly damaged. The light that had shone so vibrantly when I'd met her at the Wham Bam Club was now barely an ember.

I leaned forward and touched her gently on the arm. "Do you remember who else was down in the basement when you were there? One of those people could well be Eddie's killer."

Lilly's brow furrowed in concentration. "Mr. Fairchild was there for a while, and the guy who works for him, Joe Quincy. When Mr. Quincy saw me in the basement that night, he said Eddie had told him about me being an orphan. He said he could help me find my real father."

"How on earth was he going to do that?" I said.

"Mr. Quincy said he could get hold of my birth certificate," Lilly replied. "I wanted to believe him, but in my heart, I knew he was lying. What he really wanted was to go to bed with me." She looked down at the table for a minute. "He got on my last nerve, to be honest. Telling me how beautiful I was, following me around like a lost puppy. The man was a total nuisance. I told Eddie to keep him away from me. Joe Quincy and that pathetic girlfriend of his."

"Abigail Everleigh?" I asked.

"That's right," Lilly said. "Everybody knew about her. Silly little college girl who drank too much for her own good."

"Abigail Everleigh told the police she saw you and Eddie fighting," I said. "The way she tells it, you were waving the gun at him, not the other way around."

Lilly put down her teacup and scowled. "The girl is lying," Lilly said. "She may have seen us fighting in the hallway outside Eddie's dressing room. But I never waved a gun at Eddie, and that's the truth."

Abigail hated Lilly, and blamed the girl for her failed romance with Joe Quincy. It made sense that Abigail would do everything in her power to pin Eddie Smooth's murder on the girl.

"Where were you when the fire broke out, Lilly?" I said. "I was waiting for you outside, but you never showed up."

"I was in the kitchen," Lilly said. "Looking for some ice to put on my black eye, when I started to smell the smoke. People were running around every which way, shouting and screaming. I ran outside and hid in that old toolshed out back. I figured the fire wouldn't get me in there, and it turns out I was right."

I nodded. I'd been waiting for Lilly at that exact spot not ten minutes earlier.

"I heard the police rounding people up," she continued. "But nobody thought to look in that beat-up old toolshed. After the police drove away, I remembered what you'd told me about Aunt Sarah. I didn't even know Eddie was dead until tonight."

She gave Aunt Sarah an imploring look. "Please, Mrs. Brown. I've got nowhere else to go. Can you help me?"

My aunt sat quietly for a moment, then took hold of Lilly's right hand and squeezed it tightly.

"Look me in the eye," she said. "Swear to me you did not kill Eddie Smooth."

"As God is my witness," Lilly said firmly.

After a long pause, my aunt nodded. "All right, child," she said. "You can sleep on the sofa in the living room. I'll keep you here for a few days while you figure out what to do next."

"Thanks a million," Lilly said, wiping away a tear with the back of her hand. "I won't be a bother. I promise."

"I've got some old clothes that need mending," Aunt Sarah said. "You'll be too busy sewing to get in my way."

I was not wild about Lilly moving in with us, not even for a few days. The girl was a walking Pandora's box, creating chaos wherever she went. However, I knew better than try to argue with Aunt Sarah's decision. Heaving an audible sigh, I wished Aunt Sarah and Lilly a good night and retreated to my room.

CHAPTER 17

When I got up the next morning, Aunt Sarah was sitting at the kitchen table darning an old sweater that a less frugal person would have thrown out long ago. Across the table from her, Lilly Davidson sipped a cup of tea and studied me with frank curiosity.

"Your aunt tells me you went to Mrs. Ratcliffe's house last night," she said. "I've always wanted to get inside one of those mansions on Vista Hill. What's it like?"

"Fancy," I said. I kissed Aunt Sarah on the top of her head, poured myself a cup of hot tea from the pot simmering on the stove, and sat down. "I've been out there a couple of times now. Last night, Mrs. Ratcliffe threw a dinner party for Congressman Skelton and a few of his friends."

Lilly's aura lit up like a Christmas tree. "Congressman Skelton? Really?"

"Don't get too excited," I replied sourly. "The man is not all he's cracked up to be, not by a long shot. Harry 'Happy' Skelton claims to be a friend of the colored man. The truth is, he doesn't give a fig for any of us."

Aunt Sarah nodded in agreement. "The man's a politician," she said. "All talk and no action. He's liable to say whatever will get him elected. What has Congressman Skelton actually done for us folks down here in Lincolnsville?"

"Very little," I said bitterly. "Man's a two-faced hypocrite, if you ask me." I told them what I'd overheard the Congressman say about keeping Boss Dillard in his place.

Lilly frowned. "Congressman Skelton is from one of Agate's five founding families," she said. "That's the closest thing we get to royalty around here. Perhaps you misunderstood him, Nola."

I stared at the girl in amazement. Lilly was a naive girl looking for her Prince Charming in all the wrong places, but even she could not be this clueless.

When I opened my mouth to respond, Aunt Sarah interrupted me.

"No need to upset ourselves with this election foolishness today," she said firmly. "Nola, I need for you pick up some supplies from Parnell's Market. I've got a client coming tomorrow for a Money Bath. I'll need honey, cinnamon sticks, cloves, a yard of yellow cloth, five oranges, and a small pumpkin. Put on some proper clothes while I write out my list."

As I pushed back from the table, she turned to Lilly. "I suggest you get busy darning those socks I gave you to work on last night, young lady. I got work piling up waiting for you to finish."

"Yes, ma'am," we chorused in unison. As I walked into my bedroom, I remembered the book Mrs. Constant had asked me to give to Lilly. The small leather-bound volume was sitting on top of my dresser where I'd dropped it after my visit to the Agate Public Library. *The Five Founding Families of Agate: An Illustrated History*, the cover read. *Written by Harry A. Skelton Sr.* It had been less than a week since my visit to see Mrs. Constant at the Agate Public Library. Yet, so much had happened that it felt like a lifetime. After getting dressed, I picked up the book, carried it into the kitchen, and handed it to Lilly.

"Mrs. Constant wanted me to give this to you," I said. "I forgot about it until now."

Lilly hugged the book to her chest with a radiant smile.

"At last!" she said. "This is the proof I've been waiting for."

"Proof of what?" I asked her.

"My father's real name, of course," she said. "I'm not like those other girls at the Institute, Nola. I've got a sponsor, someone who sends Mrs. Wyatt money every month on my behalf. Two months ago, I overheard her on the phone, talking to him about me. The old battle axe refused to give me his name, but obviously he's rich, and *very* distinguished. I figure he's got to belong to one of the founding families. It's just a question of which one."

She opened the book and thumbed through the pages, her brow furrowed in concentration. A minute later, she let out a delighted squeal and pointed to the photograph in the center of the page. Staring out at us was a slender man with penetrating eyes, a long patrician nose and thick, curly hair. Next to him stood a teenaged boy with the same bright eyes, long nose and unruly curls. *The Author With His Son Harry,* the caption read.

"Tell me these people don't look like me," Lilly demanded. "I dare you."

"Perhaps," I admitted. Make Harry Jr. a girl and give him a slightly darker complexion and he and Lilly could be twins. "The young boy is Congressman Skelton?"

"The very same," Lilly said triumphantly. "I always knew my father came from one of the founding families. Now I've got proof."

The fact that Lilly bore an uncanny resemblance to Congressman Skelton when he was a boy was interesting, but hardly qualified as proof. I was about to say this when Aunt Sarah shot me a warning glance. Let the girl have her fantasies, her look said. She's got little else to sustain her at the moment.

Aunt Sarah handed me a sheet of paper. "Here's my list, Nola. Have Parnell put it on my account. He knows I'm good for it."

I nodded, then turned to Lilly. "Be sure to stay indoors and out of sight," I told her. "Remember that the police are looking for you."

"Sure," Lilly replied absently. Since I'd given her the book, the girl had not taken her eyes off of it.

"Don't worry, Nola," Aunt Sarah said. "Lilly is wearing my special Protection Mojo Hand. She is going to be fine."

As I stepped outside, the wind blowing in off the Mississippi river felt heavy, almost tropical. Although the sky was clear, the air felt unseasonably sticky and humid. Rain was likely before the day was out, I thought. I considered going back to fetch an umbrella but decided against it. If I hurried, I'd be home in an hour.

The two-inch headline topping the front page of the *Agate Daily Chronicle* as I passed Mack's Corner Newsstand caught my attention. Nodding hello to Mr. Mack, the one-legged war veteran who ran the place, I stopped for a moment to read:

POLICE WIDEN DRAGNET IN SEARCH FOR WHEATLEY INSTITUTE RESIDENT SUSPECTED IN MURDER OF NEGRO BANDLEADER — "LILLY" STILL IN AGATE, AUTHORITIES CLAIM

I shook my head and continued walking. It was only a matter of time before the cops decided to go house by house through my neighborhood, knocking on doors. Once Lilly was found, her chances of beating a murder rap would be slim to none, unless I could come up with concrete evidence to prove her innocence.

I spent the next few blocks deep in thought. Abbie Everleigh, Joe Quincy, Jeff Fairchild, and Jack Cross had all been in the basement of the Wham Bam Club at the time of the murder. So had Tom Hoyt, the owner of the Wham Bam Club. According to Jack Cross, Hoyt had chased him out of the club at gun-point. The question was, which one of them had been angry enough with Eddie Smooth to kill him? At the moment, my money was on Abigail Everleigh. By her own admission, she had been furious with Eddie that night. What's more, she'd been in Eddie's dressing room, and even admitted knowing about the gun he kept there. As I turned onto Main Street, I turned this problem over and over in my mind. It was all well and good to suspect Miss Abigail of having shot Eddie Smooth. It would be another thing altogether to convince the police that the girl was guilty. At the moment, I had to admit I did not have the slightest idea how to make this happen.

Parnell's Market was located on the far end of Main Street near the docks, a half hour's walk from Aunt Sarah's house. Al-though it was not strictly in the Lincolnsville area, lots of col-ored folks shopped there because of the wide variety of fresh herbs, vegetables, and knickknacks Mr. Parnell kept in stock. If you happened to be looking for a rare variety of edible mush-room, some Saint-John's-wort or ginger root, a pink parasol or a bamboo bird house, Parnell's was the best place in town to find it.

The store's proprietor, Clarence Parnell, was an elderly man of unspecified ethnicity. His skin was the color of well-worn leather, and his accent hinted vaguely in the direction of the West Indies. I handed Mr. Parnell Aunt Sarah's shopping list. He pulled at his wispy white beard and nodded. Without a word, he disappeared into the back of his store, emerging sev-eral minutes later with a large shopping bag stuffed to the brim with fruits, herbs, and bottles.

"I'll put this on your Aunt Sarah's account," he told me. "Give her my regards."

As I picked up the shopping bag full of supplies and headed back up Main Street, I took a quick glance at the sky. Although it had been clear half an hour ago, thick clouds had begun to mass overhead. When the northbound streetcar stopped to pick me up at the corner, I heaved a sigh of relief. At least I would make it back to Aunt Sarah's without getting soaked.

"Colored in back," the conductor said, jerking his thumb toward the rear.

"I've got a legal right to sit anywhere I please," I said tartly.

"Not in my car you don't," he shot back, and clicked his change counter impatiently. Maybe I'd been away from Agate too long. Maybe it was the insolent way he looked me over as I stood with one foot on the steps and one foot on the sidewalk. Maybe it was having spent the previous night listening to the Congressman and his hypocritical friends say what they really felt about colored people. I do not know the cause. I only know that in that moment, something inside me snapped.

Before I could stop myself, I told the trolley conductor what he could do with his job, his streetcar, and his nasty-assed Dixie attitude. I was not surprised when he responded by slamming the trolley door in my face and driving away.

I picked up my shopping bag and began trudging up the hill toward Lincoln Avenue.

The first fat raindrops splattered against the top of my uncovered head minutes later. Muttering several choice curse words under my breath, I clutched the shopping bag against my body, hunched my shoulders against the rain, and picked up my pace.

The rain was coming down in buckets by the time I got to the corner of Seventh and Lincoln. I peered through the plate glass window of Richard's Café at the dry and cozy diners sipping their coffee inside. Should I go in? On the one hand, Aunt Sarah was waiting for me at home. On the other, the wind and the rain were picking up. If I kept walking, I'd get soaked to the skin for sure.

For a long minute, I hovered indecisively under the café's striped awning. When I spotted Lilly's best friend, Brenda

Washington, sitting at a table near the front window, I pushed open the front door and walked inside. The last time I'd seen Brenda was at the Wham Bam Club. It was entirely possible she had seen something that night that could help clear Lilly's name.

Brenda's broad, freckled face broke into a wide smile as I approached her table. "Nola Ann Jackson, as I live and breathe," she chirped. "Sit down and have a coffee with me."

I draped my sopping wet overcoat over the back of an empty chair, placed my shopping bag under the table, and settled myself in the seat across from her.

"I looked all over the grounds of the Wham Bam Club for you when the fire broke out," I said. "Obviously you made it out of there okay. What happened?"

"I hope you weren't too worried about me," Brenda said apologetically. "Larimer and I were down by the river when we saw the fire. Folks were running every which way, screaming their heads off. The dinghy was still moored at the boat dock, so we decided to take it and get away from all the commotion."

"Did I hear you say 'we'?" I said, raising an eyebrow. "Please don't tell me you've spent the last two days holed up with that bass player."

Brenda Washington's freckled face blushed scarlet. "It's not what you think, Nola," she said hastily. "Larimer and I went to City Hall and got our wedding license yesterday. This time next week, we will be man and wife."

"That's wonderful news," I said. "Where is the lucky groom-to-be?"

Brenda pointed toward a door labeled EMPLOYEES ONLY behind the counter at the front of the room. "He's talking to Mr. Richard about having the two of us to play music here—a little piano and bass duo during the lunch hour to brighten up the place."

"He's not planning to join a new band now that Eddie Smooth is out of the picture?" I said.

Brenda shook her head. "Now that we're getting married, Larimer intends to stay home more. We plan to have a real family someday," she told me. A combination of gentle pink and orange hues glowed softly in Brenda's aura as she spoke. "We want to have at least two kids."

"Sounds lovely," I said wistfully. Before he died, Will Jackson and I had planned to do exactly the same thing. Would I ever meet another man I wanted to start a family with? Once again, my mind turned to Jim Richardson. The man was handsome, witty, and sophisticated. Courageous, too. Yet somehow, he did not strike me as a family man.

As if she could read my thoughts, Brenda Washington said, "Don't ever give up on true love, Nola. Even when it's hard to find, it's still there. You just have to know where to look for it."

I nodded as Brenda sipped her coffee and looked pensively out the window.

"Lilly didn't know the difference between true love and the kind you read about in fairy tales," Brenda continued. "She was looking for love from a man who couldn't give it. I tried to talk her out of running off with Eddie Smooth, but she wouldn't listen. We argued about it the night she decided to run away from Wheatley Institute."

"Eddie Smooth was a rotten apple," I said. "I don't believe she killed him, but if she did, I could understand why."

"Lilly would never do something like that, Nola. She loved Eddie Smooth more than anything."

I gave Brenda Washington a skeptical look. "Even though he was cheating on her? Mrs. Wyatt made a point of telling me Lilly had a terrible temper. She said Lilly fought with the other girls."

"Only because they made fun of her birth parents," Brenda said. "She grew up in an orphanage, you know. Her mother was a colored woman who died in childbirth. Lilly doesn't even know her real last name. Davidson is just the name they gave her at the orphanage. Because of Lilly's light complexion, we all assumed her father was a white man. The girls used to pick on her, call her a half-breed and such."

"It must have been terrible for her," I said softly.

Brenda nodded in agreement. "Somehow Lilly got it into her head that her real father was from one of the five founding families." She took another sip of coffee, then put her cup down with a sigh. "That was just like Lilly. Always the romantic. She couldn't have just any white man for a father. He had to be the richest man in town."

"Do you think there is anything more than fantasy to this idea?" I asked.

"Maybe," Brenda said slowly. "A few months ago, Lilly overheard Mrs. Wyatt talking to someone on the phone about giving a large donation so long as Lilly remained at Wheatley Institute."

Now we're getting somewhere, I thought. "Did she ask Mrs. Wyatt about this?"

"Of course," Brenda answered. "Mrs. Wyatt said that it was not nice to snoop, and that Lilly would learn all about it when she turned seventeen."

"This conversation took place before Lilly started going to the Wham Bam Club?"

"Yes," Brenda said. "When she started seeing Eddie Smooth, I thought Lilly might forget about trying to find her real father, but Eddie egged her on. He said he'd help her look for her daddy, that he had some rich white friends who he could approach to help with the search."

"Do you know if Eddie actually contacted anyone?" I asked.

"I doubt it. He was always making promises he had no intention of keeping," Brenda said. "Poor Lilly. It said in this morning's *Daily Chronicle* that the police are still looking for her. I hope she's all right."

"Me, too," I said. I thought it best not to mention that Lilly was less than a mile away, hiding in my house at this very moment. Brenda Washington was a good soul, but she was no keeper of secrets. "Mrs. Wyatt has asked me to investigate, dig up evidence that will prove Lilly is innocent of this crime. Did you see her at the Wham Bam Club that night?"

"I wish I had seen Lilly that night," Brenda said, "but I didn't. After you and I went outside, I stayed down by the river with Larimer the whole time."

"When you see Mrs. Wyatt again, you might want to keep the part about Larimer to yourself," I said wryly. "Good thing you two are getting married soon."

CHAPTER 18

It was nearly six according to the clock on the wall behind the counter. Even though it was still raining heavily, it was time for me to head for home. Aunt Sarah was probably wondering what had happened to me. I stood up and shrugged into my coat, which was a bit less damp than when I'd taken it off half an hour ago. Hopefully, the shopping bag I'd carried here from Parnell's Market had also dried out some.

"It's been good to see you, Brenda," I said. "Let's talk again soon."

As I bent down to pick up my bag, the front door of the café banged open to admit Miss Eleanor Constant, accompanied by a brisk gust of wind. Her belted trench coat was dripping wet, as was the matching felt hat she wore. She shut the door, closed her umbrella and dropped it in the umbrella stand by the door.

"Good evening, ladies," Miss Eleanor said. "Mind if I join you?"

"Of course not," Brenda called out gaily. "Nola has to go, but I'd love to chat with you for a while. Come and sit down."

"Good to see you again, Miss Eleanor," I said. "I wish I

could stay and catch up with you, but I really must get going. I was supposed to bring this bag home to my Aunt Sarah hours ago."

"It's pouring cats and dogs at the moment," Miss Eleanor replied. "You should wait till it lightens up a bit."

When I turned to look outside the window, the rain was coming down in sheets, buffeted by a furious westerly wind. The woman had a point. The minute I stepped out the door, I'd be soaked to the skin, for sure.

"It's downright miserable out there," I agreed. I put down my shopping bag and took off my coat. "Perhaps I will sit here just a little bit longer."

Miss Eleanor summoned the waiter and ordered a cup of coffee. "How have you been, Brenda?" she said. "Mrs. Wyatt tells me you're no longer living at Wheatley Institute. Are you all right?"

"I'm perfectly fine," Brenda answered cheerily. "As a matter of fact, I am getting married next week."

Miss Eleanor Constant's eyebrows shot up in surprise. "My goodness," she said. "Who is the lucky gentleman?"

"Larimer Betts," Brenda said proudly, "the sweetest, kindest, and handsomest man in the whole wide world."

Miss Eleanor pulled her spectacles down to the tip of her nose, tipped her head to one side and studied Brenda in silence for a minute. "Mrs. Wyatt tells me that you're a very talented musician, Brenda," she said. "I hope you won't give up your music after you are married."

"Of course not," Brenda said with a serene smile. "Larimer is a musician, just like me. We plan to have our own jazz orchestra someday."

"If you're happy, then I'm happy," Miss Eleanor replied. "I hope I didn't overstep my bounds just now. I don't want to be a busybody."

"It's fine," Brenda reassured her. "You're only doing it

because you care about me. I want you to be proud of me, Miss Eleanor. Mrs. Wyatt, too. I'm going to wait until everything is legal between Larimer and me before I tell her about the wedding."

As Brenda spoke, Larimer Betts walked up behind her and kissed her on the cheek. "Tell who?" he said. The minute she heard his voice, Brenda's aura lit up like a Christmas tree.

I had to admit they made an adorable couple. Brenda was tall, light skinned, and lanky. Larimer was short, dark, and built like a fireplug.

"I was just talking about our wedding plans, darling," Brenda said. "How did your meeting go? Is Mr. Richard going to hire us?"

Larimer Betts grinned. "This Saturday, Richard's Café will present a live performance by the Café Crooners, otherwise known as Mr. and Mrs. Larimer Betts."

"Ooh!" Brenda said, letting out a delighted squeal that turned heads in our direction. "Wonderful news. Our first real gig!"

"Congratulations to you both," I said, lifting my coffee cup in a ceremonial toast.

"Larimer, this is Nola Jackson," Brenda said. "She came to the Wham Bam Club with me, remember?"

"Of course," he said, reaching over to shake my hand. "Good to see you again."

"And *this* is Miss Eleanor Constant," Brenda added. "Miss Eleanor is the librarian I've been telling you about."

"Brenda raves about your lectures," he said as he shook Miss Eleanor's hand.

"I'm just a sucker for a good story," Miss Eleanor replied, and turned to me. "How's your investigation going, Nola? Turned up any new evidence yet?"

There were several things I could have said. I could have told her about my meeting with Boss Dillard and Jack Cross. Or, I could have told her about my visit to Jim Richardson's office, and the way he had taken me in his arms and kissed me. Instead of saying any of these things, I simply said that my investigation was moving forward. "I'm expecting something new to turn up any day now," I told her.

I was saved from further interrogation when a bespectacled young man burst through the front door, slamming it loudly behind him. He dropped his umbrella in the umbrella stand, hung his rain-soaked overcoat on the peg next to the door, and marched over to our table.

"'Tis a foul and stormy night," he declared in a dramatic baritone. His spectacles, tweed suit, and the pipe he smoked lent the man a literary air. "Good evening Miss Eleanor," he continued. "Are these lovely people coming to join our writer's group?"

Miss Constant smiled. "Nola, Brenda, and Larimer, this is Ben Langford. Ben is a talented author and a founding member of the Negro Writers Circle."

"'Good friendship, good wine and good welcome' to you all," Ben said cheerfully. "The great William Shakespeare wrote that line three hundred fifty years ago, and it still applies today. Good wine is not as available as it once was, thanks to Prohibition. Still, I wish you all a very good welcome."

Ben Langford's blustery good humor was hard to resist. "It's a pleasure to meet you," I said. "Even on this dark and stormy night."

"The feeling is mutual," Ben replied, puffing contentedly on his pipe. "Won't you consider coming to our writers circle tonight? Four authors will be reading from their work. At the risk of sounding ridiculously arrogant, I will say that we are all very talented."

"Thanks for the invitation," Larimer Betts said, "but Brenda and I have some shopping to do."

"Can't it wait?" Ben Langford said. "Shakespeare would

describe this night as being 'most unruly.' In more prosaic language, it's raining buckets outside. Definitely not a night for window shopping."

"Normally I would agree with you," Larimer replied, "but my future wife is making her show business debut next Saturday. She's going to need a new dress." With a genial farewell nod to the rest of us, he pulled his umbrella from the stand, threw a protective arm around Brenda Washington, and piloted her out the door.

"What about you, Nola?" Miss Eleanor said. "We're getting ready to start in just a few minutes. Won't you stay and listen for a while?"

I shook my head. "I was supposed to bring this bag to my Aunt Sarah hours ago," I replied, and nodded toward the shopping bag at my feet.

"I doubt if your Aunt Sarah wants her bag to get soaked clear through," Miss Constant replied. "If you'll stay and be an audience for my writers group, I promise to drive you and your shopping bag home when we're done. I'll even buy you a bowl of Mr. Richard's split pea soup if you'll agree to stay. How does that sound?"

"It sounds wonderful," I admitted. It had been hours since I'd eaten anything, and Mr. Richard made the best soup in the city. "If you don't mind me eating while you read, I'll join you for a little while. Don't know how much help I'll be, though. I've never written anything."

Ben Langford winked at me. "I get the feeling you've got a fascinating story inside you, an amazing tale just waiting to be told."

"I doubt it," I replied. "I'm just an ordinary girl, nothing special."

"No you are not," Ben said. Behind his wire-rimmed spectacles, his dark brown eyes sparkled with good-humored mischief. "I know for a fact that you used to live in New York

City. You moved back to Agate a few months ago, and now you live with a hoodoo woman. There is nothing ordinary about any of this, my dear."

"Not when you put it like that," I admitted. "How do you know all this? Have we met before?"

"I am a writer," Ben Langford replied. "I make it my job to study people. In addition, I just happen to live on Upper Fifth Street." Langford's aura was bright gold with tiny flecks of purple. According to Aunt Sarah, these colors only appeared in the auras of people who were natural born leaders. "You may not know it, but I've had my eye on you for some time, Nola Ann Jackson."

"Is that so?" I said. I suddenly found myself wishing I'd worn a nicer dress. The serviceable gabardine I had on did little to flatter my shape, and my hair was still wet from my long walk in the rain.

"I'm writing a short story about our neighborhood," Ben continued. "I'm going to read an excerpt from it tonight. I think you'll like it, Nola. In fact, I know you will."

As it turned out, Ben was right. I ended up staying for the full two-hour meeting. The stories were wonderful. Aaron Troutman, a lumbering teenager with a thick Southern accent, read a chapter from his novel, a biting satire about the relationship between a white plantation owner and the sharecropper who farmed his land. Doris Kaye, a skinny teenager who didn't seem old enough to know about such things, shared a poem about lost love. A fair-skinned boy named Philip read from the novel he was writing about Toussaint Louverture and the Haitian revolution. The most riveting piece I heard that night came from Ben Langford. His story about a middle-aged colored man struggling to buy Christmas gifts for his family moved me to tears.

There was a lively discussion after each piece was read. To my surprise, I found myself joining in along with everyone else, giving my impressions about the plot and the characters. It had been a long time since I'd been around a group of people my own age, and I had to say, it felt good.

After everyone's piece was read, Ben regaled the group with episodes from his time as a student at Atlanta University under the great Negro scholar W. E. B. Du Bois. You wouldn't think a Negro college would be a hotbed of humor, but Ben's comic timing and deadpan delivery kept us all in stitches.

The four writers were still deep in conversation when Miss Eleanor Constant stood and put on her coat.

"Let me take you home, Nola," she said. "I've got to go to work in the morning. This crew is likely to stay here talking all night."

As I stood up to leave, the four writers chorused "goodnight" in unison.

"Shakespeare once wrote, 'thy friendship makes us fresh,' which is just a fancy way of saying it's been great to meet you," Ben Langford said. "We're here every week. I hope you'll come back."

The rain was finally beginning to let up. Only a few drops spattered against the windshield of Miss Eleanor's Model T as we drove along Lincoln Avenue toward Aunt Sarah's house.

"Thanks for inviting me tonight, Miss Eleanor," I said. "It was nice to meet some new people, and do something else other than worry about Lilly Davidson."

Miss Eleanor nodded, and turned left onto Upper Fifth Street. "I had a long talk with Mrs. Wyatt this afternoon," she said. "She's very impressed with you, you know."

I looked at her in surprise. "Really?"

"She told me she thought you were exceptional. That's why she got so angry when you ran off to get married. She has great faith in you, Nola. You're going to find Lilly, bring her back to Wheatley Institute, and prove that she is not a murderer."

As we pulled to the curb in front of Aunt Sarah's house, it

was on the tip of my tongue to tell Miss Eleanor I knew where Lilly was. Instead, I simply thanked Miss Eleanor for the ride and watched as she drove away. Finding Lilly was only part of the job. My work would not be finished until I discovered the true identity of Eddie Smooth's killer.

Aunt Sarah was waiting for me in the front room as I walked in. " 'Bout time you got home," she said tartly. "You get those things I asked you to pick up from Mr. Parnell?"

"Yes, ma'am," I said, and handed over the shopping bag. Aunt Sarah peered inside, then grunted in satisfaction. "I'm glad to see you had the good sense not to let them get soaked through," she said. "Have you had your dinner? Let me fix you something."

When I told Aunt Sarah that I'd already eaten at Richard's Café, she raised an eyebrow. My aunt refused to believe that anyone else's cooking, even Mr. Richard's, could hold a candle to her own. "You had his split pea soup, I suppose," she said. "Was it any good?"

Richard's soup had been fantastic, but I knew better than to ruffle my aunt's feathers by praising it too highly. "It was all right," I said carefully. "I ran into Miss Eleanor Constant and she offered to buy me dinner. So of course, I couldn't say no."

"I suppose not," Aunt Sarah agreed reluctantly. "Come back in the kitchen and let me fix you some tea."

While the kettle heated up, I told Aunt Sarah about seeing Brenda Washington at Richard's Café, and about the interesting people I'd met in the Negro Writers Circle.

"I had more fun with those writers than I thought I would," I said. "This fellow Ben Langford is quite something. He quotes Shakespeare all the time, can you imagine?"

As I continued to share my experiences, a shadow of worry fell across Aunt Sarah's face. "You didn't tell anyone about Lilly staying here, did you, Nola?"

I shook my head. "I wanted to say something to Miss Eleanor

when she brought me home just now, but then something told me to keep quiet."

"No one must know that Lilly is hiding here," Aunt Sarah said firmly. "Not until we can find out who really killed Eddie Smooth." Aunt Sarah set out two cups and filled them to the brim with chamomile tea. "Did you ask Brenda Washington what she saw the night of the murder?"

"I did, but I don't think she's going to be much use to us," I said. "At the time of the murder, Brenda was walking by the river with her boyfriend."

"Did she see or hear anything unusual while she was down there?" Aunt Sarah asked.

I gave my aunt a wry smile. "Brenda Washington and her new boyfriend are very much in love," I said. "I think an entire brigade of soldiers in full uniform could have passed through those woods without the two of them noticing."

Aunt Sarah patted me gently on the arm. "You sound a bit jealous, Nola Ann," she said. "Your time is coming, my dear. I promise you."

I looked down at the table as I felt a flush of embarrassment creep over my face. There were definitely times when I wished my Aunt Sarah were just a little bit less psychic.

Hastily, I changed the subject. "What did you and Lilly do today?" I said.

"This and that," Aunt Sarah replied. "After you left, Lilly curled up with that book you gave her. She was supposed to be darning socks, but I could see the book contained something she was hungry for, so I let her alone. I went out to the yard to get some fresh lavender for my next batch of Supreme Peace Potion. When I came back inside, Lilly was gone."

I felt as though I'd been punched in the stomach. In all my plans and calculations, the idea that Lilly would leave the safety of Aunt Sarah's house had never occurred to me. "Gone?"

"That's what I said," Aunt Sarah told me. "I figured she'd

come home when it started to rain, but she hasn't returned as of yet."

"What in blazes is wrong with that girl," I fumed. "Doesn't she know police are looking for her?"

"Apparently, she's got something more important on her mind," Aunt Sarah replied. "All she could talk about was her birth father, about how he belongs to one of the five founding families."

"Most likely, the man does not even know he has a daughter," I said. "Even if he does know, he probably doesn't care."

"You know that and I know that," Aunt Sarah said, "but Lilly believes with all her heart that finding her birth father is going to solve all her problems. She's got this fairy tale stuck in her head and does not want to give it up."

"I can't believe she's run away again," I said bitterly. "Can't the Spirits just tell you where she is?"

Aunt Sarah got very still and closed her eyes. When she spoke again, her voice sounded different, as though she'd been away on a long journey.

"Some things are just not meant for us to see," she told me. "When the time is right for us to see into what is going on with Lilly Davidson, our Spirit Helpers will show us."

"Let's just hope the right time comes soon," I said. "Lilly is not safe out there. She could be picked up by the police at any minute."

For the next hour, I paced around the house, peering out the window every few minutes to look for Lilly. When I looked out the front window for what seemed like the hundredth time, Aunt Sarah told me to stop fidgeting and sit down.

"I'm getting a headache just watching you," she told me. "Go to bed and get some sleep. The Spirits are not going to help us one minute before it's time."

I tossed and turned restlessly that night, waking up every time I thought I heard footsteps outside. Where could Lilly have gone? All the respectable businesses in Agate had closed hours ago. The only places that stayed open this late were the gambling dens, the sporting houses, and the Black Rooster Pool Hall. If Lilly had gone to one of these places, there was little anyone could do to help her. The girl was going to need every ounce of help the Spirits could muster.

CHAPTER 19

When I got up the next morning, Aunt Sarah was kneading bread dough in the kitchen. "Good morning, Nola," she said. "And before you ask me, the answer is no. Lilly has not come back yet." My aunt took a clean red and white checked dish towel from the sideboard and draped it over the bowl of dough and set it to rise on the countertop.

I was about to open my mouth to say something about Lilly Davidson's irresponsible, no-account nature when Aunt Sarah put a finger to her lips. "Do not speak ill of the girl until you've walked a mile in her shoes," she said firmly. "She'll come back when she's good and ready."

"We can only hope that happens before she winds up being arrested for murder," I said sourly.

"Why don't you sit down and let me make you some breakfast," Aunt Sarah said gently. "You're looking a bit peaked."

Aunt Sarah had just poured me a cup of tea when we heard a loud knock at the front door.

"Open up! Police!" a man's voice shouted.

Seconds later, the front door flew open. Three white policemen charged into the house with their guns drawn. As Aunt Sarah and I stared at them in shocked amazement, the biggest of the three men grabbed me roughly by the arm.

"Where is she?" he shouted. His eyes were alive with malice as he stuck his gun in my face. "Where is Lilly Davidson?"

I was weak in the knees with terror, but knew I could not show fear. "Lilly is not here," I said.

A second officer took hold of Aunt Sarah's shoulder and shoved her against the wall. Judging from his ruddy cheeks and baby fat, the man was little more than a teenager. His disrespectful manner made me want to punch him, but I knew better than to lose my temper while white men pointed guns at me.

"Please, Officers," I said quietly. "We've done nothing wrong. We're happy to cooperate. Just tell us what you want."

The policeman tightened his grip on my arm. "Jeffrey Fairchild's been murdered," he said. "He was shot in the back outside Congressman Skelton's house yesterday night."

"That's terrible," I said, "but what does it have to do with us?"

The third policeman was older than the other two. He had side whiskers, a hefty gut, and onions on his breath.

"Mrs. Skelton saw a girl fitting Lilly Davidson's description running from the scene just after the shot was fired," he said. "The girl's been staying with you, so we figure you know where she is." He stuck his face inches from my own, and sneered. "Before we leave here, you're gonna tell us everything you know."

When I opened my mouth to speak, the policeman shook a finger in my face. "No use you making up some lie about not knowing this girl," he said. "Artie Mack at the corner newsstand saw the girl leaving your house at three o'clock yesterday afternoon."

I kept my expression neutral, but resolved never to shop at Mack's Corner Newsstand again. Mr. Mack was a small-time bookie who took bets on the races now and then. Apparently, he was also a police informant.

My heart thumped wildly in my chest. *Think*, I told myself. *There has to be a way out of this.*

"Lilly was staying here," I answered carefully, "but she left. She didn't tell us where she was going, and that's the truth."

The older policeman stepped back, rubbed a thick hand over the stubble on his chin, and turned to his two younger colleagues.

"You believe her, boys?" he said.

The two younger men, uncertain of what answer would please their boss the most, said nothing.

"Let me share some wisdom with you here," the older man continued. "All nigras lie, especially to the police. This little girl is lying." With a smirk, he caressed the knob of the nightstick hanging from his belt and turned to face me. "You can tell us nice and easy or we can beat it out of you, little girl. What'll it be?"

"You can see for yourself that Lilly is not here," I answered. "She left here yesterday afternoon just like Mr. Mack told you. Isn't that right, Aunt Sarah?"

My aunt nodded, her dark face expressionless. The red-faced boy looming above her narrowed his eyes and looked around the room.

"The Davidson girl may have left her things here, Sergeant Sullivan," he said. "If we search, we might find an important clue."

"Good thinking, Patrolman Miller," the older policeman said with an approving nod.

"You won't find anything," I said quickly. "Lilly had nothing but the clothes on her back when she showed up here."

The older policeman gave no indication that he'd heard me. "We'd better take a look around," he told his men. "Be real thorough, boys. Make sure you don't miss anything."

For the next hour, the three policemen systematically trashed Aunt Sarah's small haven. They dumped the contents of every drawer in her dresser onto the floor. They rifled through her kitchen cabinets, upending the bowls of herbs steeping on the counter. As Aunt Sarah and I watched with stony faces, the policemen rifled through her closets and smashed her bottles of medicines and potions.

Perhaps a colored policeman would have recognized the signs: the fact that Aunt Sarah's jaw was silently working as if chewing something; the fact that the gnarled fingers on her left hand were tracing small circles against the gingham cloth of her apron.

I did not turn to look at her. I didn't have to, because I knew full well what she was doing. Sergeant Sullivan had just started to pry open the locked cabinet where Aunt Sarah kept her most powerful potions when his legs buckled underneath him.

"Jesus, Mary, and Joseph," he said, and steadied himself against the kitchen sink.

Patrolman Miller stopped in the middle of throwing a pile of Aunt Sarah's bedclothes onto the floor and looked at the man in alarm. "You all right, Sergeant Sullivan?"

"Just a little dizzy," Sullivan replied, mopping the sweat from his forehead with the back of his sleeve. "It's hotter than Hades in here." His jowly face was beet red as he gasped for breath. "That's enough, boys," he said suddenly. "Let's go. It stinks to high heaven in here. I need some fresh air."

As Sergeant Sullivan and his policemen stumbled outside into the street, I gave my Aunt Sarah a knowing look.

"Do as I say and not as I do," she said crisply. "Those men were about to upset my entire herb cabinet. I couldn't have them getting ahold of the jars where I keep the hexing powders. Poor fools might have hurt themselves. They had to be stopped, so I stopped them. And don't you keep looking at me like that, Nola Ann Jackson." She turned away and picked up a broom and dustpan from the corner next to the kitchen sink. "Help me get this mess cleaned up."

"Yes, ma'am," I said, suppressing the urge to grin.

"Wipe that grin off your face, young lady."

"I'm not grinning," I replied. "Honest, I'm not."

"You're grinning on the inside," my aunt replied. "I can tell."

For the next hour we cleaned and straightened. We swept up shards of broken glass and crockery. We put the dishes that had not been broken back on the shelf in the kitchen, and refilled the drawers whose contents had been unceremoniously dumped on the floor. I was in the process of folding the tattered afghan Aunt Sarah kept on the living room couch when the doorbell rang.

Praying that Sergeant Sullivan and his men had not returned for another visit, I opened the door a tiny crack and peered out. I let out a sigh of relief when I saw Mr. Layton, dressed, as usual, in a black three-piece suit, standing on the doorstep.

"What in heaven's name is all this?" he said, stepping carefully around the heaps of clothing and bits of broken glass littering the floor.

"The police were here," I said. "Congressman Skelton's assistant has been murdered. The police think Lilly Davidson did it."

Mr. Layton nodded. "The story is in all the papers," he said. "What has this got to do with you?"

"Lilly was here last night," I told him.

Mr. Layton looked at me and Aunt Sarah in surprise. "The girl was hiding here?"

"Not for long," Aunt Sarah answered. "She was here, but then she left. We haven't heard from her since yesterday."

Mr. Layton surveyed the mess in the living room, then grunted. "If you're lucky, it'll stay that way," he said. "Are you ladies all right?"

"Right as rain," Aunt Sarah said with a grim chuckle. "Thanks for asking, though. What brings you by here, Edward?"

Mr. Layton bent down to help Aunt Sarah straighten an

armchair that had been knocked on its side. "We got a last-minute call this morning for a big catering job," he said. "I was hoping Nola was available to work this afternoon."

I waved a hand at the piles of clothes, food, and broken dishes scattered on the floor. "I don't see how I can," I said. "I'm in the middle of helping Aunt Sarah get the house back in order."

"Don't be silly," Aunt Sarah said briskly. "I'll be fine. You run along."

Aunt Sarah was as tough as they come. Still, the home in which she took so much pride had just been brutally invaded. Sweeping up the broken glass was easy. Healing the damage the police had caused to my elderly aunt's psyche would be a lot more difficult.

"Sure you don't need me to help clean up this mess?" I persisted.

Aunt Sarah frowned. "Don't fuss over me, Nola," she replied. "Go on, get out of here. After all this commotion, I need some time alone."

"If you say so," I replied. I walked into my bedroom and dug through the pile of clothes the police had dumped on the floor until I found my DeLuxe Catering uniform. I told my aunt I'd be home by early evening, kissed her goodbye, and followed Mr. Layton outside.

CHAPTER 20

Minty greeted me as I slid onto the front seat of the DeLuxe Catering delivery truck next to her. "Glad you could come with us, Nola," she said. "This job came up at the complete last minute. Edward and I were going to handle it by ourselves, but I suggested we stop by your house on the way, just in case you were free."

"It's been a difficult day so far," I said. "Hopefully this afternoon will be an improvement."

"Nola and her Aunt Sarah received an unexpected visit from the police this morning," Mr. Layton said. "They think Nola knows where the murderer is. Tore the house apart looking for evidence."

Minty Layton stared at me in amazement. "Didn't I warn you about keeping your nose clean, Nola? Mr. Layton and I cannot afford to be seen associating with criminals. You're lucky the cops didn't take you both down to the station house."

"I know," I said hastily. "And I'm sorry, Minty. Truly. It will not happen again."

"You've said that before," Mr. Layton said. "Mrs. Layton

and I like you, Nola. But if this pattern continues, we're going to have to let you go."

"It won't continue, I promise," I told them.

Mr. Layton grunted, downshifted his truck into second gear, and turned onto Main Street. After several minutes of awkward silence, Mr. Layton told me we were headed downtown to Hastings Hall to cater a fundraising luncheon for Congressman Skelton's campaign.

"The event was supposed to be held at Mr. Fairchild's house," Minty explained. "Mrs. Fairchild is too distraught to supervise anything, what with her husband being murdered and all. At the last minute, Mrs. Skelton decided to move the lunch to Hastings Hall. She called us early this morning."

"It's going to be a buffet lunch," Mr. Layton said. "We cook the food, put it out, then allow the guests to help themselves. You'll serve the beverages, just like you always do, Nola."

"Mrs. Skelton wants me to make the same sweet potato casserole I fixed for Mrs. Ratcliffe," Minty said. "Fortunately, we still have all the supplies."

Mr. Layton turned to his wife and smiled. "You see, my dear? Instead of losing customers, we are gaining them. With any luck, Mrs. Skelton will have us back to cater even more parties in the future."

"Maybe," Minty said darkly. "Or maybe whoever is sending Mrs. Ratcliffe hate mail will find out Mrs. Skelton has hired us, and start sending her hate mail as well."

"No use in speculating," Mr. Layton said brightly. "For the moment, the only thing that matters is that we do a good job."

Hastings Hall was a small gray building built out of rough-hewn granite in the style of a medieval castle. A square tower topped by a stone parapet overlooked the front entrance, a heavy wooden door with iron handles in the shape of lions. I had passed the building many times, but had never been inside the place. Hastings Hall did not welcome Negroes either as customers or employees. As we approached the building, I had to admit I was curious to see what forbidden opulence the place had to offer.

The service entrance at the back of the building, however, was considerably less fancy. Mr. Layton squeezed his delivery truck into the small parking space in the alley behind a plain metal door, and rang the bell.

The man who answered the door was thin, balding, and white. He wore a dark blue janitor's uniform and frowned when he saw us standing there.

"You must be the new caterer," he said. His aura pulsed with jagged red waves of indignation. "Most irregular, hiring coloreds like that. It's never been done before. We're only making an exception to our regular policy on account of Mrs. Skelton."

Mr. Layton did not reply. His aura remained an impenetrable blue as he continued to stand unmoving in the doorway. After a long minute the janitor, still muttering under his breath, turned and walked away. Once we were inside Hastings Hall, I was surprised by how ordinary things looked. The kitchen had white walls and a white tiled floor. In addition to a long butcher-block table in the center of the room, there were two sinks, two stoves, and a walk-in pantry. Nice, I thought, but nothing we hadn't seen before. Mrs. Ratcliffe's kitchen was equally well equipped. Funny how places you're not allowed to enter can acquire a luster that is completely unjustified by reality, I thought.

As I pondered this insight, Minty Layton told me to get a move on. "Help us get this truck unloaded, Nola," she said. "Mrs. Skelton expects lunch to be ready at one o'clock. No ifs, ands, or buts."

We spent the next half hour carrying boxes, bottles, and crates of cooking supplies inside. When the ham had been rubbed with ginger, cloves, and dry mustard and placed in the oven, Minty and I peeled a dozen large yams and set them in a large pot to boil.

Minty Layton's butter-pecan sweet potato casserole was one of her most popular dishes. Sweet enough to be a dessert, yet savory enough to serve as a tasty side dish, the melt-in-your-mouth casserole was as light as a feather. The secret to its success was the dozen eggs it took to make it. The yolks, blended with mashed sweet potatoes, a pound of butter, cinnamon, nutmeg, and a pinch of clove, gave the casserole a velvety richness. The whites, when whipped into a meringue, gave the dish the illusion of being light as air. Topped with a crumble of crushed pecans, butter, and brown sugar, Minty's sweet potato casserole was out of this world.

While Minty continued to work her magic in the kitchen, I went out to the banquet hall to help Mr. Layton set up the buffet table. The banquet hall featured parquet floors, oak-paneled walls, Tudor-style leaded windows, and a massive stone fireplace. Comfortable leather armchairs and small circular dining tables had been placed around the room so the guests could easily mingle, standing or sitting as they chose. Once the food was laid out in the large stainless steel warming trays arranged along one side of the long, wood-paneled room, I would circulate among the guests, serving hot cider and clearing away the dirty dishes as needed.

Two hours later, Hastings Hall was filled with expensively dressed white women, most of them well into their middle years, chatting, mingling, and helping themselves with gusto to baked ham, creamed spinach, and Minty's heavenly sweet potato casserole.

I was carrying a small silver tray filled with cups of hot cider when I spotted Congressman Skelton's wife, Millicent, standing next to the fireplace. Although she wore an elegant tweed suit that must have cost upwards of one hundred dollars, the woman looked as dreary as a sunless day. As I hovered near the fireplace offering cider to the guests, Mrs. Ratcliffe walked up and kissed Mrs. Skelton on the cheek.

"My condolences, Millicent," Mrs. Ratcliffe said. She was attired with typical flamboyance in a pink chiffon dress, a long rope of pearls, and her usual diamond hair clip. "I know how close Jeff Fairchild was to your family. How are you and the Congressman holding up?"

"As well as can be expected," Mrs. Skelton replied. "I was going to cancel today's luncheon, but Penny Fairchild insisted her husband would have wanted us to go ahead with it." She smiled ruefully. "Every woman at this luncheon has donated generously to Harry's campaign. We need to keep them energized and excited. The election's only two weeks away."

"How is Penny doing?" Mrs. Ratcliffe said. "I've been thinking about her."

"To be honest, the poor woman is in a terrible state," Mrs. Skelton said. "She keeps saying that her dead husband is calling to her. Not in her mind, and not in her imagination, but out loud."

Mrs. Ratcliffe nodded sagely. "That is not as unusual as you would think. As a Spiritualist, I've seen this sort of thing many times before," she said. "Jeff Fairchild's spirit is restless and wishes to communicate."

"I wish you would tell Penelope that," Mrs. Skelton said. "The poor girl is nearly out of her mind. Her husband's photograph keeps falling off the mantelpiece, even though no one has touched it. When she puts the photo back, it falls back on the floor within minutes."

Holding on to my tray of cups filled with hot cider, I hovered as close as I could to the two women, eavesdropping shamelessly as they continued their conversation.

"Has anything else unusual happened?" Mrs. Ratcliffe said, in the manner of a doctor listening to the complaints of a patient.

Millicent Skelton inched closer to Mrs. Ratcliffe and said, "In the wee hours of the morning, Penny heard someone knock at her front door. When she went to look, there was no one there." Mrs. Skelton looked around to make sure no one was listening, but did not notice me as I hovered behind her. "I'm worried Penny may be losing her sanity," she continued. "The last thing Harry's campaign needs is for Penelope Fairchild to have some kind of public breakdown. That idiot Joe Quincy wanted to have her put in a sanitarium until after the election. He said she was 'weak,' and should be 'removed' from the campaign. He made the comment like it was a joke, but none of us thought it was at all funny. Harry nixed the suggestion immediately."

"Penny Fairchild is definitely not crazy," Mrs. Ratcliffe said firmly. "In my work as a Spiritualist, I've seen this happen many times before. Her husband was snatched from this material world abruptly, without the chance to say goodbye. It makes all the sense in the world that he would return to pay her a visit. Once I've contacted his spirit directly, we can find out what he wants."

Mrs. Skelton stared at Mrs. Ratcliffe in surprise. "You mean, have a séance?" she said. "Here?"

"Of course," Mrs. Ratcliffe said. "We should begin as soon as possible. It will do Penny Fairchild a world of good."

"I don't know, Portia." Millicent Skelton's voice held a small note of panic. "The Congressman is very skeptical about these sorts of things. I don't know if he would approve. In fact, I am sure he wouldn't."

As I watched the two women, I saw Mrs. Portia Ratcliffe's aura turn a brilliant orange, the colors of a woman on a mission. "Is the Congressman here?"

"Not now," Mrs. Skelton replied. "This luncheon is for women only. Harry's out somewhere with Joe Quincy. Drumming up votes on the West Side, I believe."

Mrs. Ratcliffe smiled triumphantly. "Then there's no reason why we can't have our séance this afternoon. Bring Penelope to my house when this luncheon is finished."

"There are reporters here," Mrs. Skelton said anxiously. "Don't look now, but Rosemary Scott is standing right over there." She pointed her chin in the direction of a fat, round-faced woman helping herself liberally from the buffct table. "Mrs. Scott is the gossip columnist for the *Agate Daily Chronicle*. The woman has been following me all over town. I'm supposed to appear at a campaign dinner with Harry at five. If I deviate one jot from my schedule, that blasted woman is going to write about it."

"So what if she does?" Mrs. Ratcliffe said grandly. "You cannot be worried about petty gossip at a time like this."

"Easy for you to say," Mrs. Skelton replied. "You are not in politics. I can't afford to do anything even the least bit unconventional, not with the election just two weeks away. If my husband finds out, he'll be furious."

"Of course, dear," Mrs. Ratcliffe said in a softer voice. "Do what you must. But I'm telling you—Penelope's situation is critical. You can see that for yourself. When the Spirits start calling a person in this way, immediate action is required."

Millicent Skelton sighed and looked away for a moment. "Do you think we could do it here? There's a private sitting room upstairs. We could go there right after the guests go home. If anyone asks, I shall say we are planning our next Ladies Auxiliary board meeting."

"Perfect," Mrs. Ratcliffe said firmly. "Go take care of your guests, and let me speak with Penelope. If she approves of the idea, I will make all the arrangements."

Holding my tray aloft, I trailed behind Mrs. Ratcliffe through the crowd of chattering, gray-haired white women to the opposite side of the room where Penelope Fairchild sat looking out the window. The grieving widow's red-rimmed eyes had the haunted look of a small animal caught in a trap. Her fingers picked nervously at the lace handkerchief she held, twisting and untwisting it in her lap.

Mrs. Ratcliffe touched her gently on the arm. "I'm so terribly sorry for your loss, Penny," she said. "Do you mind if I join you?"

I sidled closer, hoping the glasses of cider on my tray would not run out before I could snoop on their conversation. With any luck, Penelope Fairchild might say something about Lilly that might help to prove the girl's innocence.

"Millicent tells me that you haven't slept a wink since your husband's death," Mrs. Ratcliffe said. "I think I can help, if you'll let me."

"There's no one in the world that can help me," Penny said wearily. "Nothing you say or do will ever bring my Jeffrey back."

"That's not entirely true, my dear," Mrs. Ratcliffe said softly. "From what Millicent Skelton has told me, your dear Jeff has already come back a few times to say hello."

Penelope Fairchild turned pale as a sheet. "Millicent told you?"

"Of course," Mrs. Ratcliffe said. "Otherwise, how could I possibly help you? I'd like to conduct a small séance for you, Penelope. If I'm successful in bringing your husband through, you'd be able to talk to him yourself."

Penelope Fairchild's eyes widened. "Could you really do that?"

"Of course," Mrs. Ratcliffe said grandly. "We can connect with your husband this very afternoon, if you'll allow it. Mrs. Skelton tells me there's a sitting room upstairs where we can hold a private séance."

CHAPTER 21

An hour later, as the last of the guests headed out the front door, Mrs. Ratcliffe approached me as I carried a tray of dirty glasses into the kitchen. "Have Mr. Layton send a vase filled with flowers, a bowl of water, and an unlit candle to the private meeting room upstairs," she said. "If anyone asks where Mrs. Fairchild and I are, Mr. Layton is to say he does not know. Is that clear?"

"Yes, ma'am," I said, and hurried back to the kitchen.

Minty Layton responded irritably when I relayed Mrs. Ratcliffe's request. "Doesn't the woman know we're in the middle of cleaning up here?" she said.

"I'll take the things upstairs myself," I said. "It'll only take a minute."

"One minute and no more," Mr. Layton told me. "I need your help washing up these dishes."

"Yes, sir," I said.

"Better bring them some hot coffee too, just in case," Minty said. "Be careful going up those stairs, Nola. This bowl of water is heavier than you think."

I sighed inwardly. Minty was a good boss, but there were moments when her tendency to lecture got on my very last nerve. I was about to carry a tray loaded with china cups, a carafe of hot coffee, a bowl of water, a vase of roses, and a candelabra up a steep flight of stairs. Why would I be anything but careful?

"Yes, ma'am," I said, and headed up the back stairs.

The private sitting room at Hastings Hall was considerably more elegant than the banquet hall downstairs. As I walked in, Mrs. Ratcliffe, Penelope Fairchild, and Millie Skelton sat in matching chairs at a round mahogany table whose curved legs had been carved to resemble lion's feet. A thick Oriental carpet covered the hardwood floor.

"Put the coffee and cups on the sideboard," Mrs. Ratcliffe told me. "Set the flowers and water on the table. Light the candle, and place it next to the water."

I took my time setting my tray on the antique walnut sideboard that ran along the back wall. I could only stay for a minute, but wanted to take advantage of this opportunity to snoop on their séance. Penny Fairchild's aura had an interesting silver tinge I'd never seen before. And unless I was mistaken, the spirit of her husband, Jeffrey, was already beginning to make his presence known. The temperature in the room felt strangely cool, despite the fire burning in the fireplace across from me.

As I placed the vase of flowers carefully in the center of the table, Penny Fairchild turned toward me. "Thank goodness you've brought coffee," she said. "I'll take a cup right away, please. I am chilled right through."

I felt the chill as well. For some strange reason, I was finding it very difficult to focus clearly. It wasn't that I felt dizzy exactly. It was more as if a part of me was floating, observing the room and the people in it, including myself, from a point high on the ceiling. *Concentrate*, I told myself. *The last thing you need to do is spill hot coffee on one of these white women.*

MURDER AT THE WHAM BAM CLUB   189

As though I were moving through water, I watched myself put the cup in a saucer, fill it with coffee, and carry it to the table. My ear had begun to buzz with a ferocity and volume I had never experienced before. My hands felt cold as ice as I set Mrs. Fairchild's coffee cup on the table.

When I returned to fetch the candle, I felt my knees begin to buckle. Despite my best efforts to remain upright, I sank to the floor, my head swimming in dizzy circles. I could hear that Mrs. Ratcliffe was speaking to me. But for the life of me, I couldn't make out the words. It was as though I were deep underwater, in a place of profound darkness.

Suddenly, I began to sing. I thought it was only another sound buzzing in my head at first. Then I realized that I was singing out loud:

> *You used to be my dearest friend*
> *Buddies till the bitter end*
> *Then you stole my gal from me*
> *You double-crosser you*
> *All this time I trusted you*
> *In return what did you do*
> *Cheated, lied, and stole from me*
> *You double crosser you*
> *As you reap you're surely gonna sow*
> *Whatever you have got will surely go,*
> *'Cause comeuppance time is comin' round for you*
> *Just deserts—you're gonna eat them too*
> *You think you've won the day my friend*
> *But your good day's about to end*
> *Comeuppance time is comin' round for you."*

The singing voice was not my own, but that of a man. Through the foggy haze that surrounded me, I could tell that Penny Fairchild recognized it. I could also tell that my singing the song bothered her, but for the life of me, I could not make myself stop:

> *"You think you've won the day my friend*
> *But your good day's about to end*
> *Comeuppance time is comin' round for you."*

The crazy song felt like a swarm of bees buzzing around my head. The intensity of emotion I felt while singing it was overwhelming—grief, anger, and a strange sense of urgency, all rolled into one. I don't know how long I kept singing or what else I said before I lost consciousness completely.

When I came to, I was sitting on the floor with my back propped against the wall.

"She's coming round," Mrs. Ratcliffe said. She leaned over and peered into my face. "Can you stand on your own, or shall I tell Mr. Layton to come up and assist you?"

The thought of Mr. Layton finding me sprawled out on this expensive Oriental carpet was enough to snap me back to reality.

"I'm all right," I mumbled groggily. I staggered to my feet and shook my head. "I'm terribly sorry. I have no idea what just happened."

"You went into a mediumistic trance," Mrs. Ratcliffe said. She dipped a cloth napkin in the bowl of water on the sideboard and handed it to me. "Put this on your forehead and sit down. Rest over there in that chair by the window until you have fully recovered your senses."

I nodded groggily. While I was aware of my body and physical surroundings, part of me still floated in another dimension.

As I sat down, Mrs. Ratcliffe turned to Mrs. Fairchild and said, "Your husband's spirit was definitely with us this afternoon. Why he has chosen this colored girl as his vehicle is a mystery to me, but I suspect it has something to do with the song. Do you recognize it?"

"'Comeuppance Time,'" Penny Fairchild said softly. "It's not the most romantic of numbers, but it was Jeffrey's favorite song. Eddie Smooth used to play it for him every night at the Wham Bam Club."

"The girl even sounded like Eddie when she sang it," Millicent Skelton added. "The same gravelly Negro voice. Gave me the chills when I heard it."

Mrs. Ratcliffe squeezed Penny's hand. "Never doubt that your husband's spirit is with you, my dear," she said. "He had the colored girl sing that song in order to let you know that he is here."

"Yes," Penelope Fairchild said, wiping away a tear with the back of her hand. "I thought the same thing. If there was any song Jeff would have wanted me to hear, it would have been that one."

Forgotten in my chair by the window, I floated in and out of consciousness as the women continued their conversation.

"My husband hated that song," Millicent Skelton said. "He gave me a real scolding when he caught me singing it around the house last week." She stared pensively into the fire. "Harry has not been himself recently," she said softly. "At first I thought it was just politics. There's a presidential election in two years, and he's been under a lot of pressure to make sure he can deliver the State of Illinois to the Republicans. But Harry has been under pressure like this before without completely changing his personality. Strange men have been coming out to the house to speak to him. Tough men in loud suits and big hats. Not our normal sort at all. Not only that, but there have been Negroes as well, lots of them. That man Eddie Smooth even came by here two weeks ago. Upset my husband terribly."

"Funny you should mention this," Penny Fairchild added. "The same thing was going on at our house. Last week my husband told me that as much as he liked Eddie's music, the man was getting way too big for his britches. When I asked what he meant, Jeffrey said for me not to worry my pretty little head, meaning it was men's business."

Millicent Skelton shook her head sadly. "Funny how little things that you don't notice in the moment take on a greater significance later on."

Mrs. Ratcliffe turned to face her friend. "Such as?" she asked. "Whatever you remember might well hold a clue to this whole mysterious business."

"All these coloreds coming to the house," Millicent Skelton said. "Eddie Smooth. Tom Hoyt, the owner of the Wham Bam Club. Boss Dillard and that thuggish lout that works for him, Jack somebody."

Penelope Fairchild nodded. "They came by our house as well. Most unusual. At the time I assumed it all had to do with getting out the Negro vote for the election next month. Now I'm not so sure."

"Then there was that young colored girl who came to the house last week," Mrs. Skelton added. "Light complexion and long hair, but still a colored. Rather pretty if you like the type, I suppose. Walked up to the door bold as brass, wanting to talk to my husband."

Lilly, I thought to myself. Suddenly I was wide awake. Hoping the three women would continue to ignore my presence, I kept the wet cloth over my eyes and listened intently.

"Of course, I sent the girl away," Millicent Skelton continued, "but she hung around outside the house for the rest of the day. Even in the pouring rain, I caught her peeking through the window. When I sent the butler to tell her to leave, do you know what she said?"

Penny Fairchild shook her head.

"She said that she had every right to be there," Mrs. Skelton continued. "She told my butler that Congressman Skelton was her father. She demanded to be recognized as his lawful heir."

"Ridiculous," Penelope Fairchild said. "I assume you sent her packing?"

"She ran off when I threatened to call the sheriff," Millicent Skelton replied. "She said she'd be back the next day with proof."

"Proof?" Penny Fairchild said. "What kind of proof could a girl like that possibly be able to offer?"

Millicent Skelton sighed and stared out the window. "If Harry did stray, this would not be the first time," she said quietly. "He doesn't know I know, but he's got a colored mistress he keeps in an apartment up in Washington, and a string of girls he sees when he's traveling on business."

"Men can be terrible that way," Mrs. Ratcliffe said. "I've been keeping a close eye on my husband ever since I caught him kissing that pea-brained blond secretary of his last year."

"Boys will be boys, they say," Millicent Skelton said sadly, "but a mulatto child is a different matter altogether. If the press gets hold of this story, the scandal will destroy us."

Penelope Fairchild nodded in agreement. "The Congressman would lose the colored vote and many white supporters as well. This is Illinois, after all. We're not in Mississippi, where such things are more common. Have you spoken to him?"

"Yes," Millicent Skelton said. "When I confronted my husband about the girl, he denied it at first, but eventually he had to admit the truth. This colored girl really is his daughter. He got his father's Negro maid pregnant when he was just a teenager. To avoid a scandal, the Skelton family paid for the child to be raised in an orphanage at the other end of the state. No one ever imagined this girl would find out that Harry was her real father."

"Surely she doesn't expect the Congressman to acknowledge her," Penelope said.

Mrs. Skelton sighed heavily. "I don't really know what she expects. I only know we cannot afford this kind of scandal. Not now, not in an election year." She pushed back from the table and stood up. "Harry is expecting me to be home any minute. It will definitely not do for us to be seen cloistered away like this for too long. Do you think the colored girl is all right, Portia? I'm sure Mr. Layton could use her help in the kitchen."

As the three white women turned to look at me, I opened my eyes and got to my feet.

"She looks fine to me," Mrs. Ratcliffe said. "Call me if you need to talk about this further, Penelope. Better still, come to my next séance. Your husband is eager to communicate with you from the Spirit World."

As the three white women left the room, I picked up my tray and got back to work.

CHAPTER 22

Mr. Layton was washing dishes when I returned to the kitchen. "You were supposed to come right back," he said irritably. "Where have you been?"

I didn't think Mr. Layton would appreciate me saying that I'd been overtaken by the spirit of Jeffrey Fairchild. Instead, I offered a simpler explanation. "Sorry, Mr. Layton," I said. "I fainted. It was awfully hot up there."

Mr. Layton grunted in response, then dried his hands on a dish towel. "It's nice and cool down here, young lady," he said. "Time for you to get back to work. There's a large pile of dishes in the sink that need your urgent attention."

Two hours later, as we pulled out of the alley behind Hastings Hall, Mr. and Mrs. Layton permitted themselves a rare moment of self-congratulation. "I thought things went well today," Mr. Layton said. "We only had a few hours to pull everything together, but Mrs. Skelton seemed pleased."

"She *should* be pleased," Minty said proudly. "My sweet potatoes were even better than usual, if I do say so myself. I added a little shredded coconut to the recipe. Just a sprinkle, but it really made a difference."

"Brilliant as always, my dear," Mr. Layton said, giving his wife an affectionate pat on the knee.

"I was surprised to see Mrs. Fairchild at the luncheon this afternoon, weren't you, Edward?" Minty said.

"Election's in two weeks," Mr. Layton replied. "She probably felt she had to be there, in spite of her husband's death."

"This murder is going to be bad business for the whole Negro community," Minty said darkly. "Lilly Davidson didn't murder just anyone. The silly girl killed an important white man. It's going to bring trouble down on all of us, believe me."

"We don't know for sure that Lilly Davidson killed that man," I said. "What if she is innocent?"

Minty Layton shot me a pitying look. "Grow up, Nola," she said. "The girl's as guilty as sin."

"You don't know that," I replied stubbornly. "I believe Lilly Davidson is innocent, and I am going to prove it."

"Knock yourself out," Minty said. "As long as you keep out of trouble. No more hanging out in speakeasies, and no more run-ins with the police. Understand?"

I nodded, and brooded silently for the rest of the trip. The more I thought about the events of the afternoon, the surer I was that the song "Comeuppance Time" was Jeffrey Fairchild's way of sending a message about the identity of his killer. Jeff Fairchild had barely known Lilly Davidson, and the girl had certainly not betrayed him. However, there were plenty of other folks around the Wham Bam Club who might fit that category. I wondered what Congressman Harry "Happy" Skelton was doing the night of the murder. What about Tom Hoyt, or Fairchild's aide, Joe Quincy? I made myself a mental note to find out whatever I could about these possible suspects in the morning.

When we arrived at my Aunt Sarah's house, Mr. Layton offered to walk me to my front door. "What with all the crime going on around here, you can never be too careful," he told me. As we got to Aunt Sarah's front porch, he slipped a small envelope into my hand.

"I found this taped to the screen door of Mrs. Ratcliffe's kitchen yesterday," Mr. Layton said. "It's another hate letter, but this time it is addressed to me. Whoever's writing these things wants our company to keep away from Mrs. Ratcliffe's house. The letter says that if we don't, there are going to be consequences."

As my hand flew to my mouth in alarm, Mr. Layton shot me a warning look. "For God's sake, stop looking so terrified, Nola. I haven't said a word about this to Minty, nor do I intend to do so. My wife is frightened enough as it is," he said. "I still think these letters are just a sick joke, written by someone in the neighborhood with a grudge against Mrs. Ratcliffe. In case I am wrong, could you ask your Aunt Sarah to make us a banishing potion?"

I suppose I should have been surprised to hear that the staid and conservative Mr. Edward Layton was looking to get some hoodoo work done, but after the events of the past two weeks, my capacity to be surprised was at an all-time low. My world was becoming a dark and scary place, and I was hard-pressed to figure out what, if anything, could be done about it.

"Of course, Mr. Layton," I said, and shoved the envelope into my pocket. "I'll talk to my Aunt Sarah about your letter tonight."

When I walked inside, I observed with pleasure that all traces of our encounter with the police were gone. If anything, the house felt safer and more comfortable than before Sergeant Sullivan's visit. Aunt Sarah was placidly darning a pair of socks in her favorite rocker in the living room next to the fireplace. I closed the front door and hung up my coat.

"The house looks great," I said. I walked into the living room and kissed my aunt on the cheek. "I hope it didn't take you too long to put everything right."

"It took a little bit of time," she admitted, "but it gave me an excuse to throw away some old things I didn't need anymore. How was your day?"

"Very strange," I said, and took a seat across from her on the couch. "Mrs. Ratcliffe and her friends had a séance while I was there. I was in the middle of serving coffee when I suddenly fell into a trance."

She put down her sewing and studied me. "Are you all right?"

"I think so," I said. "I blacked out for a while, though. Next thing I knew, I was singing a song." When I told her about Eddie Smooth's spirit coming through me to sing "Comeuppance Time," my Aunt Sarah nodded approvingly. "Well done, Nola," she said. "You eased Mrs. Fairchild's burden of grief, and let her know that her husband is still with her." She put her sewing back in the basket next to her chair and leaned forward. "Not only that, but this spirit message could be an important clue to the identity of Mr. Fairchild's killer."

I nodded. "Why else would he come back from the Spirit World with a song about getting back at your enemies? His wife told me 'Comeuppance Time' was his favorite song."

"Anybody who did the Congressman's wheeling and dealing would have folks waiting in line to send him on to the next world," Aunt Sarah said. "We just need to figure out which one of them did him in."

"Do you think the same person who shot Eddie Smooth killed Jeffrey Fairchild as well?" I asked her.

"Stands to reason," Aunt Sarah replied. "The two Spirits came from the afterlife together. Eddie Smooth sang the song, but the message was from Mr. Fairchild."

I gave my aunt a puzzled look. "How can you possibly be sure?" I asked her. "What if Eddie just popped in to sing his song and say hello. What if his message had nothing at all to do with Mr. Fairchild?"

"No, child," Aunt Sarah said calmly. "The Spirits are intelligent. They are people, just like you and me. The only difference is they don't have physical bodies the way we do. Mr. Fairchild's spirit knew his wife was sitting there, devastated by grief and hoping for a message. He used Eddie's 'Comeuppance Time' song as a way to say something important about who killed him and why."

At moments like these, I was so glad to have Aunt Sarah in my life. Her expertise on these matters was not to be denied. "It's not an accident that Mr. Fairchild and Eddie Smooth came through together," she continued. "The message they gave you also says that betrayal is involved in this thing somewhere. Someone double-crossed someone, and the murder was some kind of payback. The song was a clue, Nola. I'm sure of it."

I shook my head in frustration. "When you put it like that, the killer could be anyone," I said. "Jeff Fairchild probably had hundreds of enemies."

"Don't forget that the killer had to be someone who knew both Eddie Smooth and Jeffrey Fairchild well," Aunt Sarah told me. "These murders were not just about business. The motive for them feels personal to me. We need to be looking for someone who had a serious grudge, Nola. Someone who felt betrayed by both these men."

"But who?" I said. "Lilly went out to the Congressman's house yesterday. She confronted Mrs. Skelton and told her that she was going to come back. When Jeff Fairchild was killed in Congressman Skelton's driveway just a few hours later, Mrs. Skelton saw her running away from the house. If she didn't shoot Fairchild, she must have seen the person who did. If only we could talk to her!"

Aunt Sarah looked at me and smiled. "Stop fretting, Nola. Get some rest. Things will seem a lot clearer tomorrow after you've had a good night's sleep."

That does not seem likely, I thought, *considering the letter*

Mr. Layton just showed me. I pulled the envelope from my pocket and placed it on the end table next to Aunt Sarah's chair. "Would you mind taking a look at this?" I said. "Mrs. Ratcliffe has been getting hate mail. Yesterday, Mr. Layton received a threatening letter as well. Do you think he needs a banishing potion?"

My aunt passed her hand over the letter without opening it. "How many of these has Mr. Layton received?"

"Just this one," I said. "But Mrs. Ratcliffe has been getting them for a while. The letters started coming after she invited a colored medium to give a séance in her home."

"Humph," Aunt Sarah said. She picked up the letter, walked into the kitchen and took a bottle of Justice Oil from her herb cabinet. Her eyes had a faraway look when she returned. She placed the letter in a cast-iron skillet and began to chant in a low monotone:

> *Big John stand*
> *Ten feet tall*
> *Beat the devil*
> *Watch him fall*

As her eyes stared vacantly off in the distance, Aunt Sarah muttered the tuneless chant over and over again. With each repetition, she poured another dose of Justice Oil onto the letter until it was dripping wet. After continuing this process for several minutes, she lit a match and dropped it in the skillet. Instantly, a jet of blue flame shot up, burning the letter to a crisp in seconds. When the process was finished, Aunt Sarah carried the skillet full of ashes into the bathroom. Minutes later, I heard the toilet flush. When she returned, she nodded in satisfaction.

"God don't like ugly, Nola," she said. "He will take care of this in His own way and time. Tell Mr. Layton that his problem has been resolved."

"So quick?" I had seen my Aunt Sarah do a lot of amazing things, but this topped them all. A tiny hint of skepticism crept into my thoughts. "Isn't there something else he needs to do?"

My aunt gave me an impatient shake of her head. "What did I just say, Nola?"

"That Mr. Layton's problem had been resolved?"

"Exactly," she said firmly. "There is no need to mention it again, understand?"

"Yes, ma'am," I said. Shaking my head in wonder, I kissed her good night and headed off to bed.

CHAPTER 23

I tossed and turned much of the night, tormented by strange and vivid dreams. When I finally got up the next morning, Aunt Sarah was standing in front of the cabinet next to the kitchen sink. On the countertop in front of her was an unruly pile of dried herbs and a glass jar filled with blue liquid.

"Good morning, Nola," she said, without looking up. "I'm going to make you a new Protection Candle."

I kissed my aunt on the cheek and put some water in the kettle to boil. "I need all the help I can get," I replied. "I had a really weird dream last night."

Aunt Sarah stopped her preparations and sat down across from me at the kitchen table. "Tell me about this dream," she said. "It could be very important."

"I dreamed that Congressman Skelton, Jeff Fairchild, and Eddie Smooth were all floating in an enormous pool of melted butter," I told her. "They were singing Eddie's 'Comeuppance Time' song in three-part harmony, while Boss Dillard kept time on a beat-up tin washtub."

Aunt Sarah studied me in silence for a moment. "And now your head hurts, right?"

"Like the dickens," I said. "How did you know?"

My aunt offered me an enigmatic smile. "The Spirits are trying to reach you through your dreams," she explained. "The messages may be a bit jumbled at the moment, but they'll clear up in time. Once your new Protection Candle is lit, you are going to be fine."

When the kettle came to a boil, I fixed myself a strong cup of black tea and sat down at the kitchen table to watch her work. Aunt Sarah made her own candles from scratch, chanting special prayers as she poured the wax into a mold to cool. Once the candle was formed, it still had to be prayed over, sprayed with gin, and rubbed with powdered garlic, Saint-John's-wort, and oregano oil. By the time the candle was lit, it contained all the magical properties needed to summon the Spirits when help was needed.

"The fact that Boss Dillard was in your dream is significant," Aunt Sarah told me. "My Spirits say that you need to pay him another visit. There is something important Boss Dillard hasn't told you."

"Did your Spirits tell you what this thing is he's not telling me about?"

"No," she replied. "Just that you will need to go back to the Black Rooster Pool Hall and find out."

I sipped my tea in thoughtful silence for a moment. One of the most frustrating things about being psychic was that the Spirits tended to reveal their messages in dribs and drabs— breadcrumbs on the path to truth. Why the Spirits did this, I had no idea. Perhaps they thought mortals incapable of handling the whole truth all at once.

"I keep remembering the way Congressman Skelton talked about Boss Dillard at Mrs. Ratcliffe's dinner the other night," I said. "The Congressman claims to be a great friend of the colored man. In fact, the man is a total hypocrite. Do you think that's why Eddie Smooth was singing 'Comeuppance Time' in my dream last night?"

"Perhaps," Aunt Sarah said. "And Jeff Fairchild was also in the dream?"

"Yes. It was all very strange," I said. "The three of them singing in harmony like that. Made no sense at all."

"That's where you're wrong," Aunt Sarah said. "Your dream is a message from the Spirit World. A message telling you Eddie Smooth's murder and Jeff Fairchild's murder are somehow connected. Eddie Smooth, Mr. Fairchild, the Congressman, and Boss Dillard. Each man has a part to play in this story."

"If you say so," I said doubtfully. "Seems like a big jumbled mess to me."

"Have faith, Nola. We just need to put the pieces together. We know Mr. Fairchild was a big fan of Eddie Smooth. And we know Boss Dillard's bodyguard, this Jack Cross fella, was with Eddie Smooth at the Wham Bam Club the night of the murder."

"That's right," I said. "Jack Cross said Tom Hoyt pulled a gun on him and chased him out of the place before he could get his money."

"That's what he told you. But what if he's lying?" Aunt Sarah said. "Jack Cross had a very good reason to return to the Wham Bam Club. He said himself that Eddie Smooth owed him money."

"I was waiting for Lilly in the woods when Jack Cross ran past me," I said, "but there's a second path in the woods that leads to the Wham Bam Club. He could have circled back to Eddie's dressing room afterwards."

Aunt Sarah placed a handful of dried oregano on a cutting board and began chopping it into tiny pieces. "You heard the

Congressman encourage Mr. Fairchild to keep supporting Tom Hoyt, Boss Dillard's biggest rival?"

"That's right. The Congressman said as much to Mrs. Ratcliffe at the dinner the other night."

"Boss Dillard is working so hard to help the Congressman get elected," Aunt Sarah said. "He can't be happy about the way Mr. Fairchild has been treating him. Perhaps Boss Dillard told his bodyguard to have a little talk with Jeffrey Fairchild, a talk that ended up in gunfire?"

"It could have happened that way," I said. "Jack Cross could have killed Eddie Smooth in an argument over money, then shot Jeffrey Fairchild on orders from Boss Dillard."

"It's just one possible answer, Nola. It might not be the way it really happened, but we've got to investigate it."

She wiped her hands on her apron and turned to face me. "I want you to go see Boss Dillard today, Nola. Ask him a few questions."

I stared at my aunt in amazement. "Boss Dillard is a dangerous man," I said. "When I spoke to him before, he was quite clear about not wanting to see me again. I can't just waltz into the Black Rooster Pool Hall and accuse the man of murder."

Aunt Sarah offered me a serene smile. "You'll find a way," she said. "You will have to be subtle, of course, trick him into revealing something useful. My Spirits say that time is growing short. The police are bound to find Lilly soon. If we don't have some evidence that proves her innocent, they are going to put that girl under the jail, you hear me?"

"Yes, ma'am," I said. I knew from experience that when Aunt Sarah got her mind made up in this way, there was no stopping her. Somehow or other, I would have to find a way to talk to Boss Dillard, and find out what he knew about Jeffrey Fairchild's murder.

"All right," I said, and pushed back from the table. "I'll go see Boss Dillard this morning. And please—get that Protection candle up and burning as soon as you can."

"Don't you worry, baby," Aunt Sarah told me. "Nothing is going to happen to you. Not if I can help it."

Chapter 24

It was nearly noon when I headed down Upper Fifth Street toward Lincoln Avenue. The sky was clear and brilliant blue, not a cloud to be seen, which was more than what could be said for my mood. The more I thought about it, the less optimistic I felt about Boss Dillard being willing to talk to me again. One word from Boss Dillard could get you an appointment with the mayor. Another word from Boss Dillard could get you killed. For me to walk into the Black Rooster Pool Hall uninvited seemed the height of madness. The only reason I'd gotten to speak to him at all was because of Jim Richardson.

As I joined the stream of pedestrians moving along Lincoln Avenue, I suddenly got a brilliant idea. What if I got Jim Richardson to come to this meeting with me? He and Boss Dillard were old acquaintances, after all. Perhaps, with Jim Richardson to smooth the way, Boss Dillard would be willing to open up about his relationship with Jeffrey Fairchild. I'd have to be very careful, of course—ask gentle questions and not make any wild accusations. But with Jim Richardson in my corner, there was a chance, albeit a small one, that I could find out something useful.

With this new plan in place, I turned off Lincoln Avenue and headed up Gray Street toward Jim Richardson's office in the basement of Shiloh Methodist Church. As I left the hustle-bustle of Lincoln Avenue, the neighborhood became more residential. Shrieking children played barefoot in the street, moving only when honked at by irate motorists. Small, carefully maintained wooden homes fronted by tidy yards alternated with unpainted wooden tenements that looked like they would fall down if you blew on them.

Shiloh Methodist Church stood at the top of the hill overlooking Lincoln Avenue, giving the street a sense of dignity in spite of its dilapidated tenements. Built by freed slaves at the end of the Civil War, the imposing solid granite church was a testament to Negro perseverance in the face of overwhelming odds.

I walked around to the side door of the church and rang the bell. My heart beat faster in anticipation as I waited for Jim to answer the door. The last time I was here, Jim Richardson kissed me. Would he kiss me again? What would this next kiss feel like? Would it be long and deep? Quick and passionate?

As I mulled over these delicious alternatives, the back door of the church swung open to reveal a sloe-eyed brunette wearing a surprising amount of lipstick. Her skin tone was golden brown, her hair was thick and curly, and her abundant bosom threatened to escape the confines of her tight-fitting red dress.

We studied each other silently for a moment.

"I'm here to see Jim Richardson," I said. "Is he around?"

The brunette looked me up and down and sucked her teeth. "Maybe," she said. "Depends who's asking."

"I don't see how that's any of your business," I said. I pushed past her and marched down the stairs. When I burst through his office door, Jim Richardson was sprawled behind his desk with his feet up and his tie undone. Sitting in front of him were two plates piled high with fried chicken. A homemade pound cake wrapped in wax paper and a pitcher of ice tea sat off to the side. As I took in this remarkable scene, I came to a dead stop, at a complete loss for words. Judging from the expression on his face, Jim Richardson felt the same way.

As we looked at each other without speaking, the brunette sidled past me, propped her generous behind on the edge of Jim's desk and cooed, "Sorry your lunch got interrupted, Jimmy. This rude little girl barged in before I could stop her."

Jim Richardson cleared his throat and stood up. "Nola," he stammered. "What a surprise. This is Miss Hicks from the Negro Women's Missionary Society. We were just discussing some business matters over lunch."

My cheeks flushed with embarrassment. From the looks of things that wasn't all they'd been doing. The top two buttons at the back of Miss Hicks's dress had been undone, and there was a telltale smudge of red lipstick on Jim's collar. What on earth had I been thinking, showing up at Jim's office unannounced?

"I can see you're busy," I said, with as much dignity as I could muster. "I'll talk to you another time."

I marched up the stairs and slammed the door on my way out. As I stomped back down Gray Street, tears of humiliation stung my cheeks. In spite of his kisses, Jim Richardson was not serious about me, not at all. *He probably kisses every new girl he meets*, I thought bitterly. What a fool I'd been!

When I got to the bus stop at the corner of Lincoln Avenue, I sat down on a wooden bench and sobbed like a baby. Miss Eleanor had warned me to guard my heart, and she had been right. Fool me once, shame on you, I told myself. Fool me twice, shame on me.

I pulled a handkerchief from my pocket and blew my nose. I'd been through far worse times than this. I'd lost both my parents to yellow fever. I'd lost my husband in the war. I was not going to let myself get down in the dumps over some no-account playboy. You are nearly twenty-one, I told myself sternly. You're a full-grown woman now. Way too old for this kind of nonsense. The fact was, I had a murder to solve. If Jim

Richardson was not going to help me, I was just going to have to tackle Boss Franklin C. Dillard on my own. There was still a chance I could convince him to answer a few more questions, if I played my cards right. I blew my nose and wiped the final residue of tears from my cheeks.

I did not notice the man coming toward me until it was too late.

"Somethin' wrong, sugar?" he said. The man was light complected with a pencil-thin mustache and predatory eyes. "You shouldn't be out here like this, crying on the street alone," he said, and slid onto the wooden bench next to me.

I stood up and glared at the man. "Get lost," I said.

"Aww, now, sugar," he insisted. "Is that any way to treat a fella?"

I ignored him and set off at a brisk pace down Lincoln Avenue. For the next two blocks he trailed along behind me, filling the air with catcalls and suggestive comments. When I got to the front door of the Black Rooster Pool Hall, he turned and walked away.

To my surprise, the anxiety I'd felt about confronting Boss Dillard alone had vanished. In the space of the past hour, I'd been accosted by a creep and disappointed by someone I thought cared about me. Surely that was enough bad news for one day. Lilly Davidson needed me to be strong. Mrs. Wyatt needed me to be strong, and most important, I needed me to be strong.

I took a deep breath, squared my shoulders, and walked into the Black Rooster Pool Hall.

Inside the dimly lit room, a dozen musicians dressed in top hats and star-spangled red, white, and blue uniforms milled about on a makeshift stage at the back of the room. A larger-than-life picture of Congressman Harry "Happy" Skelton, sporting a toothy smile, hung above the stage. In front of the stage, Boss Franklin C. Dillard stood with his legs spread wide and his arms akimbo. As usual, Boss Dillard was impeccably attired in a gray three-piece suit and matching fedora. A pink carnation peeked from the buttonhole of his jacket.

"It's after twelve, Danny," he said. "Congressman Skelton is going to be speaking from this stage at exactly two o'clock. When are you going to rehearse my song?"

A potbellied man holding a trombone responded wearily, "Don't worry, Mr. Dillard. We'll have your song ready in plenty of time. I promise."

"It damn well better be," Boss Dillard snapped. "The Congressman's right-hand man has been gunned down by a cruel and heartless killer. I want Congressman Skelton to know he can still count on our support. This rally has got to be the biggest and best rally in the history of Agate."

"It will be," the potbellied man said enthusiastically. "My band will give your rally the razzle-dazzle it needs to shine. Folks are going to be wowed, Mr. Dillard. Just you wait and see."

Boss Dillard nodded and turned away from the stage. When I walked up to him, I didn't need to use my psychic skills to know that Boss Dillard was less than pleased to see me.

"Miss Jackson," he said. The frost in his tone was impossible to miss. "I should never have let Jim Richardson talk me into seeing you in the first place. Why didn't you tell me this Lilly Davidson was the type to go around shooting people?"

I willed myself not to wilt under Boss Dillard's angry stare. "Lilly is no murderer," I told him. "Your bodyguard, Jack Cross, is a far more likely suspect."

Boss Dillard frowned. "Keep your voice down, Nola. Even the walls out here have ears." He took me by the elbow and steered me toward the door leading to his private office. "Follow me."

Once inside his private office, I took a seat in the plush green leather armchair across from his desk, and waited expectantly.

"For your information, Jack Cross is no longer my

bodyguard," Boss Dillard announced. "I have terminated his employment. The man is a complete idiot."

I gave Boss Dillard a skeptical look. I had overheard the Congressman's wife say that she'd seen Jack Cross at her house on more than one occasion. "If the man was such an idiot," I said, "why did you send him out to meet with Congressman Skelton in the first place?"

Boss Dillard's eyes narrowed. "If I sent Jack Cross anywhere, it is certainly no concern of yours," he said irritably. "In fact, I don't even know why we're having this conversation."

"We're only having this conversation because you are a civic-minded man," I said. "Take, for example, the rally you're holding for the Congressman today. Would someone who did not care about our community spend the time and money to put on such an elaborate event?" I paused for dramatic emphasis, then shook my head. "No sir," I told him. "A less civic-minded individual would never even think about doing such a thing."

Boss Dillard nodded silently, taking it all in. I was flattering him shamelessly, of course. But, as my mother used to say, you catch more flies with honey than with vinegar.

"A girl from Phyllis Wheatley Institute, the only shelter for homeless Negro girls in all of Southern Illinois, has been unjustly accused of murder," I said. "If her name is not cleared soon, the Ku Klux Klan supporters on the City Welfare Board will fire Mrs. Wyatt and shut down Wheatley Institute forever. You're a leader in this community, Mr. Dillard. Surely, you would not want to see the Klan succeed in closing one of the few institutions available to us."

When I finished speaking, Boss Dillard stared at me silently for what felt like an eon. Then he sighed and looked away.

"All right, Miss Jackson," he said. "Because I do have an interest in this community, it's possible I may be able to answer a few more questions. What do you want to know?"

I nodded my appreciation, and took a deep breath. I'd succeeded in getting Boss Dillard to talk to me. To get the information I needed, I was going to have to choose my words carefully.

"Did Jack Cross go out to the Congressman's house to meet with Jeff Fairchild?" I asked.

"Jack Cross did run occasional errands for me," Boss Dillard admitted. "Errands that took him out to Congressman Skelton's house. But he was nowhere near the Congressman's house the night Jeff Fairchild was killed."

"Jeff Fairchild was actively supporting your archrival, Tom Hoyt," I said. "Didn't that make you angry?"

I could tell by the way Boss Dillard looked at me that I was treading on very thin ice, but I found myself unable to stop. The uneasy yellow spots flickering at the edges of the man's aura told me I was on to something.

"It must have made you angry that Jeff Fairchild showed up at Hoyt's place night after night," I continued. "It must have made you even more angry when Mr. Fairchild told you he would not support legislation to close the loophole that allowed Hoyt's nightclub to function in the first place."

As Boss Dillard continued to glower at me, I took a deep breath and looked him in the eye. "Yes, Mr. Dillard. I think Jeff Fairchild made you very, very angry. Did you send your bodyguard out to his house to set the record straight? To even the score once and for all?"

To my absolute surprise, Boss Franklin C. Dillard suddenly burst out laughing. "That's rich," he said. "You oughta write a novel or something, little girl."

His sudden good humor was disconcerting, to say the least. Even more disconcerting was the fact that the yellow band of anxiety I'd noticed in his aura earlier had completely disappeared.

"Let me set your mind at rest once and for all," he said. "Jack

Cross was nowhere near the Congressman's house when Jeff Fairchild was killed. What's more, he wasn't even in the State of Illinois. At the time of Jeff Fairchild's murder, my former employee was sitting in a Pullman car on the Sunset Limited, bound for sunny California. I know this for a fact, my dear, and I can prove it. I'll even show you my receipt for his ticket if you like."

"No thanks," I said. Boss Dillard's smug grin told me everything I needed to know. "I'll take your word for it." My carefully constructed theory about Jack Cross having murdered both Eddie Smooth and Jeff Fairchild had just gone up in smoke. Still, I could not resist one final jab.

"Jeff Fairchild and the Wham Bam Club have both disappeared from your life in the space of a single week," I said. "You've got to admit it's a remarkable coincidence."

Boss Dillard's eyes narrowed. "Watch your mouth, little girl," he said softly. Though his tone remained mild, steely gray arrows tipped with red danced in the aura around his head. "You are still a child. There's a lot in life you don't understand."

I *hate* to be patronized. I lifted my chin and faced Boss Dillard with a challenging stare.

"Like what?" I said.

"This week, the state legislature is considering a bill that would require Negroes to be off the streets of downtown Agate by sundown," he replied.

My heart sank. "A sundown law? I know Agate can be a bit backward, but I can't believe they'd pass a sundown law here."

"Don't be naive, Miss Jackson. Negroes in Agate will always be vulnerable until we have representation in the state legislature," Boss Dillard said. He leaned forward and looked me in the eye. "That is why I intend to run for the Illinois State Senate next year."

I stared at the man in open-mouthed amazement. "We've never had a Negro in the state senate before," I said. "Do you really think you could win?"

"I'll win if I get Congressman Skelton's support," he said. "If the Congressman thinks I had anything to do with Jeff Fairchild's murder, I can kiss my political career goodbye."

"Is that why you sent Jack Cross away?" I asked. "Are you afraid he might say or do something to embarrass you?"

Boss Dillard's dry chuckle was anything but warm. He stood and pressed a button on the side of his desk. Seconds later a man with a scarred face, a muddy-brown aura, and a gun tucked into his belt stepped into the room.

"Show Miss Jackson the way out, Fred," Boss Dillard said.

Stubbornly, I remained in my chair. "What about Lilly Davidson?" I said. "What about Mrs. Wyatt and the Wheatley Institute, Mr. Dillard. Shouldn't you be trying to help them?"

Boss Dillard gave me a bland smile. "Let me offer you some advice," he said. "Leave this investigation to the police. Dangerous men play dangerous games, Miss Jackson. I'd hate to see you get hurt."

More patronizing, I thought. Since it looked like Boss Dillard was going to throw me out of his office any minute now, I decided there was nothing to be lost in speaking my mind.

"If you really cared about this community, you'd do something about the pimps recruiting girls on Lincoln Avenue," I said. "They're a menace to every woman in the neighborhood. This is the second time this week that I've had some creep follow me around."

"You need protection?" Boss Dillard said. "Why didn't you say so in the first place? If you want, I'll have Fred walk you home. God forbid a sweet little girl like you should be harassed on the street."

Although Fred was scary enough to strike fear in the heart of anyone foolish enough to bother me, I didn't want to be beholden to either him or Boss Dillard.

"Thanks but no thanks," I told him. "I'll just have to take my chances alone."

Boss Dillard shrugged. "Suit yourself," he said, "just trying to be helpful."

Outside Boss Dillard's office, the musicians on the stage at the back of the pool hall had begun to rehearse. A dapper young man with processed hair and a megawatt smile stood in front of the group. "Can we do this tune one more time, Danny?" he said plaintively. "I missed my cue where to come in for the finale."

The potbellied trombone player I'd seen earlier frowned. "Make sure you don't miss it again," he said. "Boss Dillard wrote all the words to this song. If we mess it up, God only knows what he'll do to us." He picked up his trombone and nodded to the group. "One more time from the top, boys."

As I walked out of the Black Rooster Pool Hall, the cheery strains of Boss Dillard's campaign song followed me out into the street:

> *"Happy Harry, he's the one*
> *To fight for you in Washington*
> *He will never let you down*
> *So give a cheer and rally round*
> *Hip Hip Hooray for Harry!*
> *Harry Skelton, he's the one!"*

CHAPTER 25

Aunt Sarah was sitting in the living room when I got home. A thin, weary-looking woman in a blue cotton dress sat on the living room sofa across from her.

"For the life of me, I don't know what's gotten into my husband lately," the woman said. "The man's been acting downright crazy. Secretive, like he's hiding something from me." She looked at my aunt and sighed heavily. "Do you think he is seeing another woman?"

Aunt Sarah gave her guest a sympathetic look. "You should have come to see me much sooner, Freedia," she said gently.

"I know," the woman replied. "I was afraid to come. I love him so much. If he's seeing someone else, I almost don't want to know."

"You should never be afraid of what the Spirits tell you," Aunt Sarah told her. "They only want what's best."

I hung up my coat and closed the front door quietly, not wanting to disturb what was clearly an intense conversation. Aunt Sarah spotted me as I tiptoed down the hallway toward the kitchen. "Come in here, Nola," she said. "I want you to meet someone."

I walked into the living room and nodded toward the woman on the couch. She looked to be in her late thirties, with a dark complexion and wisps of gray showing in her hair.

"Freedia Cleeves, this is my niece, Nola Ann Jackson," Aunt Sarah said. "Nola is a powerful psychic. I'm going to ask her to help me consult the Spirits regarding your problem."

Freedia looked me up and down for a minute without speaking, then shook her head. "Your niece looks awfully young. Do you really think she'll be able to help advise me?"

"I'm certain of it," Aunt Sarah replied calmly. "Nola is wise beyond her years."

"If you say so," Freedia said dubiously.

"Try her out and see for yourself," Aunt Sarah insisted. "Go ahead, Freedia. Tell Nola what is going on."

The woman heaved a resigned sigh and turned to face me. "I'm worried about my husband, Peter," she said. "The last week or so, he's been acting very strange, like he's doing something he don't want me to know about. He leaves home early and don't come back till late. When I ask him where he's been, he says it's none of my business. I've been with this man for nearly ten years. Until recently, we've always been the best of friends."

"And now you're scared," Aunt Sarah said softly. "Scared of the man you thought would be your life companion, a man who for years has been your very best friend."

Freedia Cleeves pulled a handkerchief from the sleeve of her dress and wiped away a tear. "That's about the size of it," she said. "Do you think he's seeing another woman? And if he is, do you think I can get him to come back to me?"

"Let's see what the Spirits have to say," Aunt Sarah told her. "Nola, go in the kitchen and pour out the grounds from this morning's coffee onto a clean white plate and bring them to me."

When I returned to the living room a few minutes later with

the plate of coffee grounds as requested, Aunt Sarah told me to set the plate on the coffee table and sit next to our visitor on the couch.

"Take hold of Freedia's hand, Nola. Look carefully into those coffee grounds and tell us what you see."

I had only read coffee grounds once before, and never for someone as distraught as the woman sitting next to me. I wasn't at all sure I could help Freedia Cleeves, but as she and Aunt Sarah looked on expectantly, I could think of no graceful way to refuse. Despite my inexperience, I was just going to have to do my best. I took hold of Freedia's hand and slowed my breathing until it became deep and regular.

Soon, I felt an electric current begin to run back and forth between the two of us. Taking another deep breath to steady myself, I let my eyes go slightly out of focus and gazed into the plate of coffee grounds. Now that Freedia's hand was in my own, the coffee on the plate seemed to come alive, almost as though the grounds were rearranging themselves into pictures, letters, numbers, and shapes.

As these images danced through my mind, I began to speak. "Your husband has a secret that he does not want to share with you. Every day he gets dressed, puts on his uniform, picks up his lunch box, and goes to work. Or at least, that's where you think he's going. Your husband is lying to you, Mrs. Cleeves. He's not cheating on you, but he is lying."

I felt her hand tighten in mine as I spoke. At the same time, I felt strangely detached, both from Freedia Cleeves and from the story unfolding in the coffee grounds on the table in front of me. "Your husband was laid off from the Wells Coal Mine last week, and has been trying to find a way to tell you ever since," I said. "He's scared to death he can't support his family, and he's scared to death that when you find out he's unemployed, you will leave him. Instead of going to work every day, he's been pounding the pavement looking for another job."

When I was finished, Freedia's entire body sagged with relief.

"Thank God it's only that," Freedia said softly. She gave my hand a squeeze, then released it.

"There's more," I said suddenly. "The Spirits tell me your husband will find a new job within the week. If you want to sweeten your marriage, they say you should fix him a pineapple upside-down cake. When you make the cake, add five extra tablespoons of honey and a tiny pinch of cinnamon to the batter. Things are going to sweeten up between the two of you, I promise."

Aunt Sarah nodded approvingly. "Nola is right," she said. "Fix him that cake tonight. Tomorrow, I'll make a Love Candle for you to use as well. Keep the candle in your bedroom. Light it every night at five o'clock and let it burn for exactly fifty-five minutes. Within a week you are going to see a big change in your situation."

When Freedia Cleeves had gone home, Aunt Sarah gave me a hug. "I'm so proud of you," she said. "You look hungry, though. Come on back in the kitchen and let me fix you something to eat. Were you able to see Boss Dillard today?"

"He told me his bodyguard was on the train bound for California at the time of Jeff Fairchild's murder," I said. "He also said the Klan is trying to get the state to approve a sundown law here in Agate."

Aunt Sarah shook her head sadly. "That would be a big step back for the colored folks here," she said.

I nodded. "Boss Dillard wants to run for the Illinois State Senate," I said. "He thinks he can fight for Negro rights there."

"Boss Dillard is a complicated man," she said, pulling a jar of leftover collard greens out of the icebox. "He can be a devil and an angel, depending on what's going on in his mind at the time. One thing is certain, though—Boss Dillard is always looking for a way to stay ahead of his competition."

"In other words, he's not to be trusted," I said bitterly. "Just like the rest of the men in this pathetic little town."

Aunt Sarah put the jar of greens on the countertop and looked at me. "There's more to this than just Boss Dillard," she said quietly. "It's that Jim Richardson fella, isn't it?"

I nodded bleakly. "I've made a complete fool of myself. The way he spoke to me, the way he looked at me. The way he kissed me," I said. "I actually thought the man cared for me."

"He probably does," Aunt Sarah said, "but it was a mistake to assume he was interested in you and you alone." She bent down to kiss the top of my head. "Don't be too hard on yourself, Nola. Jim Richardson is the type that needs attention from women, lots of women. Not just now and then, but all of the time."

"He sure got attention out of me," I said ruefully. "I'm such a fool."

"*He's* the fool, believe me," Aunt Sarah said. "The Spirits say that Jim is not going to learn his lesson any time soon. Best to forget about him, Nola Ann. The right man will come when it's time. I will burn an Attractor Candle for you tonight. See if that doesn't turn your luck around."

CHAPTER 26

Aunt Sarah was already awake when I got up the next morning. In the kitchen, the air was rich with the smell of cornbread baking in the oven. Six rounds of thick Canadian bacon sat cooling on the countertop. "Morning, sleepyhead," she said. "You had such a rough day yesterday, I thought you could use a nice hearty breakfast."

"You're the best," I said, and kissed her on the cheek. "If there's anything that can put me right, it's a piece of your cornbread. Of that I am certain."

Using a dish towel as a potholder, she pulled a pan of fresh-baked cornbread from the oven and set it on the counter to cool. Light as air, yet rich and deeply soul-satisfying, Aunt Sarah's cornbread was a meal all to itself. In addition to the usual flour and cornmeal, her recipe included mixing creamed corn, tiny chunks of chopped onion, and bell pepper into the batter. As the bread cooled on the countertop, the smoky, spicy smell of down-home goodness filled the house.

"That sure smells good," I said. As I poured myself a cup of tea and sat down at the kitchen table, I could already feel my stomach rumble in anticipation.

"It smells good, but it's gonna taste even better," Aunt Sarah said with a self-satisfied air. "My cornbread is the best to be had anywhere outside New Orleans."

During breakfast, a respectful silence prevailed. The golden wedge of spicy cornbread was the perfect temperature—hot enough to melt the large chunk of butter I'd slathered on top, yet not so hot that it burned my tongue as I wolfed it down. When I'd gobbled down the last crumbs on my plate and drained a second steaming mug of hot ginger tea, my aunt tilted her head to one side and looked at me.

"When are you going back to Wheatley Institute?" she said. "You haven't spoken to Mrs. Wyatt in days."

"I know," I said. "The problem is, I've made absolutely no progress. Two people are dead. Lilly Davidson remains the prime suspect. I haven't been able to find her, and I still haven't been able to turn up any solid evidence that will clear her name. I hate having to tell Mrs. Wyatt I have nothing new to report."

"Go and see her anyway," Aunt Sarah said stubbornly. "Tell her about Boss Dillard, about that 'Comeuppance Time' song, and about having seen Brenda Washington. You may not have this thing all wrapped up the way you'd like, but you're closer to solving these murders than you think. Keep after it, Nola. Go out to Wheatley Institute and do some more investigating."

I poked at the last remaining crumbs of cornbread on my plate. "You're right," I said slowly. "At the very least, I owe Mrs. Wyatt some kind of explanation to sum up what I've found so far, insignificant as it is."

"Nothing is ever insignificant," Aunt Sarah told me. "Everything on God's green earth happens for a reason. Things just seem insignificant when we don't understand what that reason is. I'm convinced the solution to these crimes is hidden in plain sight, Nola. Right under our noses. We just have to do a bit more digging, and the answer will turn up. You'll see."

After breakfast, I took the Tyler Avenue trolley to the end of the line and walked the rest of the way to Phyllis Wheatley

Institute. Before I could even ring the bell, Miss Clark opened the front door. The expression on her long, horsey face was as gloomy as the long black dress she wore.

"We've been waiting for you to show up, Miss Detective," she said sourly. "I sure hope you've got some good news for us. Follow me."

I heard the sound of the girls laughing and chatting in the parlor as I followed Miss Clark down the hallway. I'd been sitting in that same room with those same girls only four days ago. So much had happened, and yet, I felt no closer to finding Lilly Davidson than when I started my investigation.

I waited next to the portrait of Booker T. Washington while Miss Clark tapped discreetly on Mrs. Wyatt's door, then told me to go inside. Mrs. Wyatt, dressed in a brown tweed suit and crisp white blouse, sat reading at her desk as I entered.

"Thank you, Miss Clark," she said without looking up. "Please close the door on your way out."

Mrs. Wyatt took off her reading glasses and massaged the bridge of her nose for a moment. When she raised her eyes to greet me, they were red and lined with dark circles.

"These are messages from donors," she said, pointing at the pile of paper slips in front of her. "They've been reading about the murders in their local newspapers. They've seen the stories in the *Agate Daily Chronicle* linking Lilly Davidson and Wheatley Institute to this horrible business. Do you have any good news for me? Anything at all?"

I told her about my conversation with Boss Dillard, about having seen Brenda Washington, and about my theory that whoever killed Eddie Smooth had also murdered Jeff Fairchild.

"I wish I could say I'd found something definite," I said, "but I intend to keep looking. Lilly is obsessed with getting Congressman Skelton to acknowledge her as his daughter. We know she went out to his house to confront him once. The only good thing about this news is that she will probably remain nearby in the hopes that she'll be able to get him to talk to her."

Mrs. Wyatt stared pensively out the window for a minute before turning to face me. "When Lilly came here, I should never have accepted that anonymous donation," she said softly. "I should have known there'd be strings attached."

"Congressman Skelton must have made that donation," I said. "A salve to his conscience for what he'd done to Lilly and to her mother."

Mrs. Wyatt nodded in agreement. "When I saw Mr. Fairchild's picture in the paper, I realized who he was," she said. "Mr. Fairchild was the man who paid the money and made the arrangements for Lilly to come here in the first place. He made me swear on a stack of Bibles never to tell Lilly the name of her benefactor. Looking back on it now, it seems so foolish of me not to have asked more questions." Mrs. Wyatt fell silent, her aura wreathed in a heavy blanket of gray.

"I wish I could have been more help to you," I said.

"You tried," she answered. "That's all anyone can do. It's all water under the bridge now anyway. I have a meeting with the City Welfare Board next week, and a large fundraising event at Shiloh Methodist Church this Sunday. The way things look at the moment, there's nothing I can do now but pray."

"Perhaps," I said. "But as you know, the Lord helps those who help themselves, Mrs. Wyatt. We know Lilly was at the Congressman's house the night Jeff Fairchild was murdered, because the Congressman's wife saw her run away. It's quite possible that she actually saw the killer that night. If we can find her, get her to talk to us, we may be able to solve this thing. We know she's not staying with Brenda Washington and we know she's not staying with Miss Eleanor Constant. Is there anywhere else she could have gone? It's possible one of the other girls on the field trip the night Lilly ran away might know something."

"It can't hurt to try," Mrs. Wyatt said. She pushed back from her desk, strode to her office door, and opened it.

"Would you come inside, Miss Clark?" she said.

"You need me, Mrs. Wyatt?" Miss Clark said. Although her aura bubbled with curiosity, her long, dark face remained impassive.

"Fetch Darlette Wilson, Minerva and Marcia Williams, and bring them to my office right away," Mrs. Wyatt said. "Send them in here one at a time, and don't tell them what it's about. Miss Jackson and I are going to ask them some questions."

"Yes, ma'am," Miss Clark said, and closed the door behind her.

Ten minutes later, Marcia Williams glared at me as she sat on the edge of her chair. If Mrs. Wyatt had not been in the room, I am sure the girl would have left the room without a word. As it was, she offered a stony stare when I asked her to walk me through her experiences on the night that Lilly disappeared.

"Do I have to, Mrs. Wyatt?" she said. "My sister and I have already been over this with Mr. Richardson at least twice."

Mrs. Wyatt's expression wiped the sulk off the girl's face in an instant. "If you and your sister wish to continue your stay here, you will answer," she said bluntly. "Go on, now. Tell us exactly what happened and don't hold anything back."

"Yes, ma'am," the girl said. Though her expression remained sullen, she took a deep breath and launched into her story. "Mr. Richardson picked us up at six. But we didn't leave for the reading until six fifteen because Lilly was late, as usual."

"What do you mean by 'as usual'?" I said.

"That's just how Lilly was," Marcia explained. "She was always late for everything. Always taking extra time to fix that curly white-folks hair she was so proud of. Primping and preening, calling attention to herself, as if she was the only girl on the planet."

"You didn't like her much, did you?" I said.

"Hated her guts, to be honest. My sister felt the same way. Lilly was always putting on airs, telling the rest of us what to do. Going on about how her white daddy was a member of the five founding families of Agate."

"Tell us what happened when you arrived at the YMCA that night," Mrs. Wyatt prompted.

"When we finally got there it was nearly seven," Marcia said. "There were no seats left in the front of the hall, so we had to find places in the back. I could tell Mr. Richardson was upset about this, even though he pretended not to be angry with Lilly for making us late."

"Did you notice Lilly doing anything unusual during the event itself?"

Marcia shook her head. "We all just sat there and listened to James Weldon Johnson give his lecture. When it was over, Mr. Richardson told us to get in the receiving line so we could shake Mr. Johnson's hand."

"And did Lilly go with you?" I asked.

"Maybe," Marcia said. "To be honest, I wasn't paying much attention to her. There were coconut macaroons on the table next to the stage, and I was hungry. My sister and I helped ourselves to a few cookies before we joined the line."

"And then?" I said.

"That's it," Marcia said. "We shook Mr. Johnson's hand. Then we waited around with Darlette Wilson while Mr. Richardson talked to Mr. Johnson and his other friends. Finally, he told us to get in the car. That's when we realized Lilly had disappeared."

"You didn't see Lilly talking to anyone outside of your group or making eye contact with anyone?"

"Not that I saw," Marcia said.

"Did she ever mention having friends or family outside of Wheatley Institute? Somewhere she might be using as a hideout?"

"Like I told you, Lilly and I were not close. I didn't see any reason to talk to her, so I didn't. Ever. Neither did my sister."

Mrs. Wyatt leaned forward and fixed Marcia Williams in a steely gaze for several seconds before speaking. "That's all you can tell us?"

"Yes, ma'am," Marcia said. Under the force of Mrs. Wyatt's gaze, she lowered her eyes. "That's all there is, I swear. You can ask Mr. Richardson. I told him the same thing."

"Very well," Mrs. Wyatt said. "You may go. Tell your sister to come in."

Minerva Williams was every bit as sulky and unfriendly as her twin sister. Under Mrs. Wyatt's stern gaze, she told us almost word for word what her sister had said. Lilly was "snobby and stuck-up," Minerva said, always lording it over the other girls. She had no idea where Lilly might be hiding, and had little sympathy for the girl's predicament.

"It's just like Lilly to stir up trouble like this," Minerva said. "Mr. Richardson was chatting it up with someone from his church. The lady had on a fancy dress and a lot of makeup for a church lady, so I guess he got pretty distracted. Anyway, when they were done talking, that's when he realized Lilly was gone."

Darlette Wilson was the last of the three girls Jim Richardson had taken to the YMCA the night Lilly disappeared. Unlike the Williams twins, she had a gentle demeanor and offered me a shy smile as she entered the room. When asked by Mrs. Wyatt to describe what happened that night, she repeated what the twins had told us about Lilly keeping everyone waiting while she got dressed.

"After about fifteen minutes, Mr. Richardson asked me to go upstairs and see what was keeping her," Darlette said. "He was worried we'd miss the beginning, and we very nearly did. As it was, we had to sit in the back."

"What was Lilly doing when you went to get her?"

Given the fact that Lilly was getting ready to run away with the man she considered the love of her life, I expected Darlette to say she'd found Lilly in front of the mirror, fixing her hair or adjusting her hat. Instead, her answer surprised me.

"Funny you should ask that," Darlette Wilson said. "She was writing. Sitting in her bed hunched over a piece of paper scribbling like a madwoman. When I told Lilly that she was keeping everyone waiting, she barely looked up. She said she'd be right there and kept on writing."

As my clairvoyant senses kicked in, I could see Lilly clear as day. Biting her lip, her brow furrowed in concentration as her pen flew across the page.

"Did she say what she was writing?" Mrs. Wyatt asked. "Think carefully, Darlette. It could be important."

"No, ma'am," the girl replied. "Like I said, she barely spoke to me. Just said she'd be down in a minute and kept on writing."

"Did she have the paper with her when you went out?" I asked.

"I don't think so," Darlette said. "All she had was a small beaded purse. No room in there for much of anything."

After Darlette Wilson left the room, I told Mrs. Wyatt I wanted to go through the clothes Lilly had left behind, to search for clues.

"I suppose you might as well," she said wearily. "Though I can't imagine it'll do much good."

"I understand, Mrs. Wyatt," I said. "But my left ear is buzzing something fierce. I know it sounds strange, but when that happens, my psychic senses are trying to tell me something. Perhaps if I can touch the things that Lilly touched just before she ran away, I will get a sense of what she was thinking and feeling."

Mrs. Wyatt gave me a skeptical look, but nodded reluctantly. "Whatever you say, Miss Jackson. I suppose we should leave no stone unturned."

Mrs. Wyatt opened the door and summoned Miss Clark. "Miss Jackson would like to look through Lilly's things," she said. "Take her upstairs and help her find anything she needs."

CHAPTER 27

"On to something, are you?" Miss Clark said as we climbed the broad wooden staircase up to the dormitory. She took the stairs two at a time as I struggled to keep up.

"I hope so," I said. When we got to the top landing, I stopped for a moment to catch my breath.

"That Darlette Wilson is a tricky one," Miss Clark said. "Acts all sweet as if butter wouldn't melt in her mouth, but I've seen her punch and kick other girls when she thought no one was looking."

"Darlette said Lilly was writing something right before she left on the field trip. Do you think she's telling the truth?"

"Can't rightly say," Miss Clark told me. "If Mrs. Wyatt had let me question the girl, I can assure you I'd have gotten the truth out of her one way or another."

"I bet you would," I said. "I've still got a bruise on my arm from where you grabbed me the day I first arrived here. I don't know what it is you've got against me, Miss Clark. I'm trying to help Mrs. Wyatt, too, you know."

"Call me Maybelle," Miss Clark said. "Sorry if I hurt you,

Nola. I'm just a country girl from Holly Springs, Mississippi. I was broke, hungry, and headed for a life on the streets when Mrs. Wyatt found me. If she hadn't cleaned me up and brought me with her to Wheatley Institute, I'd be dead by now." Her dark eyes bored into me with ferocious intensity. "This place means the world to me. I will do whatever it takes to protect it. When Lilly first went missing, I begged Mrs. Wyatt to let me look for her. For some strange reason, she chose you to find her instead."

"Understood," I said and looked away. The steely energy projecting from her aura was almost more than I could bear. Maybelle Clark would either make a valuable ally or an implacable enemy.

I walked into the dormitory and looked around. During my stay at Wheatley Institute, I'd spent little time there. Five narrow beds were arranged on each side of the room with a narrow aisle that ran down the middle. Next to each bed was a small night table. A small cedar chest secured with a padlock stood at the foot of each bed.

Miss Clark pointed to a bed in the center of the row of beds along the right-hand wall.

"As you know, Lilly slept here, next to Brenda Washington," she said. "The two of them were thick as thieves, always up to something. I had to reprimand them several times for whispering together after lights-out."

"You had no idea they were sneaking out at night?"

Maybelle Clark's steely aura shifted to a pale yellow as she looked down at the floor.

"Not much of a detective, am I," she said softly. "The girls fooled me completely. Maybe if I were a psychic like you, I could have prevented this entire disaster. When the story hit the papers, I offered to resign, but Mrs. Wyatt insisted I stay on."

"Mrs. Wyatt needs you," I said gently. "Now more than ever. Truth is, we've both made mistakes, but there is still time to find Lilly before the fundraising gala this weekend."

Each girl had a small table next to her bed. While the other girls used the space for their hairbrush and toilet items, Lilly's was piled with library books: *Oak and Ivy*, by Paul Lawrence Dunbar; *The Book of American Negro Poetry*, by James Weldon Johnson, and *A Brief History of Agate, Illinois*, by Alvin Sparr. A newly sharpened pencil and Big Chief composition book rested precariously on the top of the pile.

"Has anyone moved any of these things since Lilly left?" I said.

When Maybelle Clark shook her head, I sat down on Lilly's bed and leafed through the notebook. The first several pages had been torn out and the rest of the book was empty. The minute I touched it, a series of clairvoyant images flooded my mind. Lilly's passion for Eddie Smooth and her excitement that they would soon be together; Lilly's wish that she could share her excitement with Brenda, and at the same time, Lilly's absolute resolve to keep her plan to run away a secret.

"You're picking up something, aren't you," Maybelle said.

"Nothing particularly useful so far," I told her. "I was hoping to find whatever it was Lilly was writing before she ran away. Do you think she might have locked it in her storage chest?"

"Let's take a look," Maybelle said. She walked out of the room, returning minutes later holding a heavy iron crowbar. In one smooth motion, she levered the crowbar between the lock and the hasp of the chest. Grunting, she pressed down on the hasp until it broke open with a satisfying crack.

We peered inside eagerly. The trunk contained only a worn cotton summer dress, a winter scarf, some mittens and an unfashionable but sturdy woolen cap that looked like it had seen better days. Though Maybelle Clark upended the trunk in the hope that we had missed something, it soon became apparent that whatever Lilly had written was not hidden inside.

"Nothing," Maybelle said with a disgusted shake of her head. "Now what do we do?"

I sat down on Lilly's bed to think. "Is there any chance she took the letter with her?" I said.

"She was carrying a white beaded clutch purse, a light shawl, and a yellow print dress with no pockets," Maybelle said.

I studied her in amazement. "How can you be so sure?"

"I pride myself on my powers of observation," she said. "I may not be psychic like you, but I'm a pretty good detective in my own way."

There was no doubt about that, I thought. Maybelle Clark was surprisingly complex for a self-described "simple country girl."

"She must have left the letter here," I said. "It also seems logical that whatever she was writing was important enough that she had to finish it before she left." Suddenly an image popped into my head. Whether it was a true psychic insight or not, I couldn't say. At this point in my search, I could not afford to be picky. Whatever the source of my inspiration, I was going to have to run with it.

"Has Brenda Washington been back here to collect her things?" I said.

"Not yet. She telephoned Mrs. Wyatt earlier this morning, though. Explained that she was getting married and said she'd be by to pick them up tomorrow."

"Let's take a look through them, shall we?"

Before I had a chance to explain the reason for doing this, Maybelle Clark pried open Brenda's storage trunk and dumped the contents on the floor. Like Lilly, Brenda Washington had few possessions—a tattered copy of Homer Rodeheaver's gospel songbook, *Victory Songs,* a threadbare woolen overcoat, a stash of nickels hidden in an old sock, and a packet of letters bound with twine.

I untied the twine and flipped through the stack. All the letters were from a Mrs. Elva McKenzie in faraway Minneapolis.

> *Dearest Bren,*
> *How are you? Didn't get to talk to you much at*
> *your mama's funeral. I loved your mama like she*
> *was my own sister. If it weren't so far and I*
> *weren't so broke, I'd come down to Agate and get*
> *you. But with corn prices down and all, Mel and I*
> *are struggling to put food on the table. Not a day*
> *goes by I don't think of you. Will write when I*
> *can.*
> *Love, Miss Elva*

Although Brenda had taken the trouble to save the letters, they did not appear to have been read recently. As Miss Clark watched me with questioning eyes, I shook my head.

"Nothing useful here," I said. "Is this everything?"

"Everything except for the sheets of piano music she kept hidden under the mattress. She's had them with her ever since she got here," Miss Clark told me. "Piano music for that straight-from-the-devil blues music Brenda loves so much. Mrs. Wyatt told her to throw them away, but of course she didn't."

Maybelle Clark's hawklike face softened slightly at the memory. "Music means the world to that girl. Even though it was against the rules, I let her think she'd hidden the sheets from me."

As Maybelle described the sheet music, the hairs on the back of my neck stood up. "Let me see them," I said.

Grunting, Miss Clark slid a long arm between the thin mattress and the iron springs on Brenda's bed. Seconds later, she handed me a thick manila envelope. The minute I touched it, I felt Lilly's energy.

"Here it is," I said, extracting a carefully folded sheet of paper from its hiding place inside a worn copy of the piano sheet music for Mamie Smith's "Crazy Blues."

Maybelle Clark peered impatiently over my shoulder as I unfolded the paper and began to read:

> *Brenda*
> *By the time you read this I will be a married*
> *woman! I know you don't believe it, but Eddie is*
> *really swell. He's promised to give me a church*
> *wedding, with a white dress and everything, just*
> *as soon as he finishes up next week at the Wham*
> *Bam Club.*

Poor little fool, I thought sadly. Not for the first time in the last two days, I wished I'd had a chance to talk some sense into Lilly Davidson before she ran away. I sighed heavily and continued to read.

> *Eddie has picked out a house for us, just over the*
> *county line in Craigsville. I can't wait to see it!*
> *Even the address is romantic—33 Clover Lane.*
> *Isn't that sweet? When you escape the clutches of*
> *Mrs. W., you can come and visit me.*
> *Your Friend Forever, Lilly*

My left ear began to buzz as I passed the letter to Miss Clark and stood up. "I need to see this place as soon as possible," I said suddenly.

Miss Maybelle Clark shoved the letter in her pocket and sprang to her feet. "Let's go," she said. "We can take my car."

CHAPTER 28

Five minutes later, Maybelle Clark and I climbed into her car, a sporty Dodge roadster that seemed far too jazzy for her dour personality. Neither of us spoke as she peeled out of the driveway and onto the highway. Though the drive should have taken much longer, we were rolling down Route 247, the main street of Craigsville, Illinois, in fifteen minutes.

I'd never been to Craigsville before, but from the looks of the unpainted wooden shanties lining both sides of the road, I hadn't missed much. Maybelle Clark slowed down to peer at the names of the narrow winding streets that branched off the main highway.

"Read me that address again," she said, the first words she'd spoken since leaving Wheatley Institute.

I pulled out Lilly's letter from the pocket of my coat. "Thirty-three Clover Lane," I said.

"That's what I thought." Maybelle Clark yanked the steering wheel all the way to the left, cutting off a slow-moving truck and dodging in front of an oncoming Pierce-Arrow sedan. As we turned down a winding dirt road, we passed the

Say Hey Pool Hall and a row of tumbledown frame houses with bare yards and shuttered windows.

"Looks like we're in a colored neighborhood," I said, "and not the nicest one, by a long shot. You sure we're in the right place?"

"I'm sure," Miss Clark said. She continued driving at a brisk clip, swerving this way and that to avoid potholes. As we rattled toward the end of Clover Lane, I told her to pass number 33 without stopping so I could take a look. Maybelle nodded and jerked the steering wheel all the way to the left. Her tires kicked up dust as she made a U-turn and circled past 33 Clover Lane for the second time.

The curtains of the house were pulled shut. The front yard was filled with weeds, and a pile of mail lay uncollected on the doorstep. But houses, like people, have an aura, a sense of color and energy around them that is readily visible if you know how to look. Despite its deserted air, there was someone inside number 33 Clover Lane. I was sure of it.

"Park around the corner and wait for me," I said. "If I don't come out in ten minutes, send for the police."

Maybelle's eyes widened with curiosity. "Are you getting some kind of psychic message?"

"I won't know for sure until I go inside," I said, "but I think Lilly is in there. I've got chills running up and down my spine."

"I should come with you," Maybelle said.

I shook my head. The last thing I wanted to do was drag someone else into what was likely to be a dangerous situation.

"No," I said firmly. "You wait here. I don't want you to get hurt."

Miss Clark glared at me and sucked her teeth. "You're making a mistake, Nola. But all right, we'll do it your way. After all," she added with heavy irony. "*You're* the detective."

I nodded and walked away. My psychic senses were on full alert, and I had no time for arguments or hurt feelings.

As I approached 33 Clover Lane, I scanned the front window for signs of movement. The curtains were drawn, but for a brief moment I thought I saw something move behind them. Was it the wind? A trick of the eye? Or, was it my clairvoyance trying to show me something?

My ear buzzed furiously as I pushed open the rusty front gate, picked my way through the weedy front yard and climbed onto the sagging front porch. Despite its air of disuse, there were footprints on the muddy floorboards by the front door. From the looks of things, there were at least two people inside this house.

For an instant I wanted desperately to run away. It was still not too late to go back to Maybelle Clark's car and drive to the nearest police station. *It's now or never, Nola*, my inner voice said. *Lilly's life is in danger.*

I took three deep breaths in a vain attempt to calm my pounding heart. And then, with shaking hands, I knocked on the front door.

"Who's there?" a muffled voice called out.

"I'm from Phyllis Wheatley Institute," I said. "A registered letter came for Lilly Davidson yesterday. It's from some lawyer in Chicago."

I had no idea where this lie came from, but as the words rolled off my tongue, I knew they would do the trick. Registered letters are not the kind of thing people ignore, no matter who they are.

"Lilly's not here," the voice replied. "Go away." Although the voice was definitely that of a man, it was high in pitch, like that of a girl.

"Do you know when she's coming back?" I insisted. "It's important. Mrs. Wyatt told me not to leave until I'd given it to her personally. She'll have my hide if I walk away without giving it to her."

"Leave it in the mailbox." The voice was louder now. It

sounded like its owner was standing on the opposite side of the door.

"You want me to lose my job?" I replied in a whiny little-girl voice. "Please, mister. Just open the door so I can give this letter to Lilly. Please. It won't take but a minute, I promise."

After a long pause, I heard the bolt slide back. As the door swung open, I used my shoulder as a battering ram to push my way inside.

"I should have known you'd try to louse things up," Joe Quincy said. His expensive suit was wrinkled and disheveled. His light brown hair hung down around his ears and his shirt was stained with what looked like blood.

The main thing that got my attention was the .38-caliber revolver he held in his right hand.

He grabbed me roughly by the arm. Twisting my arm behind me, he shoved a gun into my back, kicked the door shut with his foot, and marched me into the front bedroom. The room was empty of furniture except for the spindly wooden chair where Lilly Davidson sat, bound by rope around her hands and feet. A rag had been stuffed in her mouth to silence her. When she saw me, a tiny glimmer of hope appeared in her eyes. Despite the gun jabbing into my back, I offered her a reassuring smile.

"Don't worry," I told her. "The police will be here any minute."

Of course this was a lie, but I could feel that saying it rattled Joe Quincy for a minute.

"Shut up," he snarled. He waved his gun toward the opposite side of the room. "Go over there and stand with your back against the wall." His aura reminded me of a mirror that had been dropped down a flight of steep stairs. Seven years of bad luck fractured into a thousand little pieces.

"Let the girl go," I said. "You'll never get away with this."

Joe Quincy whirled and pointed the gun in my face. "Didn't I tell you to shut up?"

I nodded and backed up to stand against the wall. Although

it was chilly inside the house, Joe Quincy was sweating. If I could get him distracted enough, there was a chance I could somehow wrestle the gun away. Or better still, perhaps Maybelle Clark would return soon with the police.

"If you let Lilly go, the police will go easy on you," I said. "I won't tell them anything, I promise."

"You're lying," Joe Quincy said. "Even if you were telling the truth, I will never let Lilly go. I love her, don't you understand? I've wanted her from the moment I first saw her. Eddie Smooth said he would set me up with Lilly if I helped him to open a nightclub in Chicago. I might have done it, too. That is, if Eddie hadn't made fun of me in front of the other nigras. Eddie thought I didn't know about the way he laughed at me behind my back, but I saw him with my own eyes. Outside the kitchen door with the other coloreds, making fun of my accent, calling me a spoiled little mama's boy."

"It was wrong of him to insult you," I said gently. Perhaps if I let Joe Quincy think I was on his side, he'd stop waving that gun in my face. "Eddie Smooth is not half the man you are."

"He was a louse who did not deserve to live," Quincy said bitterly. "He *hit* my Lilly, did you know that? I'm glad I exterminated him."

"You should get a medal," I said. Keeping my eyes on Joe, I moved a couple of inches closer to Lilly's chair. "You did the world a favor."

He nodded smugly. "Exactly. Did Lilly thank me for protecting her from that scumbag? Did she reward me with her love?" His already girlish voice went up another octave. "She did not. Instead, she ran from me. If she hadn't turned up at Congressman Skelton's house, I would never have found her."

"Quite a coincidence," I cooed. I was laying it on a bit thick, but Joe Quincy did not seem to mind. In fact, he seemed to be enjoying the conversation. "Lilly was at the Congressman's house? Did she see you shoot Jeff Fairchild?"

Joe Quincy's already jittery aura darkened. "Don't mention

that loathsome man to me," he said. "I'd been asking Jeff to give me a promotion for months. I asked politely, mind you. I was always polite. And still, that rotten bastard stood in the way, blocking me with that supercilious smile of his." In a remarkable imitation of Jeff Fairchild's slow and measured speech, Quincy intoned: "'The Congressman has asked me to inform you he'd like you to stop your work on the campaign,' Fairchild tells me. 'You're hurting rather than helping, Joe,' he says." Quincy's thin face twisted in fury as he recalled the incident. "Jeff Fairchild had the absolute nerve to mock me. Told me I was a boy trying to play a man's game."

"That's why you shot him?" I spoke as if this were the most reasonable response in the world.

"Of course," he replied. "The lovely Lilly saw me do it. The tricky little minx was hiding in the shrubbery and ran away before I could catch up with her."

"But you found her again, didn't you," I said. "How very clever of you."

"The Congressman was worried that Tom Hoyt's ledger books might have survived the fire, revealing the true ownership of the club."

I'd been stringing Quincy along, lying through my teeth in the hopes of distracting him enough to get Lilly and myself out of there. But suddenly I stared at Joe Quincy in genuine amazement. "Congressman Skelton owned the Wham Bam Club?"

"Exactly," he replied, "a fact he did not want to share with the voters. Especially two weeks before the election. Congressman Skelton sent me out to the Wham Bam Club to pick through the rubble. He told me to make sure the ledgers had been safely reduced to ashes."

"Did you find anything?"

"Sure did." Joe Quincy's demonic grin sent shivers up my spine. "Little Miss Brown Sugar here, hiding in that old toolshed in the woods. That's when I got the idea to bring her here. Brilliant, don't you think?"

I offered Joe Quincy a phony smile of encouragement as I inched along the wall a tiny bit closer to Lilly's chair. "But why here?" I asked him. "What's so special about Craigsville?"

"My family owns this godforsaken mining town—lock, stock, and barrel," Joe Quincy replied. "From time to time, I'd let Eddie Smooth use this place to entertain his female friends." Quincy's barking laugh was utterly humorless. "Mr. Smooth's entertaining days have come to an end. Pretty clever of me to take the key out of his pocket after I shot him, don't you think?"

As I scanned the heavy clouds of dark energy oozing from his aura, I began to see pictures in my mind's eye. Quincy as a boy being teased for his pretty looks and high voice. Quincy trying desperately to impress a father for whom nothing was ever good enough. *Flatter him*, my inner voice said. *Joe Quincy is desperate for approval.*

"You're very smart," I cooed. "I think Congressman Skelton should give you a promotion."

"The man doesn't value me nearly as much as he should," Quincy muttered. He stopped pacing for a moment and stared at the wall in silence. I was about to make a run for the door when he whirled around and leveled his gun at me.

"Don't even think about it," he snarled. "I'm a lot tougher than folks give me credit for. Trifle with me, and you will get burned. That arrogant bastard Tom Hoyt found that out the hard way."

I looked at him in horror. "You started that fire, didn't you?"

"Did you know there was a leaky gas main down in Tom Hoyt's basement?" Joe Quincy said. "The stupid nigra was too cheap to get it fixed. I knew he kept a kerosene lantern in the storage closet. All I had to do was make sure no one saw me take the lantern and pour a trail of kerosene from that leaky pipe to the back stairs. I simply lit the wick, kicked the lantern on its side and walked away. With all those barrels of hooch down there, a fire was inevitable, don't you think?"

The man was a true monster. There was not even a hint of remorse in his aura for what he'd done. My only hope was to continue flattering him and hope Maybelle Clark had gone to the police to get help. "Well done," I said. "You've defeated all your enemies." I batted my eyelashes and sidled a little closer to Lilly's chair. "A true victor is also merciful, Joe. If you let Lilly go, I can promise you she will never tell a soul about what happened here."

Joe Quincy shook his head. "Lilly saw me kill Jeff Fairchild," he said. "I cannot allow her to live." Still holding the gun in his right hand, he gave Lilly's shoulder a wistful caress. "You understand, don't you, sweetheart?"

Lilly cringed and turned her head away. "I hoped we could spend a little quality time together here beforehand," he continued. "Your busybody little friend here has spoiled everything."

Joe Quincy grabbed me by the collar of my coat, shoved me against the wall, and pointed the gun at my head. Jagged whorls of red and orange shot from his aura like lightning bolts.

This is what it is like to die, I thought. A dozen images flashed through my mind in quick succession: My mother's face. My father's careworn hands. Aunt Sarah's impish grin.

Lilly screamed, her eyes wide with terror. With the handkerchief stuck in her mouth, it sounded like a dying animal's strangled cry. Startled, Quincy dropped his arm and swung around to look at her.

Still distracted, he turned back to face me. The gun was in his hand, but no longer pointed at me. My inner voice shouted, *Now!* I charged forward, shoved my knee into Quincy's groin and pushed against his chest with all my strength. Taken by surprise, he stumbled backward and fell, his gun skittering across the floor. As I dove to grab it, there was flash of light and a loud bang. When I looked up, Quincy lay whimpering on the ground, bleeding profusely. Above him stood Maybelle Clark, a 12-gauge shotgun cradled in her arms.

"Don't even think about getting up, you sorry-ass bastard," she said through clenched teeth. "I will blow you in so many bits that your own mama will not recognize you." She turned to face me. "Are you all right, Nola?"

I nodded dumbly and stood up.

"Lucky for you I always keep a shotgun in the car. You never know when it will come in handy," she said. "I knew this was gonna be a two-person operation, and I was right."

"You didn't go for the police?" I said.

Maybelle Clark's laugh was deep and rich.

"Of course not," she said. "What we need those fools for?" As she continued to point the shotgun at Joe Quincy with her right hand, she pulled a knife from her coat pocket with her left. "Here you are, Nola. Cut Lilly free so we can get out of here."

"What about Joe Quincy?" I asked.

"I don't care one way or the other," she said with a shrug. "If you want, we can stop by the station house on our way out of town. We'll say we heard shots while we were driving by. They'll send somebody up here to look into it sooner or later."

CHAPTER 29

The last Sunday in October dawned clear and cold. Having slept in to the luxuriously late hour of nine a.m., I was enjoying a cozy breakfast in the kitchen with Aunt Sarah when the doorbell rang. When I went to see who it was, Edward Layton stood outside our front door with a broad grin on his face and a copy of the *Agate Daily Chronicle* in his hand.

"I came by personally to make sure you heard," he said. "Reverend Gonsails has issued a public apology to Mrs. Ratcliffe for the hate letters he sent. He's giving up his weekly cross-burning service and he's resigned from the Ku Klux Klan. Take a look for yourself."

"That's amazing news, Mr. Layton," I said. I took the newspaper from his outstretched hand and waved toward the kitchen. "Care to join us for breakfast? I'm sure Aunt Sarah will want to hear all about this."

"I can't stay," he replied. "I've got to start getting things ready for the Wheatley Institute fundraising gala. Minty is making a seven-layer chiffon pound cake with orange blossom frosting as a special tribute to Mrs. Wyatt."

"I completely forgot I was supposed to work today," I said. "Give me a minute to get dressed and I'll come with you."

Mr. Layton smiled and shook his head. "No, my dear. Mrs. Wyatt has requested that we give you the day off. She wants you to come to the gala as her special guest," he said.

"Really? I hardly know what to say, Mr. Layton. I can't think when I've been to a party without my waitress uniform on."

"Consider it our way of saying thank you, Nola Ann. If your Aunt Sarah hadn't stopped Timothy Gonsails in his tracks, who knows what might have happened." Mr. Layton flashed me a grin, then turned away. "The gala starts at four," he called out over his shoulder. "Don't be late."

When Mr. Layton had gone, Aunt Sarah asked me to read the article about Timothy Gonsails in the *Agate Daily Chronicle* out loud. "My eyes are not what they used to be," she said. "You don't have to read the whole thing. Just read what it says about why he changed his mind."

I poured myself another cup of tea and began to read:

SPIRITUALIST PASTOR GIVES UP THE FIERY CROSS TO PREACH TOLERANCE

After an opening paragraph spent describing the size of Rev. Gonsails's church, the popularity of his rallies, and his close ties to the Ku Klux Klan, the article quoted a letter Rev. Gonsails had recently written to the editor:

"'In an effort to discourage Mrs. Portia Ratcliffe from hiring Negroes of any sort, I put malicious notes in her mailbox,' the letter stated. 'I even threatened the Negro catering company that worked for her. I accused Mrs. Ratcliffe of sullying the name of Spiritualism and threatened to blow up her home.

"'As a Spiritualist minister, I am accustomed to receiving visitations from the Spirit World,' the letter continued, 'but a dream I had two nights ago shook me to my very core. I have received a visitation from the Spirit of Abraham Lincoln. He stood looking down at me with fire in his eyes. "I did not free the colored man from the chains of slavery only to have you persecute him," the Spirit told me in a loud and terrible voice. He stretched forth a gaunt and bony hand and touched my forehead. "Repent, Reverend. Repent and embrace the Brotherhood of Man."

"'When I awoke, my body was on fire. My face was covered in red blisters. Blisters for which my doctors had neither explanation nor cure. Every night thereafter, I had the same terrible dream. Every day thereafter was a living hell. I could not sleep. I could not eat. My entire body itched and burned.

"'On the seventh day, the Spirit of Abraham Lincoln returned with the Angel of Death by his side. "This is your last chance," the Spirit told me. "Repent, Reverend. Repent." Fearing that I would surely die, I got down on my knees forthwith.

"'From that moment onward, I became a new man. The blisters on my face have vanished, and I am full of the spirit of Christian Love for all men.'"

I put down the newspaper and looked at Aunt Sarah over the rim of my teacup. "Did your Spirits have anything to do with this?" I asked her. "Is this why you told me not to worry about those hate letters?"

My aunt shrugged. "When you ask the Spirit World for help, you never know what may happen. It's all water under the bridge now." She pushed back from the table and stood up. "We need to get you ready for your fancy dress party, Nola Ann. Show me the dress you plan to wear."

For the next several minutes, I tried on different outfits and combinations, turning this way and that so Aunt Sarah could offer her opinion. As I went through my closet, I pulled out a burgundy long-sleeved dress that set off my caramel skin tone and thick brown curls to perfection. As I looked at the dress, I was overcome by a wave of sadness. The last time I'd worn it was when Will had taken me out to celebrate our first wedding anniversary. I was about to put the dress back in the closet when I felt Will's spirit hovering by my shoulder. Strangely enough, he seemed to be encouraging me to wear the dress. I could almost hear him whispering in my ear: *It's been nearly four years, Nola Ann. We'll always have the time we spent together. But I want you to be happy. It's time to let people see how beautiful you are.*

When I looked over at my Aunt Sarah, she gave me an encouraging smile. "You heard the man, Nola. Put that dress on. It is going to look beautiful on you."

By four o'clock that afternoon, it had begun to snow. Neither the unseasonably cold temperature nor the thick flakes of snow covering the sidewalk outside did anything to dim the festive atmosphere inside the basement of Shiloh Methodist Church.

Mrs. Wyatt, wearing a royal-blue wool skirt and matching jacket, hurried over to shake my hand as I walked in.

"Won't you join me with the other guests of honor at the speaker's table?" she said, waving toward a table placed on a small raised platform at the front of the room. Jim Richardson was sitting at the table with his back to me. From the sound of things, he was regaling the folks at the table with anecdotes from his trip to the Pan African Congress in Paris in 1919. An expensively dressed high-yellow woman sat next to Jim with her hand on his arm. As he spoke, she leaned in close, soaking up every word, gazing up at him with doe-eyed admiration. *Ugh!* The last thing I wanted was to have another embarrassing encounter with that awful man.

I gave Mrs. Wyatt an apologetic smile. "Thank you for the

offer," I said. "But if it's all the same to you I'll stay down here with the rest of the guests."

"Of course," Mrs. Wyatt replied. "At least say hello to Lilly. She's been asking for you."

Lilly Davidson sat at the opposite end of the speaker's table from Jim Richardson, with her head bowed and her eyes downcast.

"How are you feeling?" I asked.

"Better," she replied, "but still not quite myself. This is the first time I've been out of bed since . . ." Her voice trailed off and she stared into space for a moment.

"You've been through a major ordeal, Lilly," I said. "What you need is a good dose of my Aunt Sarah's Soul Restoring Potion. Stop by the house tomorrow. I'll ask her to fix you something to take home."

"I'll try to do that before I leave," Lilly said.

"Leave?" I said. Her voice was so soft, I thought maybe I'd misunderstood. "Where are you going?"

"This time next week, I will join the freshman class at Monrovia University in Liberia," Lilly told me. "That's in Africa, in case you didn't know." Out of the corner of my eye, I saw a thin strip of gold glimmer at the edge of her aura.

At a loss for words, I stared at the girl as if she had grown two heads. "I didn't know you were planning a trip," I said. "Africa is awfully far away."

"Liberia is the only country in the world founded and governed by American Negroes," Lilly said proudly. "They have an excellent educational system over there."

"I suppose," I said. "What made you decide to leave so soon?"

Lilly Davidson looked at me and smiled. "My father, the Congressman, had a long talk with Mrs. Wyatt yesterday," she said. "He wants to support me overseas for the next four years so that I can pursue my degree in English literature."

The timing of the Congressman's sudden generosity was suspicious, to say the least. It was surely no coincidence that he'd arranged for his illegitimate Negro daughter to leave the country five days before the election. At the same time, the gold strip at the edge of her aura grew larger each time Lilly mentioned Liberia.

I bent down and gave her a hug. "Congratulations, Lilly," I said. "Be sure to stop by and see us before you go."

Funny how things have a way of working themselves out, I thought. Who would have ever guessed that Lilly Davidson would emerge from this situation with a brand-new start and a free college education?

I stepped off the platform and mingled with the crowd of well-dressed colored folks sipping fruit punch and talking animatedly in small clusters around the room. When I spotted Larimer Betts carrying his bass fiddle, I followed him to the corner where Brenda Washington sat behind a large upright piano. Her freckled face lit up as I approached.

"So very good to see you, Nola," she said. "Larimer and I will be playing music during dinner. Isn't that wonderful?"

"When the two of you get rich and famous, don't forget about us folks back here in Agate," I said with a grin.

Brenda's easy laugh was infectious. "How could I ever forget you, Nola? Anyway, we're not going anywhere. We're going to be playing at Richard's Café right down on Lincoln Avenue."

Larimer Betts rested his instrument on its side next to the piano and walked over to shake my hand. "Starting next week, we'll be at Richard's every Wednesday night. Please come down and say hello."

"Yes," Brenda said, giving Larimer an affectionate peck on the cheek. "I'll even play Honeyboy Logan's 'Hot Dog Blues' for you."

Larimer turned to Brenda and said, "Have you told her yet?"

"No," Brenda replied. "You should be the one to do it."

"No, darling," Larimer said, resting an affectionate hand on her shoulder. "You do it. You know, woman-to-woman."

"As long as somebody tells me soon," I said with a smile. "Don't make me turn on my psychic powers to find out what's going on."

Brenda giggled. "All right then—here goes: Larimer and I are getting married on Christmas Eve. Right here at Shiloh Methodist Church. I'm hoping you will be my maid of honor, Nola. Now that Lilly will be over in Liberia, I want you to take her place."

"Yes," Larimer chimed in. "I hope you can join us. After all, you were there at the Wham Bam Club for our very first date."

"Of course," I said. "I wouldn't miss it for all the tea in China."

"Oh dear," Brenda said, stealing a quick glance at her watch. "It's time for us to start playing."

As Brenda began playing the piano, I gave her a wave and walked back into the crowd. Everyone seemed to know each other. Everyone but me, that is. I wandered over to the punch bowl, where Minty Layton stood, holding aloft a tray filled with dirty glasses. She gave me the once-over, then nodded appreciatively.

"That dress suits you," she said, "but don't get too used to the high life. Mr. Layton and I will expect you for your regular shift tomorrow afternoon."

"No place on earth I'd rather be," I said wryly. Though we both knew this was not strictly true, Minty laughed anyway, and carried the tray back toward the kitchen.

Now that I'd said hello to the few people I knew, I was at a loss what to do next. As I stood awkwardly in the center of the room, Maybelle Clark walked up behind me and tapped me on the shoulder.

"Have you heard the latest, Miss Detective?" she said. "Congressman Skelton is creating a scholarship to help girls from Wheatley Institute to go to college."

I raised an eyebrow. "I don't suppose his generosity has anything to do with Mrs. Wyatt staying mum about the fact that Lilly is his daughter."

"Not a thing," Maybelle Clark said, and gave me a knowing wink. "Mrs. Wyatt is making a bargain with the devil, of course. If it helps to send colored girls to college, perhaps it's worth it."

"It's good to know Wheatley Institute will get something good out of this whole episode," I said. "My Aunt Sarah always says that God puts a rainbow in every cloud."

"Let the church say 'amen,'" Maybelle Clark said wryly. She paused for a moment, then leaned in closer, her intense dark eyes sparkling. "If I tell you something, will you promise not to tell anyone?"

"Depends what it is," I said warily.

"Busting through that door to rescue you was the most fun I've had in my entire life, Nola."

"That maniac Joe Quincy would have killed me if you hadn't," I said. "If it wasn't for you, Lilly and I might very well be dead."

"I told you it was a two-person job, and I was right," Maybelle Clark said with a satisfied air. "Now I'm gonna tell you something else." She stuck out her chest and drew herself up to her full height. "You and I would make a great crime-fighting team, Nola Ann Jackson. If you ever need backup on another caper, I'm available. Think about it."

Before I could respond to this surprising offer, Maybelle Clark turned on her heel and walked away.

From his place on the raised dais overlooking the rest of the hall, Reverend Leonard Jones, the pastor of Shiloh Methodist Church, tapped the side of his glass with a spoon. "Ladies and gentlemen, please take your seats," he announced. "Our program is about to begin." As Brenda and Larimer broke into a lively version of "Shall We Gather at the River?" designed to put the audience in a gathering mood, I heard someone calling my name.

"Nola," Eleanor Constant shouted, waving to me from a table in front of the stage. "Over here, Nola. Come and sit with us."

I hurried to the last empty seat at her table and sat down just as the music stopped.

"You remember Ben, Aaron, and Doris," Miss Eleanor said, gesturing to the three members of the Agate Negro Writers Circle seated around the table.

"Of course," I said, and nodded at the trio. "I heard the three of you read at Richard's Café. Nice to see you again."

"The pleasure is entirely mutual," Ben Langford said. "I sincerely hope you'll join us again, Miss Jackson." He leaned forward and looked me in the eye. "To be honest, you made a really strong impression on me. Any chance you'd consider having dinner with me tomorrow night?"

I stared at Ben Langford in amazement. Was this man serious? His manner was light, but behind his wire-rimmed spectacles, there was passion in his eyes.

"Give the girl a minute to catch her breath," Doris said, nudging Ben in the ribs.

"Can't help myself," Ben Langston replied. Keeping his eyes on mine, he ignored the rest of the group and spoke as if we were the only two people in the room. "Please say you'll come out to dinner with me, Nola. I'm a good person. Truly I am. You can ask Miss Eleanor. She will vouch for me."

Miss Eleanor smiled. "Ben is a brilliant writer and as you can see, a very passionate soul," she said. "I've known him since he was a little boy, and I have to say I've never seen him act like this around a woman before."

"Help a struggling writer, Miss Jackson," Doris added. "He needs to stop mooning around and get some work done."

"He hasn't stopped talking about you since he met you at the reading," Aaron chimed in. "He is totally smitten, so please: Do us all a favor and let him take you out for dinner."

"See?" Ben said. "I'm a straight arrow, Nola. Now that you know I'm on the up-and-up, please consider coming out with me."

My face felt so hot I must've been blushing bright scarlet. I was rescued from the necessity of having to respond when Reverend Leonard Jones stood up at the podium and began to speak.

"Let us pray," he intoned. After a lengthy prayer in which he thanked God for the food, the weather, and the Phyllis Wheatley Institute, the reverend thanked the Agate City Council for supporting colored institutions. Since this was a celebratory occasion, Reverend Jones left unmentioned the City Council's initial reluctance to provide a home for what one councilman had referred to as "shiftless negroes." What mattered was that Wheatley Institute would continue to help colored girls in need. The reverend wrapped up his remarks by reminding us to vote on Election Day. "Our ancestors fought and died so that we could be full citizens of this country," he said. "Be sure to honor them by exercising your legal right to vote. And now, while we are on the subject of politics, our Republican Ward Committee Chairman would like to say a few words."

As the audience applauded heartily, Franklin C. Dillard stood and waved to the crowd. "What I've got to say is not going to take long," he said. "I know how hungry you are. The first rule of political speaking is never to get between his audience and their dinner." Boss Dillard waited until the laughter had died down, then continued. "Ever since poor Jeb Hayes was taken from his jail cell and lynched five years ago, I've been advocating for a greater Negro presence in the halls of government."

"Amen to that," a grizzled old man shouted from the back of

the room. "Time we stood up for ourselves. Time we made our voices heard."

"Indeed, Brother Ferris," Boss Dillard replied. "I could not agree more. That's why I am pleased to share some important developments with you." He paused and looked around the room. Like the rest of the audience, I sat on the edge of my seat and waited for him to spill the beans. From the silver arrows hovering around his aura, I knew that his news was going to be something big.

After a brief pause to allow the suspense to build, Boss Dillard took a deep breath and said, "Congressman Skelton has asked me to run for a seat in the Illinois State Senate in 1924." As the applause began, Boss Dillard extended his arms in a gesture of benediction. "I'm here to ask for your support, ladies and gentlemen. It is time we had a voice in the legislature. With your help, I intend to be that voice—your man in Springfield."

The audience continued to applaud as Boss Dillard acknowledged them with a final wave, and sat down.

As a small army of waiters ferried steaming platters piled high with baked chicken, collard greens, and potato salad to each table, Miss Eleanor leaned over to me.

"Last I heard, Congressman Skelton was supporting a white candidate for that job," she said. "I wonder what changed his mind?"

"I'm guessing Boss Dillard threatened to tell the world about Lilly," I replied.

A slow grin spread across Mrs. Eleanor's face as comprehension set in. "Boss Dillard blackmailed the Congressman?"

"Seems likely," I said. "Looks like we're finally going to get a Negro elected to the state legislature. And just think, Miss Eleanor. It would never have happened without you." In response to her puzzled expression, I continued. "Lilly would never have discovered the identity of her real father without that book you found for her. And that's what set this whole thing in motion."

Miss Eleanor speared a chicken drumstick from the platter in front of us and dropped it on her plate with a satisfied smile. "Never underestimate the power of books, Nola."

Ben Langford nodded his head in agreement. "That's why I decided to become a writer," he said. "The written word is a mighty power. Let me tell you all about it over dinner some night this week."

Was I really ready to consider being involved with someone again, after all I'd been through? I am a psychic. Quite often, I am able to see into people's hearts and foretell the future. But when it comes to my own affairs, I'm as blind as everybody else.

As I savored the last of Minty's seven-layer Celebration Pound Cake, I decided to consider the possibility that my Aunt Sarah, as usual, had been right all along. Maybe, just maybe, there really was a hidden rainbow in every cloud.

I patted my mouth with a napkin and leaned forward. "Tell you what, Mr. Langford," I said. "I'll stop by the next meeting of the Writers Circle and we can take it from there."